I0772403

WHEN STORMS AWAKEN

WHEN STORMS AWAKEN

A REALM OF ISTMERE NOVEL
BOOK ONE

MICHELLE FROHMAN

Copyright © 2023 by Michelle Frohman

All rights reserved. No part of this publication may be reproduced, distributed, or transmitted in any form or by any means, including photocopying, information storage and retrieval systems, recording, or other electronic or mechanical methods, without the prior written permission of the publisher, except as permitted by U.S. copyright law. For permission requests, contact Acorn Hill Press LLC/Michelle Frohman at www.michellefrohmanauthor.com.

The story, all names, characters, and incidents portrayed in this production are fictitious. No identification with actual persons (living or deceased), places, buildings, and products is intended or should be inferred.

1st edition 2023 published by Acorn Hill Press LLC

ISBN: 979-8-9883045-1-7 (e-book)

ISBN: 979-8-9883045-0-0 (paperback)

ISBN: 979-8-9883045-2-4 (hardback)

Cover design by MerryBookRound

Editing by EJL Editing

Formatting by Michelle Frohman

www.michellefrohmanauthor.com

Author Note

This story explores themes that may be troubling to some readers. For a full list of content warnings please visit www.michellefrohmanauthor.com

For Poppy—
Who taught me the love of writing.

PROLOGUE
THE WAR OF SIRALETH

Siraleth, Istmere
15 Years Ago

Annelise raised her sword against the oncoming witch, a Nightshade clad in black metal armor, their face masked in shadow. She plunged her sword into his chest, turning quickly to avoid another oncoming attack. Her hands shook from the effort, quickly becoming battle weary. Her sword was as heavy as a ton of bricks in her hands; it took every ounce of her energy to hold it up before her. Her strawberry blonde hair whipped back and forth as she turned, soaked through with sweat and blood.

She had been fighting for hours. Fighting for the equality of witches like her, witches who were storm born. She avoided tripping over the bodies of her comrades as she pushed her way through the battlefield, her eyes on Osiris.

The dark king battled his attackers from atop a mound of rubble, a broadsword in his hand. His long black hair pulled tightly into a bun at the nape of his neck, his armor smeared with dirt and blood.

Annelise fought and pushed to get to him, but she only made it a few feet before she was stopped again, a sword clanging loudly against hers. She pushed her newest assailant off with a grunt, swinging her sword wide and missing as the Nightshade witch ducked out of the way. As she raised her sword to try again, another sword pierced through the back of the Nightshades neck, blood squirting across Annelise's face. The Nightshade witch fell to his knees with a gurgle. The sword was pulled free with a slick, wet, sound and the witch fell to his knees. Annelise saw her oldest friend rise before her.

"Thank you, Zion," Annelise huffed, gripping his forearm tightly.

"Get to him, Anna. She will kill him. There isn't much time," he replied.

Annelise responded with a fierce nod, pushing her way through the dense crowd of fallen bodies and fighting soldiers. She pushed her slick wet hair out of her face and her forearm came away bloody. Donika may have been their daughter, hers and Zion's, but Annelise would not let Donika slay the Dark King. Her first love. Osiris. To have to choose between your daughter and your former lover, it was a choice she never thought she would have to make.

From the moment that she could walk, Donika had wanted to hold a sword, and her magic had been stronger than anything Annelise had ever seen before. She could see Donika before her now as she pushed her way through the packed bodies of the battlefield, her sword raised, her eyes dark black pits.

Donika had immersed herself in black magic, and it had twisted her soul and her very being into something foul. Something unredeemable. Something entirely unrecognizable. She was no longer the sweet white-haired girl Annelise had raised in their small cottage in Siraleth with her oldest friend. Did Zion truly understand what she had become? Annelise had tried time and time again to save her, to make her understand, but all Donika wanted was power. She would do anything to get it. Sacrifice anyone, including herself.

Osiris fought valiantly, slaying his enemies with grace, his power something to behold. He may have been on the wrong side of this war, but Annelise knew she couldn't bear the thought of him dying. He hated her kind as much as the next Nightshade, but they had been close once. In love. He had been her closest confidant. She couldn't live in a world where Osiris didn't exist. He was not as evil or cunning as everyone believed him to be. Deep down, he was a gentle soul. Perhaps too gentle to continue to rule Istmere, but Donika would not make a suitable replacement. She was only fifteen years old and despite her years entrenched in dark magic, she was still too young, too naïve. If he hadn't been pressured by his people, by his soldiers, would he still have cast her out of the stone palace? Would she still be by his side, even now?

Annelise could see Donika fighting her way to the Dark King. They were on the same side, slaying all Stormshade witches, but Donika's thirst for power had become too much. It was all she could think about, all that clouded her vision. Osiris might be on Donika's side fighting for the Nightshades, but he was the only thing that stood between Donika and the throne of Istmere. She would do everything in her power to overthrow him.

Anna was pushed from behind and she fell to her knees with a bone jarring weight, her sword flying from her hands and clanging against the rocks.

"Filthy Stormshade," a voice sneered at her back. She turned slowly, and as she opened her mouth, to beg for her life, the witch's head was detached from its body in one clean sweep of a sword. It hit the dirt before her with a resounding thud, the witch's eyes still fixed on her with a cold stare.

"Better get going." Zion's smile was sad. He had saved her, again, for the second time during this long and unending battle. Annelise scrambled to her sword, grabbing it tightly in her grip, and set forth towards Osiris once more.

A breath escaped Annelise's lips as she saw a flash of blue and white hair and a sword as dark as onyx. Osiris now battled Donika atop the mound of rubble. Annelise pushed and pushed but made no leeway, stuck between the dense bodies, the sounds of swords clashing harsh in her ears. A ball of flame whizzed past her head, close enough that she felt the tingle of her hair burning, the flame hot as it passed her face. A building fell to ruins on her left and she covered her mouth and eyes with her tunic to avoid the cloud of ash that resulted.

The rocks flew in every direction as the building fell, Anna did her best to shield her head. When she opened her eyes, all she could see before her was a cloud of dust and ash.

I need to get to him.

"Osiris!" Annelise screamed, "Osiris!" But she could not draw his attention. It had been years since they had been lovers and she had been cast out of the stone palace, but she would fight for his life all the same. Osiris was nowhere near as ruthless as Donika, having let Annelise live even after finding out she was a Stormshade herself. She tried to call on her power, to propel herself forwards faster, but the earth here had been sucked dry of all its magical tether. Her magic was only able to propel her so far, her energy was quickly becoming depleted. It would take weeks to replenish the magic that had been used here today.

A witch from Donika's army approached Osiris from behind, and Annelise watched as if the world before her was moving in slow motion. Her feet were glued to the dust as rubble littered the ground around her. She watched the witch bind Osiris' hands behind his back. A guttural scream ripped forth from him as he struggled to free himself. Another soldier joined in, pinning Osiris down with ash shackles. Donika's cold smile had a chill running down Annelise's spine.

How had she borne a witch full of such evil? Osiris might not have been Donika's father, but the idea that she would murder her mother's lover and that it would bring her such joy...she truly was too far gone. Oh, how Donika hated Annelise. She was revolted at the very thought of her own mother being a

Stormshade, and she would do anything in her power to hurt and destroy her.

With that wicked smile across her lips, Donika raised her onyx sword high, only hesitating a moment to catch her mother's eyes over the chaos of the battle. She plunged her black sword into Osiris' chest all the way to the hilt, the sword protruding from his back. His broad sword fell from his grip and clattered to the ground before him as his knees gave out, a pool of fresh red blood falling forth from his lips.

Donika, what have you done?!

She held her mother's eyes with a sinister laugh, placing her boot against Osiris' shoulder and pulling her sword free. Osiris fell to the dirt before her with a heavy thud. The dark king was dead. Osiris was dead. Donika raised her sword high above her head in victory, her eyes as dark as the black magic that had consumed her. She cast her cold glare across the battlefield. The witches sworn into her service roared and cheered; victory was theirs.

Annelise was panicked, scanning the crowd of bodies for more Stormshade allies. There were none. The Stormshade witches were dead or had already fled the battle. There were none left on the battlefield that she could see. Osiris was dead. Donika was the new queen of Istmere, and Anna needed to get out of here, now. Annelise turned, her bones cold with terror. Where was Zion? She couldn't leave without him. She wouldn't.

Anna shouldered her way through the crowd back the way she had come, hoping to put as much distance between Donika and herself as possible. The shades, the unspecialized witches, had stopped fighting. Many of them fled when they realized that the battle was lost. The army of Nightshades had won, but their king was still dead at the hands of one of their own. Annelise was pushed from behind, and she fell to her knees once more. She crawled forwards, frantically trying to locate Zion in the chaos. Where had he gone? Had he already found a way out?

The surrounding cheers were deafening in her ears, disorienting her. Hot tears streamed down her face as she clawed her hands bloody, trying to push her way through the piles of bodies. How was she going to get out of this alive? The faces before her would haunt her forever, dead lifeless eyes and faces caked in blood and dirt. Former friends, former allies. Her fellow Stormshade witches had been mercilessly slaughtered, and for what? Because the Nightshade witches were envious of their power? It was always about power for them.

The holy city of Siraleth was reduced to wreckage during the battle. Anna had never imagined that the city could fall. The air was filled with smoke and ash, and Annelise coughed as she tried to catch her breath.

A foot on her back stopped her dead in her tracks and she was afraid to turn. She knew who it would be at her back. She knew what would happen next.

"Face me," a cold voice sneered from behind her. Annelise, still on her hands and knees, turned slowly to find the end of the black onyx sword pointed directly at her. The once beautiful blue eyes of her daughter reduced to black, lifeless voids. Her blue and white hair was caked with the blood of her enemies and allies alike as she smiled down at her mother with a cold stare. She was ruthless. She used the point of the sword to turn Annelise's chin up, forcing her mother to meet her lifeless eyes.

"Annelise Kotova, you are hereby sentenced to death for the crime of being a Stormshade," she spat, her disgust plain on her dreadful face. The crime of being a Stormshade, as if anyone could control what magic they were born to. As if anyone could control the powers the earth gifted them. "Do you have any last words?"

Annelise took a deep breath and closed her eyes. Osiris was gone. Zion was nowhere to be found. Annelise swallowed hard and hoped that he had made it out, against all odds, but she would never find out. Donika was queen, and there was nothing she could do to bring back her Stormshade allies who had been slain. Siraleth had fallen. Stormshades had been completely eradicated from Istmere in one single night, and the Nightshade witches would rule. Precisely as they had always wanted. But worst of all...she had lost her daughter. She had lost her to dark magic, and to greed. She had lost her to her thirst for power.

Anna always knew her daughters' hunger for power was greater than the love she had for her own mother. It had been years since it had been different, ever since Donika had joined the king's army at the ripe age of eight years old. She had been so young, as they all were when they joined the service of the king, but it had never mattered. Annelise had given her everything. She had done everything right. She had tried her hardest to be the best mother she could be to Donika. But it had never been enough.

She opened her eyes to gaze upon her daughter's face one last time. Was there anything left worth saving? Was there a sliver of the old Donika in there, buried somewhere deep? She pictured her as she had once been, with deep blue eyes, laughing as she pushed her on the swing at the old cottage. Her blue and white hair flowed out in waves behind her in the shade of the old willow tree. The sound of her daughter's laugh was music in her ears. Donika had been happy once, but that had been a long time ago.

"Fine, have it your way," Donika hissed as she raised her black sword above her head with both hands and brought it down.

Colorado, USA
Present Day

The snow-covered mountains raced past as I floored the old green Subaru up a beaten, dirt-covered path. I wound through the twisting roads to the peak of the mountain top it had taken me years to find. I put the car in park and threw the door open, eager to get out into the fresh air. I shoved the keys into the pocket of my faded jeans and raced towards the mountain's edge. Swinging my legs over a fallen tree, I jumped the gap between two huge boulders.

The sun burned brightly overhead, and I closed my eyes against it, enjoying the warmth against my skin. This had been an unnaturally warm winter to begin with, and I couldn't wait for spring. From here I could see our small town below, from the school all the way to the new downtown district.

Sitting on the edge of the largest rock that stuck out from the mountain face, I dangled my feet in the frozen air. This was the most beautiful and secret spot in all of Colorado to watch the sun rise. It was quiet and beautiful, but most importantly, it was *mine*. Nobody knew about this spot, not my mother or my brother, only my best friend Tess. I threw my head back as a cold breeze swept across my face and stuffed my bare hands into the pockets of my velvet winter coat. I should have remembered to bring my gloves.

The chill of the morning air sent a shiver down my spine and a chatter through my teeth. Ever since moving to Colorado, I had searched long and hard for a place of my own such as this. I had grown up in New York and it had been about three years since my dad had passed and we moved to Colorado to be closer to Mom's family. It was as quick as the snap of Mom's fingers and my whole family packed up and moved across the country without ever looking back. I had to embark on my first year of high school in a new place, with no friends and family I barely knew. Here I was, a senior, and not much had changed. All I had was Tess.

I pulled out a battered copy of my favorite book. The torn and weathered pages fought against the wind to stay parted at the place where I had left off. My fingers were numb from being exposed to the cold winter air, but I wanted to take advantage of the peace and quiet and fall into my favorite fantasy.

When my eyes caught the glint of the sun as it rose higher in the sky, I knew I had to get back home before my mom started to worry. She wasn't thrilled when I took off early in the morning and was already gone by the time she woke up. I gave the sky one last glance as the pink shine of the horizon faded and I stuffed the worn book back into my jacket pocket. As I was about to open the car door, something dark in the corner of my eye caught my attention.

I turned my head and froze, I couldn't believe what my eyes were seeing. A large black wolf stood only a hundred yards from me, sauntering towards the line of the trees behind the mountaintop clearing. Its deep black coat was a stark contrast against the freshly fallen snow. The wolf stopped as soon as I did, frozen in place. Its bright blue eyes met mine, and a soft gasp escaped my lips. *How on earth could a wolfs eyes appear so... human?* The wolf was bigger than any I had ever seen before, not that I had ever encountered one in the wild. It was as tall as a horse, with thick muscles and long sharp teeth that sank below its muzzle. It glared at me, unmoving except for its tongue that made one slow sweep across its upper lip. It appeared as if it was *smiling*. I was alone.

Why was I stupid enough to think coming into the woods *alone* was a good idea? The wolf was much larger than I was; why *wouldn't* it come after me? We didn't encounter wildlife like this back in the city, and I had yet to see anything similar since I had started coming here.

I swallowed hard as the animal suddenly broke eye contact and ran full speed into the line of trees. Its body became a blur as it receded into the dense forest before it disappeared from view entirely. As fast as I could, I turned back to the car and scrambled inside, locking the doors behind me. Why had a wolf strayed this close to town? And why was it so...big? And how did its eyes, its expression, appear so...human?

I took several deep breaths, resting my head forwards on the steering wheel. *Surely, I had to have imagined this...maybe this whole thing was the product of my imagination, or lack of sleep. That had to be it. It's early, I'm tired, nothing unusual about seeing a wolf in Colorado, right? Ok, calm down, Diana.* I glanced around before turning the car on, but the peak remained how it always had been, quiet and empty.

With a deep breath, I started the car and wound back down the roads of the mountain, eager to get back home. I parked my car on the street in front of the house, realizing with a twinge of regret that I had forgotten to plow the driveway yesterday. I had parked my car on the street last night, too. I hadn't noticed it in my haste to get to the mountaintop this morning, but the driveway was still covered in a layer of wet, heavy snow.

I raced through the front yard, trying my best to stay within the footfalls I had created first thing this morning on the walkway. Despite my best efforts, my jeans were soaked up to my knees as I burst through the heavy wooden front door. The smell of pancakes filled the foyer as I closed the door behind me and kicked off my bulky black snow boots. I unzipped my jacket, shoving it into the coat closet before tearing towards the kitchen like a tornado.

"Mom!" I called as she turned from the stove with her spatula in hand, having heard me come in. "I saw a wolf. It was bigger than a regular wolf... it was practically the size of a *horse.*

I was by myself up on the mountain. It took off, but I came straight home," I blurted out, taking a deep breath and settling into one of the chairs at the kitchen table.

I wasn't sure if I had been planning on telling my mom about the wolf sighting at all, but it poured out of me as soon as I saw her. I knew she didn't think too highly of me wandering off alone in the first place, and this would only confirm her fears. We made an interesting pair, an extroverted weather woman and her quiet, artistic daughter. We had never been that close, that is, until after Dad had passed. When we had moved here and I had no friends, she was the only one I could turn to.

If I was going to tell her, the least I could do was leave out the part about it appearing almost...human. That would surely get me a lecture about my lack of sleep, daydreaming, yadda, yadda. I didn't have it in me to hear another lecture this week.

She fixed me with a skeptical expression before turning back to the stove and moving the pancakes to a plate.

"I'm not crazy, I know what I saw," I pressed, slumping down in my chair. Even without the mention of the wolf's human-like eyes, this story went into the 'Diana's been day-dreaming again' pile.

"Diana, what time did you leave this morning?" she asked, her tone light but patronizing. All I could do was roll my eyes at her back in response. Just as I had guessed...she didn't believe me.

"Why is that relevant?" I breathed, exasperated. I should have known better than to think she would believe me. Why had I even thought to tell her? Time and time again I tried to connect with her, but every single time I was met with a brick wall. Maybe we were just too different. I wanted so desperately to be close with her, but I always felt she didn't understand me. I grabbed my hat and yanked it from my head, strangling the pom-pom in a tight grip under the table.

"Because you weren't here when I woke up..." She trailed off, placing the plate of golden pancakes in the middle of the round oak table before returning to the stove.

"I left at...six. Maybe a bit earlier," I confessed.

I grabbed a fork and a plate from the stack on the table and helped myself to the pancakes. I might as well be a well-fed daydreamer if that's the card she was going to play.

"This sounds like another one of your stories," she said matter-of-factly, throwing me a sideways glance from the stove. "Please stay out of the woods when you are alone." She fixed me with a heavy glare over the brim of her thick black glasses. I suppose this wasn't the best time to tell her I wasn't exactly *in* the woods, per se.

This is why we always butted heads—she was the realist, and I was immersed in fantasy. Growing up, I had been fascinated with stories of witches and warlocks, even vampires and were-wolves. All supernatural. All made up. I would make up my own stories and share them with friends. I lived in pretend. It was no wonder I had earned myself this reputation with her, even if I was much older now and had put all that nonsense behind me.

I finished my pancakes in silence and ran up the narrow staircase to my room. I closed the door behind me and quickly assessed the damage. I hadn't quite realized how messy my room had gotten this weekend while I was busy exploring the mountains, taking pictures, and hanging out around the new coffee shop in town where my best friend had recently gotten a job. I took the piles of clothing from under the window seat and at the base of my bed and consolidated them into a laundry basket. I quickly threw the covers over my bed and fixed the pillows.

I hadn't always been one for neatness, I hoped that this version of "cleaning my room" would satisfy my mom enough that she wouldn't snap at me. Her patience was always running thin on days when I would take off without telling her. Soon I would be off to college and wouldn't have to report my every movement to her.

I grabbed my laptop from the bottom of my bed and threw it open. As soon as it was booted up, I opened a search engine and typed in reports of wolf sightings in Silver Oaks. There were so many houses in this area, and with the new shops coming in downtown, our little borough was the busiest it had ever been. I thought it odd that a wolf would wander this far into town, even if they were seeking scraps of food in the dead of winter.

The internet search proved futile; I couldn't find any reports of wolves in Silver Oaks, specifically. I would have to try the newspaper archives to see if I could find anything there.

Frustrated with the lack of information, I threw the computer back to the foot of my bed. I lay down in a huff, my auburn hair curling in torrents over the edge of the pillow. I had no other plans for today, and I would put off doing my homework for the upcoming week as much as possible on a Sunday morning.

I glanced at the clock. 9:35. How could it still be so early? The sun had risen high enough in the sky to throw a beam of light across the floor, and my chubby orange tabby Waffles had found that exact spot and curled up in the heat of the sun's rays. I wished I could take a nap too, but I hadn't been sleeping much lately. I was having a hard time falling asleep in the first place, and by the time I finally did, my dreams were all over the place. More times than not, I woke in fits and starts, restless and edgy, feeling more anxious than rested.

The school semester was well underway, and I could almost taste winter vacation. School was tedious to me, as I'm sure it was to every other eighteen-year-old on the verge of going off to college. The only thing that made it *slightly* more enjoyable was Tess, and the occasional art or photography class that I got to take between my main classes.

"Waffles, have you seen any wolves around here lately?" I mumbled absently, throwing a cursory glance at the cat, who paid me no attention from his spot on the floor.

Waffles didn't as much as twitch an ear in response. Completely useless.

My cell rang, and I leaned over the edge of the bed, fishing it off the charger on my nightstand.

"Hello?"

"Oh, so you are alive! You didn't return any of my texts."

"Hey, Tess. I was going to call but thought you had a shift at The Daily Drip today? I was going to stop by..." I trailed off, sprawling back into my spot across the bed.

"No, my shift was canceled today. The shop is closed. Something happened to Mrs. Madden," Tess sounded distracted, and I could hear the clicking of a keyboard through the receiver. Tess was never one to give undivided attention to any one person or thing, even her best friend. Mrs. Madden owned the new coffee shop downtown and was there every single day to watch over it, no exceptions.

"Well, aren't you lucky. Is she sick or something?" I asked.

"No, she's in the hospital. Something about being attacked by a wolf?" Tess sounded unconcerned, but I felt a tightening in my stomach.

"I saw one this morning up at the mountain landing," I told her, swallowing hard. "It was a big wolf, I mean *big*. Like an elk. It wasn't…normal. You probably won't believe this, and you'll think I'm completely nuts, but…its eyes looked almost…human. Full of emotion. I know that sounds crazy…" I trailed off. I didn't keep anything from Tess, even if she was going to think I was out of my mind. She was the first person to welcome me when I moved to Silver Oaks, and we've been inseparable ever since. She might be the popular girl and I was the recluse, but against all odds, she had taken me under her wing.

I couldn't believe that someone had been attacked by a wolf mere hours before I had seen one close to town. This wolf had to be one and the same; there was no way this was a coincidence.

"Oh my God! Are you serious? Are you ok? Diana?" Tess' responses came spilling forwards, now I had her attention.

"I'm fine. It ran away. But I was surprised to see one here at all. This thing was *huge,* Tess. It was the biggest wolf I've ever seen. It didn't appear to be natural. There was something…off about it."

"Are you sure?" She paused, sighing deeply. "But hey, if you want, do you think we could go check it out? The mountain landing, I mean."

"Definitely, I don't want you to think I'm the only crazy one out of the two of us." I laughed. "But what should I tell my mom? I told her this morning that I had seen the wolf."

"Why would you tell her that? Are you *trying* to be grounded?" Tess asked with a huff. "Tell her we're going to the coffee shop?"

"Won't she know that Mrs. Madden gave everyone the day off?" I asked. "She's bound to find that out soon enough." Word traveled fast in a town this small.

"That's a good point," Tess mused, "tell her we're going to study at the library?"

"…And you think that sounds remotely more believable?" I laughed.

"Do you have any better ideas? I don't hear you suggesting anything," she replied testily.

"Should I tell her we are going to check out that new bakery that recently opened up in town? I've been wanting to check it out."

"That's a good idea," Tess replied, "and surely more believable than my suggestions."

My best bet was to wait until the last possible minute to tell my mom I was going out again. I didn't want to give her time to think about it, or to say no before Tess and I were able to make it out the door.

"Be at my house in an hour and we can take my car," I offered. I could hear the light padding of my mother's footsteps
on the carpeted stairs right outside my door.

"Gotcha, see ya then!" Tess hung up with a click.

I put my phone back on the nightstand and quickly grabbed
the closest book to me and flipped it to a random page. The
door to my bedroom creaked open as my mom nudged it open
with her back, a laundry bin in her hands.

"What are you up to?" she questioned, reading the expression on my face. I sat cross-legged, the book resting between
my legs, my tangled hair falling in a mess down my back.

"Oh." I paused. "Nothing," I claimed innocently, wiggling
the book in my hands to indicate I was busy reading.

"That's got to be the millionth time you've read that one."
She laughed, bending down behind my door to grab the bin of
dirty clothes I had left.

I flipped the front of the book over to check the cover and
laughed to myself. I had to have read this one more than a
million times.

"You know…I would read different books if I could buy
more," I teased, throwing a pleading look in her direction.

"Clean out that bookshelf of yours and who knows…" She
gestured towards the messy array of books, big and small,
resting in my private library against the wall.

"Yeah…we'll see," I said, pretending to return to my book.
With a toss of her dirty blonde hair, she left, her slight figure
pulling the door half closed with a foot as she went. I tossed
the book back onto the nightstand atop a pile of other knick-
knacks and papers. I needed to clean this place up before the

clutter swallowed me whole, but I was much more interested in picking up the book I'd been reading on the mountaintop this morning.

I pulled the book out and spent the last hour before Tess arrived sprawled across my duvet, picking up right where I had left off.

The doorbell rang, and I sprang up from my bed, abandoning the book across my comforter as I ran down the stairs and flung the door open.

"Tess!"

"We have *so* much to talk about!" she said, pushing her way into the foyer.

She led the way, leaping up the steps two at a time with her long skinny legs, and closed the door of my room behind us. We sat across from each other on the bed, Tess shucking her jacket off.

"Are we actually going to search for this wolf?" she asked.

"Yes, we are. I need you to see this thing with your own eyes. You'll never believe me otherwise."

Tess appeared apprehensive, biting her lower lip and folding her hands into her lap.

"Wait a second," she said, holding her hands out as if to stop me. "What exactly are we going to do if we see this thing?"

"I don't know, Tess. Take a picture of it or something? You should have seen the sheer size of it. It has to be some kind of genetic mutation or something," I told her.

I reached over to the nightstand and picked up my DSLR camera from among the clutter. I grabbed the pocketknife, a present from my father, out of the nightstand drawer and slid it into my jeans pocket. I had no intentions of using it, but better to have *something*, even if it was dinky and possibly useless for protection against a wolf.

"Ok, but we stay close to the car and don't venture into the woods, got it?" she asked, slightly less anxious.

"There's nothing to worry about," I told her, opening the bedroom door and peering into the hallway. "We will stay out of the woods, and I promise we'll stay near the car. There are probably paw prints from this morning. What are the chances the wolf is even still there?" I assured her.

"You're right," she agreed, getting up from the bed and squeezing back into her winter coat.

Tess quietly followed me down the stairs, and as I reached for the door handle, the inevitable voice of warning came out of nowhere.

"Where are you off to?" my mom asked as she appeared in the mouth of the living room hallway, a dishtowel in her hands.

"We are going to check out that new bakery downtown. They recently opened," I replied.

I couldn't positively tell one way or the other if the look in her eyes was speculation or not, but I'm pretty sure it was.

"Ok." She hesitated. "No going back into the woods under any circumstances, do you understand? I don't need you two getting hurt."

"Sure, Mom," I called as we rushed out the door. "I promise," I called over my shoulder.

The snow may have stopped from the night before, but at this point it had left at least a foot of fresh powder on the frozen ground. I was lucky the town had already plowed the mountain pass and my Subaru had no problem with the packed dirt road we would take to the mountaintop.

We hopped into the car and slowly drove through the winding roads up the side of the mountain. The roads had already been sanded and salted, but the higher we got, the more icy patches there were. The Subaru tires slipped angrily against the ice as they searched for traction, so much for winter tires. Maybe I needed some with chains...

We made it successfully to the landing, and I parked my car in the same spot I had this morning, halfway between the tree line and the mountain's edge. The clearing was large, large enough to spot anything if it tried to approach us.

We got out of the car hesitantly, closing our doors behind us quietly. I held my camera gingerly in my hands and decided we should sit on the edge in my regular spot, just as I had this morning. Tess followed me, and we both swung our feet over the edge, dangling them in the frigid air. It wasn't exactly a drop off here. If you were to accidentally slip, the rock face below this section of mountain wasn't steep, it would catch you. The small ledge where I liked to sit gave the impression of being on the edge of the mountain, even if I wasn't.

"This place is beautiful," Tess said with a bump of her shoulder as we both stared out at the view. "It's no wonder you keep it all to yourself." She smirked. "You can see our school from here!" She pointed with her long, manicured finger and I could instantly make out the big brick building in the distance.

It was in that moment that I heard the soft padding of heavy paws on the fresh snowfall behind us. Tess and I turned towards each other at the same time. Her lips were parted, eyes wide. She had heard that too...at least I wasn't truly imagining things. We were on our feet in a split-second and at the car door even faster. With one hand slipped into the handle of the car door and the other on my camera, we scanned the area for any movement, but there was nothing. What was it that we had heard?

I slowly approached the tree line without speaking a word to Tess. I could see the imprints of large paws in the snow, looking fresher than they would have if they were from earlier this morning. The imprint was much too big, as big as my own hand. I motioned for Tess to join me with a wave of my hand, and she reluctantly trudged through the snow to my side. She knelt down in the snow and examined the footprint with big eyes.

"It's so...*big*...this can't be a wolf..." she protested, shaking her head back and forth, her cheeks pink from the cold and her hands stuffed into her jacket pockets. "Maybe a bear? But the pattern isn't right..."

"It was, Tess. I saw it with my own two eyes," I insisted.

The snap of a tree branch startled us both, and we reached for one another. There, in the woods, halfway hidden behind a tree, was the black wolf that I had seen this morning. It was far off in the distance this time, watching us silently. Tess and I both froze in place, too afraid to move an inch as we clung to each other. Adrenaline coursed through my veins, and I could hear my heart pumping thickly in my ears. I couldn't believe it, but there it was. Again. Staring at me with those *human* eyes. I hadn't expected it would be here again.

I wanted to whisper for Tess to run, to say anything at all, but my voice was stuck in my throat. We were much closer to the car than we were to the wolf, but we wouldn't be nearly as fast. What were the chances we could make it there in time if the wolf gave chase? The big black wolf had a burly stature, and it appeared even taller and larger than I had remembered from this morning. It had a long and shaggy coat the color of the blackest night. Its face was long and slim, with wide set blue eyes and long perked ears. The wolf's eyes flickered to the forest behind him momentarily, but just as quickly, his head snapped back and his eyes locked with mine again.

The wolf took a slow step forwards, then another, revealing its body fully from behind the cover of trees. Where had something this size even come from? It didn't make any sense...

The wolf continued its slow, but steady, advance and I could hear my heart beating faster and faster in my ears. We had to decide right now if it was worth turning our backs on it to try to make it back to the car in time.

As it continued to approach, I caught the glint of the sun across its razor-sharp set of teeth. Its lips curled over them in a hungry way, but not a hint of malice or aggression ever touched its human-like eyes. This wolf could easily take us both down without much effort. It started to circle around us, but Tess and I held our positions, too nervous to move and draw its attention further. He was still far away in the line of trees, and the car was only a few yards behind us. If we could make a run for it or slowly back towards the car...

I took a slow, uneasy breath. I had gotten lucky that I didn't get eaten the first time I encountered this enormous thing, but I had pushed my luck by coming back, again, *searching* for this animal a second time. I wanted to reach for the small knife in my jeans pocket, but I didn't want any sudden movements to provoke him.

The wolf continued to circle closer now, putting a smaller distance between us with each step he took. He slunk forwards, his head hung low to the ground, his shoulders hunching in anticipation. Tess gripped my arm tighter, giving it a rough squeeze. It was now or never. We needed to make a run for it and hope beyond all odds that we were faster than the wolf and we could make it back to the car in time.

As I made my decision and was about to drag Tess along with me, the wolf glanced away sharply, taking his eyes off us and searching for something in the woods. Something we couldn't hear. We didn't dare move to regain his attention. The wolf licked his lips, closing his mouth over his gleaming white teeth and tilting his head to the side. His ears were focused towards the beaten road we had taken up the mountainside. He tensed, his claws scratching the snow beneath him as he took a reluctant step back, further away from us.

Far off in the distance I could hear what I thought was heavy paws thundering against the ground. Was that a *pack* of wolves? The thundering noise grew louder and louder as it neared, the big black wolf backing away from us into the dense part of the forest. The pounding of paws against the frozen ground was all I could hear now as the wolf took one longing glance back at us and took off through the forest.

My body thawed, and my brain came back to life. Whatever had scared away a wolf of that size was obviously a threat to us, too. I didn't have any intention of sticking around to find out what it might be.

I shook my head and turned towards Tess, relaxing my hold on the camera. *The camera! Crap! Had I not come here to take a picture?* I had been frozen in place, too afraid to move. There was no time to think on it further. I released Tess' arm and we both sprinted headlong towards the car. We threw ourselves inside, locking the doors and fumbling for our seat belts. We wasted no time flooring it back down the mountain pass, never looking back.

The next morning I woke in a daze. I found myself unable to distinguish the nightmare I had with the reality of seeing the giant wolf yesterday.

The nightmare was a vivid reenactment of the afternoon, except with a much darker ending. The eyes of the wolf in my dream were piercing and intelligent, exactly how I remembered them from yesterday. The difference was...in my dream, the wolf *had* come after me. I woke with the sun peering in through my window, laying a beam of sunlight right across my face. I must have forgotten to close the shade last night. I couldn't understand how Waffles found this enjoyable; the sunlight burned the back of my eyelids.

Realizing the sun shouldn't be so high in the sky this early, I shot upright, glancing at the clock. I had overslept. Great.

I had *just* enough time to get dressed, *quickly*, and drive to school.

I bounced out of bed and grabbed the nearest pair of jeans I had, pulling them on in a haste. I fished my grey long sleeve thermal out of the pile of clothes behind the door and tugged it on as I rushed to the bathroom. I brushed my teeth and quickly ran a comb through my unruly mess of auburn curls. A ponytail would be my safest option today; there was no time to tame this mess of curls. I glanced in the mirror to make sure I was decent enough and set off to grab my backpack off the bedroom floor. I flew down the stairs with no time to spare for breakfast without missing first period.

I raced out to the car and threw my bag onto the passenger side as I slid into the driver's seat and hit the ignition. Luckily, I had parked on the street, the unplowed driveway wasn't an issue this morning. School was only about a ten-minute drive away from my house, thankfully, or I would be getting an earful this morning.

I pulled into the student lot and slid into one of the last available spots near the end of the parking row. The students had already cleared out of the lot, the first bell must have already rung.

I ran to the entrance closest to me, careful not to slip on the ice, and threw the wide glass door open. I jogged down the hallway lined by bright red lockers, my boots squeaking against the white tile. I was anxious to see Tess again and talk about what had happened yesterday. After we had caught our breath and driven home, we hadn't had any time to catch up. My mom had insisted I spend the rest of the day on homework, and Tess had gone home early. I had sat in front of my laptop with a blank page titled "To Kill a Mockingbird—Major Themes & Character Analysis" for hours before my thoughts grew tired and sleep took me. I had tried calling Tess, but she hadn't answered.

I slowed to a walk as I approached the door to my first class, English. I ran my fingers quickly through my ponytail and straightened out my shirt. Luckily, that English essay wasn't due today. When I pulled the door open all of my classmates were already in their seats and Mr. Sampson had already started his lecture. I reached my seat in the back of the room and hung my jacket across the back of my chair. I unzipped my bag and took my books out as quietly as I could. I didn't pay much attention to Mr. Sampson's lecture, I had already read this book twice. I might not have been that great with school, but English had always been my easiest subject.

While I was supposed to be listening to Mr. Sampson, I daydreamt about the wolf from yesterday. Could it have been the same wolf that had attacked Mrs. Madden? I would need to find out some details about her attack, maybe Tess would know once they reopened the coffee shop. Had she seen anything? Where was she attacked, at home, or downtown?

The bell rang, and I packed my bag, trudging to second period. These days dragged on forever, I would rather be doing literally anything else. Second period was much the same as first, history was a boring subject, and I entirely ignored the teacher while doodling on my notebook.

Next period I would get to see Tess, and I hoped she wasn't mad at me for dragging her to the mountain landing in the first place. History passed with exaggerated slowness and I speed walked to third period and sat in my usual seat near the back of the classroom next to Tess. She wasn't there yet, and my Spanish teacher eyed me speculatively. She knew the excited look in my eyes was not due to the anticipation of her forthcoming lecture.

Out of the corner of my eye I saw Tess walk in, her presence always drawing the eye of everyone in class. She was slender and fashionable, always the one to go to when I needed clothing advice. She was part of the popular crowd, and our friendship made no sense whatsoever. During my first week at school she had seen me sitting alone in the cafeteria and had asked me to join her table, the rest was history. I didn't fit in with her other friends, but I was closer with her than any of them.

"Wow," she said in a huff, throwing herself down into the seat next to mine. "I can't believe what happened yesterday, can you?" she asked, turning her body towards mine with a smile in her eyes.

"It was out of this world, I had nightmares last night I was so freaked out. I barely got any sleep, and I just had to sit through Mr. Sampson's class listening to him drone *on* and *on*. Do you believe me now?" I asked her.

"Of course!" she replied, "I saw it with my own eyes."

"So...you're not mad at me?" I asked.

"Of course not! I agreed to go, it was my own decision. I knew it could potentially be dangerous," she replied as she pushed a piece of straight chocolate brown hair behind her ear.

Well, that made one of us. I had been so wound up with excitement over seeing a wolf in the first place, I hadn't thought we would be in any danger returning to the mountain landing. I was sure the wolf wouldn't be there again.

"I will admit, I didn't believe the eyes were human-like at first. But now that I've seen it with my own eyes, I believe you. How is that possible?" She sat for a moment, turning her body towards the front of the room as the professor took her books out, feigning attention. "Do you think that was the same wolf that attacked Mrs. Madden?"

"It might be. I mean, we've never had a wolf sighting this close to town, but I'd like to find out," I responded.

Tess nodded in agreement. "I'll see what I can find out through my coworkers at The Daily Drip during my next shift."

The bell rang, signaling the start of another boring lecture. At least Tess wasn't mad at me, and we would try to find out the details of Mrs. Madden's attack. I had to know if these two incidents were related, I was awfully suspicious that they were. Was this wolf something...supernatural? I shook my head trying to toss that idea out. That was impossible. It couldn't be, I'd been watching too much TV lately. I pulled out a notebook to sketch on and let the rest of the periods before lunch slip by.

The lunchroom was crowded as usual, with brightly decorated posters covering the walls showcasing student elections, clubs, and sports meetings. Tess and I grabbed some pizza together and sat at our regular table, one of the biggest in the far corner of the cafeteria.

The table was a combination of Tess' friends, and the few that were mine, mostly other bookworms who I had met working on group projects together. I waved to Sloane as we crossed the room and took our seats. Sloane was one of the few people who had first welcomed me to Colorado when we moved here, and we had been good friends ever since. Sloane didn't hang out with anyone outside of school all that much, she was incredibly dedicated to her studies. She was trying to get a full scholarship to Yale and was always either studying or working on extracurriculars. We were friendly, but had never had the opportunity to get that close.

"Hey, Diana, how was your weekend?" she asked, nibbling on the end of a snap pea as we sat down beside her.

Tess and I exchanged a loaded glance as she took the seat next to me, and she shook her head ever so slightly. She didn't want me to tell Sloane about the wolf, which was understandable. I'm not sure anybody else would believe us, anyway. We would keep it our little secret, for now.

"Pretty boring. Homework, lots of reading, the usual," I laughed, picking up my pizza to take a bite.

Sloane was the only friend of mine here today. The rest of the table was flooded with Tess' dance friends along with an array of other girls vying for her attention. I never spoke with them much, and Tess largely ignored them in favor of talking to me, but that didn't stop them from trying.

Sloane and I chatted about the English paper that was coming due, and Sloane's time volunteering down at the animal shelter while Tess entertained her more popular friends. Sooner than I realized, the lunch bell rang. Half of the school day had already passed, thank God. My next period was art with Tess, my favorite subject by far. It was one of the few classes that I looked forward to, even if Ms. Finch was a little bit...odd.

I quickly disposed of my tray, swallowing my last bite of pizza as I slung my backpack over my shoulder and crossed the room to the large double doors that lead to the hallway. I threw the door open, Tess close on my heels with her dance friends as we made our way to the end of the hallway where the art classroom was.

The art classroom was cornered between two long hallways. The walls were painted a bright yellow and the desks were all replaced with large round tables, each with a set of chairs. The far wall was a set of big picture windows that overlooked the back-football field. The view had to be Tess' favorite thing about art class.

I took my usual seat at the table closest to the back windows and Tess followed, throwing her bag down on the ground next to mine. Without waiting for the teacher to arrive, I gathered my art supplies from the bins on the far wall. I grabbed an array of colored pencils, chalks, and a few sheets of blank poster paper. I returned to my seat and waited with my materials for the second bell to ring.

Tess didn't bother to get any art supplies, art class wasn't her favorite subject. Come to think of it...no class was her favorite. She found it hard to get the creative juices flowing when all she could look at was the gym classes being held outside the window and half of the lacrosse team running their drills without shirts.

Ms. Finch walked in appearing disheveled, her long, frizzy, grey hair tied in a bun at the nape of her neck. Her overalls were covered in fresh wet paint, a large canvas in her hands. She set the canvas down as the bell rang and the remaining students shuffled in to find their seats.

"Hello class," she began, leaning one hand against her desk to support her weight. She looked utterly exhausted. "Today we are going to work on our senior portfolios. Sketch something unique that you haven't already tried or switch up your techniques. If you have been working with chalk, try paint. If you have been working with paint, try sketching with the colored pencils." She took a deep breath, closing her eyes and steadying herself. "I will remind you that your senior portfolios are due in a few weeks. Alright get to..." She hesitated, her eyes flashing towards the open doorway.

I followed her gaze to see what had grabbed her attention, and in the doorway stood someone tall, blond, and...handsome. He leaned against the door frame, his arms crossed over his broad chest, no backpack or books in sight. He had a smirk plastered across his face and looked as though it took all of his energy to keep from bursting into a fit of laughter at the sight of Ms. Finch frazzled at the front of the classroom. Arrogant. *Not* handsome, I decided. Arrogant.

"Nikolai, how gracious of you to join us. Why are you late?" Ms. Finch asked, the entire class turning their attention towards the newcomer.

"Nik," he corrected with a nod of his head, "—I was busy." He shrugged, scanning the room lazily.

"There are no excuses, Nik. This is not the same as your last school. Tardiness at Silver Oaks Academy is *unacceptable*. You have earned yourself a detention this Saturday," she told him. She moved around her desk and sat in the swiveling chair, her eyes still focused on his smug expression.

"The hell I did," he said, his eyes narrowing at her, "I have better things to do than sit around with you on a Saturday."

"You will be at detention. If you decide not to come, you will face expulsion. What a great way to start your first day. We all have our responsibilities, and there are no excuses. *Your* responsibility is to come to class on time, and you will face the consequences if you fail to do so. You are not above the rules," she said sternly, her eyes narrowing into a hard glare. I had never seen Ms. Finch act this harsh with a student before. She was normally sweet, and a bit of a space cadet if I were being honest. She was the type of person to search for her glasses when they were already sitting on the top of her head. What had gotten into her?

Ms. Finch's admonishment hadn't affected Nik, and without sparing her a second glance he sauntered into the room and apathetically plopped himself into a chair closest to the door.

"Everyone, meet your newest classmate, Nikolai Dragovya. He is a transfer student from Seattle," Ms. Finch said with a wave of her hand. "Get to work." She sighed as she started rifling through the mound of paperwork scattered atop her desk.

Tess turned to me, leaning in so that no one else could hear. "What's his issue?" she giggled, throwing a glance towards the new kid who had put his head down on the desk, resting it across his outstretched arm.

He had dark circles under his eyes, and his mouth hung open as he fell asleep right there on top of the table. His blond hair was slightly shaggy on top, framing his forehead. He had a sharp jaw and a strong nose. He wore a black long sleeve T-shirt and jeans, apparently unaffected by the frigid temperatures outside.

"He's kind of got that whole sexy asshole thing going on." Tess smirked as she got up to gather her supplies. I couldn't help but stare. This had to be the only guy who had the audacity to openly mouth off to a teacher in front of the entire class. And on his first day of school, no less. Tess was right, he *definitely* had an issue, he was downright rude. Why on earth would anyone transfer halfway through the school year, anyway? Graduation was only a few months away...or did he not care? He had to have been a senior to have been assigned into this class. He slept for the entire duration of class, and Ms. Finch let him. He hadn't moved at all, not even twitching an eyelid. Not that I had been looking.

The bell rang and as I prepared to return my materials to the cupboard, I glanced down at my paper to find an intricate drawing of a black wolf with piercing blue eyes staring back at me. I hadn't even realized that was what I had been sketching. It appeared as if it was jumping off the page at me.

I glanced over at Tess, and she had drawn a summery fashion dress with matching heels. She glanced at my drawing and her mouth fell open. I quickly folded the drawing away and stuffed it into the smallest pocket of my backpack. This drawing was definitely *not* going in my senior portfolio. Everyone filed out of the classroom one by one to go to their last class of the day except for Nik, who was still asleep sprawled across the art table.

Final period passed quickly, and I shuffled out of biology to meet Tess by my car. She had taken the bus this morning—I wasn't exactly a reliable morning ride when I couldn't seem to wake up when my alarm went off. That is, if I remembered to actually set it. I always made it a point to try to drive Tess home or to her shift at The Daily Drip so we could spend more time together.

I made my way out to the parking lot where all the ice had melted in the afternoon sun. It wasn't as cold as it was yesterday, but I still needed my velvet jacket to keep warm. Tess was leaning against my car as I approached, a cell phone in one hand and lip gloss in the other.

"Hurry up, I'd like to get home *before* nightfall," she joked, waiting for me to unlock the doors. We both hopped in, tossing our bags into the backseat. Tess immediately took over the radio as I pulled out of the parking lot. She put on one of her favorite pop hits stations, singing along to every song as we made our way to her house. I couldn't wait until spring when we could drive with the windows down, our hair swirling around us as the car filled with warm fresh air.

I pulled up to her house and kept the Subaru on the street as she fished her backpack out of the backseat.

"Call me tonight if there's any news?" she asked, brushing her hair aside to replace it with the strap of her bag.

"Will do, and call me if you hear anything about Mrs. Madden," I told her. "See you tomorrow."

Tess' house was close to mine, we both lived on the residential side of town nestled at the base of the mountain. My house was more modest than hers, but we were lucky to be able to afford this side of town at all with my mom being the sole income with her job at the weather station. It only took about four minutes to make the drive back to my house. Luckily the afternoon sun had melted enough of the snow on the driveway, that I still hadn't shoveled, so that I could park the Subaru there.

Mom's car wasn't home, she was probably working a later shift at the station tonight. My brother always had chess practice after school, so it was just me tonight. I grabbed my bag and headed up the stairs to my bedroom. I tossed my backpack down on the black loveseat in the corner of my room along with my winter jacket.

Waffles picked his head up from my pillow to give me a cursory glance, then went right back to napping. I wanted *badly* to go to the mountain and take pictures of the melting icicles, but I knew that it was a terrible idea to return there after the events of yesterday.

I padded back down the stairs into the living room and lit a fire in the large stone framed fireplace. I plopped myself down on one of the reclining chairs with my heavy biology book. The last thing I wanted to do was read about meiosis and mitosis, but I thought I better finish my homework before Mom got home. I had neglected it all weekend. I was a procrastinator if nothing else. Biology was my toughest subject, and it always took me more effort than the rest of my classes. I opened the book and dove in, knowing the sooner I started, the sooner it would be over with.

I hadn't realized that I had dozed off, but I woke as I heard the garage door open. The biology book fell out of my lap with a loud clap. My mom came in, shaking off the snow on the bottom of her boots and stowing her jacket in the coat closet by the front door. I had wanted to start dinner before she came home, but time had gotten away from me.

Luckily, I had read most of the grueling biology chapter. I finished the last few paragraphs before whipping up some tacos for us. On nights when she worked late, I tried to cook dinner for us, my way of helping out. I made my brother a plate and put the leftovers in the refrigerator.

I trudged back to my room and changed into my pajamas, throwing myself down on the bed. I grabbed my book and allowed myself to slip away into its tattered pages.

I was running down a steep hill filled with pink and purple flowers until I came upon ruins that were set beneath a snow-covered mountain. Old and broken buildings covered the dimly lit horizon, the only remains left were piles of rubble and a few walls that still stood. It appeared to have once been a city, left over from a past life.

I approached a wooden door that still remained standing. I rested my hand on its surface as it gave a loud groan, giving way beneath my touch. The door fell inward revealing a long dark corridor. I stepped inside and complete darkness enveloped me, there was no sign of the light from where I had just come. The door slammed shut on its own volition, and the remaining ruins began to collapse around me, stone shards flying, trapping me within.

What had remained of the lost city was reduced to wreckage as I knelt, shielding my head from the falling debris. Once the rubble *had settled I stood, surveying the remains. The corridor had been reduced to ash, but the heavy wooden door remained.*

As I turned to pass through it again, I saw a wolf out of the corner of my eye, but it wasn't like the wolf I had seen on the mountain landing a few days ago. This wolf was even larger, its eyes were fathomless black pits, there was no pupil. No iris. Its coat was white as snow, a red marking of dripping blood covering its face and eyes. It almost looked like...a sigil. The wolf growled, curling its lips back, but I couldn't see any teeth. Its mouth appeared hollow. It opened its jaw to snap at me, a big red tongue came darting towards me followed closely by big black daggers. It did have teeth, I hadn't been able to see them in the darkness of the rubble filled corridor. The teeth were black, masked in shadow.

I tried to run, but I couldn't, I was frozen in place. My brain was telling my body to move, but my legs weren't listening. No matter how hard I tried to move my feet I was stuck there. The wolf appeared to enjoy watching me struggle, a glint in its eye as it prowled forwards. A scream ripped from my throat as those big black teeth sank into my shoulder, tearing at the soft flesh there.

I woke with a start, covered in sweat, my oversized T-shirt sticking to my back. I sat upright and pushed my hair out of my face, trying to catch my breath. What an insanely vivid nightmare. I felt pain in my shoulder, but as I ran my hand over the skin, there was no mark. No indication that anything had happened at all.

I glanced at the clock to see that it was only five in the morning, and it was still dark out. With a few hours left before school I wiped away the sweaty hair that had stuck to my forehead and threw the covers off the bed, heading to the bathroom to take a long hot shower. I let the water slowly relax my muscles and lathered myself in a soothing lavender body wash.

I dressed in a pair of jeans, pairing my purple thermal with a dark blue scarf. I rolled on a pair of fluffy socks and quietly made my way downstairs, careful not to wake anyone. These nightmares had started to become an almost daily occurrence, but they had never felt so real before. I was desperate for a restful night's sleep.

Mom had left early again, leaving a note for me on the kitchen counter—she got muffins for breakfast. I opened the bag and immediately spotted a double chocolate chip, my favorite. I ate the bottom half of the muffin first, saving the top half for last. By the time I had eaten breakfast, finished the leftover dishes from the night before, and cleaned the kitchen, it was almost time to go to school. Jake had already been picked up by his carpool, so I threw my bag over my shoulder and trekked out into the snow.

It couldn't hurt to be early today, seeing as I had been making it a habit of arriving late recently. There was significantly less snow than yesterday which meant not only had it not snowed at all overnight, but the temperatures were steadily getting warmer.

I threw my bag onto the passenger's seat and made my way down the twists of streets until I pulled into the school parking lot. There were about ten cars there before me, and I pulled the Subaru into a spot as close to the front door of the school as possible. With plenty of time to spare, I aimlessly played around with different radio stations, enjoying the warm heat of the car.

I jumped when I heard someone rapping on the window. Tess' familiar face greeted me, and she continued tapping until I pressed the button and rolled the window down.

"Hey silly, we better get going or you're going to be late again," she told me, opening my door from the outside and waiting impatiently.

I glanced at the clock and realized she was right. I grabbed my bag in one hand, and my book in the other. I stepped out of the car almost slipping on what surely had to be the only patch of ice left and bracing myself against the open car door.

"Graceful, Diana," Tess deadpanned as she glanced down at her own feet. Instead of snow boots Tess had donned black booties bedazzled in silver sequins with a three-inch heel that matched her sequined top.

"We can't all be as graceful as you," I told her, closing the door and testing the small patch of melting ice with the tip of my boot. With little reassurance we made our way towards the big glass doors at the school's entrance. I struggled to stay upright, the sidewalk coated in patches of melting ice while Tess sashayed her hips back and forth in an effortless walk. I would never understand how we could be so completely opposite.

I was almost to the door when I caught a patch of black ice with the toe of my boot. My arms went flying into the air as my body fell backwards. My first instinct was to grab the closest thing to me, which coincidentally was a body. Down we went, crashing to the cold ice below. I broke my fall with one hand out behind me, my bag being crushed under my weight and my book flying into the air.

"Ouch," the body responded in a low, gruff, voice as they turned to grab my book which had landed a foot from us on the ice.

I propped myself up on my elbows and saw who it was that I had taken down with me. Nikolai Dragovya, my sleepy art classmate. He ran a hand through his tousled blond hair and turned to fix his icy blue stare at me. He tossed the book onto my lap.

"Oh my gosh, Diana, are you alright?" Tess asked, leaning down to make sure I hadn't hurt myself when I braced for the fall.

"I'm fine, Tess. Nik, I'm really sorry..." I started, heaving myself into a standing position as he did the same. He fixed the hem of his shirt, the same as yesterday, and wiped off the tiny bit of mud that now stained the side of his jeans. He had no jacket, no book bag, he didn't even look cold in the biting Colorado morning air.

Without a word, he turned on his heel and passed through the glass doors never so much as glancing back at me, or Tess.

"Rude," Tess hissed at his back, the door swinging shut behind him.

"No, it's my fault," I defended, passing through the doors myself and rubbing my squeaky boots off on the doormat.

"How did you miraculously evade me as I desperately clung for something to hold on to?" I plastered on my best fake smile as I turned towards her.

"You're the one who said I was utterly graceful"—She winked at me as we started down the hallway to first period—"and don't you forget it."

Tess and I went our separate ways to first period, but I was more distracted today than usual. Surprisingly, I couldn't wait for art class to see if Nik would be there, and if he would say anything about this morning. I'd be lying if I said he wasn't attractive...that part was obvious. He had a strong jawline, muscular shoulders, piercing blue eyes and perfect blond hair. He was cocky, arrogant, and cranky...just the type of boy I needed to stay away from. He was more Tess' type, anyway.

The rest of the day I tried my hardest to catch up on the material and pay attention to the lectures, but the whole time I had an anxious feeling in the pit of my stomach. Maybe it was the nightmares that had plagued me the last few nights, they had started to unsettle me. I wanted more than anything to return to the mountain landing today, but I knew that was out of the question. I loved going there, and having to stay away felt like a punishment. I couldn't wait for this wolf incident to blow over and I could get back to my normal routine.

The lunch bell rang, and I hurried into the cafeteria, throwing my book bag down on a chair at our usual table and getting in line for food. Tess joined me and started to tell me all about Shawn from the soccer team and how he had hit on her during math class today. I returned to my seat with my food, chewing numbly, eyes glazed over in thought. Was it a coincidence that I had seen the wolf on the mountain landing and then dreamed of a wolf attacking me? Was it my subconscious?

I noticed with a pang of sadness that my lunch buddy Sloane was absent today. I ate my lunch in silence as Tess entertained her popular friends with elaborate stories about the crazy college party she had gone to last weekend. I avidly avoided that party, not feeling comfortable going when Tess was the only one I knew. I never enjoyed being a wallflower while Tess worked the room, I'd rather stay home and read. I had been to a few college parties with Tess, but I had always felt awkward the entire time.

When the bell rang, I grabbed my bag and pushed my way through the doors, leaving Tess to follow. Instead of sitting at my regular spot near the windows, I put my bag on the table closest to the door where Nik had sat yesterday. I pulled out a drawing I had started during History class and continued working on it when Tess finally joined me.

"Why are you sitting over *here*?" she asked, her face scrunched up as she glanced around, reluctant to sit down.

"I thought I would try sitting here today, is that a problem?" I asked with a forced smile. She squinted her eyes at me suspiciously before giving in and sinking down in the seat next to mine.

"Does this have to do with *Nik*?" she asked dramatically rolling her eyes and giving my arm a playful shove.

"No, it doesn't. I thought I would see how we fair without the distraction of *football practice*." I pointed meaningfully at the back windows.

She rolled her eyes and tossed her hair. She knew I was prone to crushing on the brooding, silent type. I had never had a boyfriend in high school and had never liked anyone seriously, either. I had the occasional crush here and there, but I was quiet, not outgoing, and nobody ever approached me. I had a crush on a guy named Daniel back in New York, but once I moved, we lost touch.

Tess, on the other hand, had dated about a quarter of the football team. She had plenty of experience with boys and her crushing on someone new would be no surprise. I pulled my hair in front of my shoulders letting it hang loosely to frame my face. I could see Tess glaring at me out of the corner of her eye. The rest of the class shuffled in and took their seats, followed by Ms. Finch who was equally as disheveled as she was yesterday, wearing the same paint-stained overalls.

"You. Think. He's. Cute," Tess mouthed silently, pointing an accusatory finger in my direction. I motioned with my own finger for her to shush and we turned towards Ms. Finch as she called the class to attention.

"Today, I thought we would practice our three-dimensional buildings," she said as she settled into the chair at her desk.

"I showed you how to do this exercise last week, don't forget to put the starting point at the horizon in the middle of the page. Go ahead and get started. I will walk around to see how you are all doing and answer any questions you may have," she said with a dismissive wave of her hand. These last few days she had been so...out of it. More than usual, which was really saying something.

I glanced around the room, but there was no sign of Nik. As I went to get my supplies to start my drawing, he passed through the open doorway, sitting in the chair closest to the door again. He glanced at Ms. Finch who was busying herself with her stack of papers, she didn't scold him for being late again today. He cast his glance around the room, his eyes finally resting on Tess who sat in the chair next to him. A look of confusion crossed his face.

I returned to my chair on the other side of Tess and started the assignment. I could feel his eyes on me as I picked up my pencils and began drawing. Was he mad that I took him down with me when I slipped on the ice this morning? I had said I was sorry, which he hadn't even bothered to acknowledge. I glanced quickly at Tess who had scrawled out the beginnings of a boutique and a shoe emporium on the paper I had given her.

"What are we supposed to be doing?" he asked in a smooth voice. It sounded sensual, or decadent. Like warm honey. I could still feel his eyes on me. I paused for a moment, waiting to see if Tess would answer him, but she wasn't going to take the bait. She wanted me to fall into this trap. She was waiting for me to incriminate myself. I cleared my throat and spoke up.

"We are supposed to draw three-dimensional buildings. She taught us how to do it last week...but I don't think you were here..." I trailed off in a small voice, meeting his gaze. As if he actually planned on completing an assignment, he literally slept during class yesterday.

"I just transferred into art, I took woodshop at my last school but it wasn't working out," he said with a laugh. I could only imagine what would have gotten him kicked out of woodshop. Nailing someone's hand to a piece of wood? Accidentally cutting someone's finger off with a saw? "I think I can figure it out though," he said with a wink as he got up to gather his materials.

He *was* cute. Dammit. My face flushed involuntarily, and Tess threw me a disgusted glance. The sound of a chair scratching against the tile regained my attention as he pulled the seat away from the table and sat back down. For the rest of the art period, he paid us no attention, and as the bell was about to ring, I glanced over at what he was working on.

On his paper was an intricate scrawling of broken-down buildings with a setting sun in the distance. Ruins. The ruins from my nightmare. My mouth hung open as I continued to stare. There was a large wooden door on the building to the left, it appeared to have been chopped in half by some incredible force. I couldn't be sure, but I thought it looked like the door that had been in my dream last night.

It was well done, almost better than anything I could draw. I could feel his eyes on me again as my mouth hung open. I snapped my mouth shut and shamefully brought my eyes back to my own paper, but not before absorbing his expression. His eyebrows were raised, almost in a challenge. There was no way he could have known what I dreamed last night, so what was that face about? What is that place that he drew, and why did it look so familiar? Could it be the same place that I had dreamed of? The bell rang, and I put away my drawing and materials. When I turned back to the table to retrieve my book bag, Nikolai was gone.

On the drive home from Tess' house, I felt that same pit in the bottom of my stomach that I had been experiencing all day, but I couldn't place the feeling. As I turned onto my street, my mouth dried up and I was suddenly gasping for air. It felt as if something heavy was pressing on my chest, and it wouldn't let up. Something was wrong. Was I having a panic attack? Is this what a panic attack felt like? I threw the front door open, racing into the house and leaving my jacket and bag behind in the car.

I whirled into the foyer like a tornado and slammed the door behind me. The feeling had moved to my chest, and now my throat. It felt as if someone had their hands around my neck, squeezing relentlessly. I tried to suck air in through my nose and failed, my vision started to go blurry.

I fell to my knees in the foyer and crawled towards the side table next to the couch. I had to get to the phone, I had to call for help. My arms felt like they weighed a ton and I struggled to grab the receiver. I could feel gravity taking over as I slumped to the ground. My chest felt heavy, and my head swam. Everything was a blur, the hardwood floor cold against my cheek. *I had to get up, I had to get help.*

Was I having a heart attack? An asthma attack? I tried one last time, putting all of my effort into standing and I managed to make it onto my hands and knees. My face was hot, and my lungs felt strained as I gathered up a scream in the back of my throat. Whatever this heavy, strangling, feeling was, it wanted out.

I cried out and my head fell back, my arms flung out behind me from the force of it. I heard a loud shatter, and I collapsed down on all fours again. I took a deep steadying breath as hot tears rolled down my cheeks. *I could breathe.* It was as if the panic had been building in my chest and the scream had released all of that pent-up energy. *It's alright Diana, you're alright. It was a panic attack. Deep breaths. You are ok. Deep breaths, In and out. Everything is ok.*

I wiped the tears from my cheeks and stood, finally opening my eyes. Every light bulb in the room had shattered and lay in a pile of broken glass across the hardwood. The sliding glass door that lead out to the back porch had shattered as well, leaving a spray of glass shards across the floor and the threshold. A fire roared in the fireplace, and I could have sworn it hadn't been there when I walked in. How did all of this glass break? I heard a loud crack of thunder outside and left the broken shards of glass on the floor before me as I moved towards the back door.

I stepped over the threshold carefully, taking in heavy gulps of fresh air, my hand on my chest. I swallowed hard as I saw the storm that was brewing in the distance. Over the field in back of our house was a heavy, angry, black thunder cloud. Thin blue bolts of lightning burst down from the clouds striking the snowy ground beneath. The storm had to be only a few miles away. How had it moved so fast? Thunder cracked again in the distance as a single raindrop fell from the sky onto my cheek. It was too cold to rain...would it be turning to more snow? Or worse—ice?

Had *I* done that? Had *I* shattered the glass? Had *I* started the crackling flames in the fireplace? Tears came again, rolling silently down my cheeks as I did my best to wipe them away with the sleeve of my shirt. What had just happened? How would I explain this to my mom? To Tess? I walked across the porch and had my cell phone in hand before I was even settled down onto the deck chair.

"Hello?"

"Tess...it's Diana. We need to talk."

"What's wrong, is everything ok?" Tess asked, "did something happen?"

"Yes…" I replied, my breathing becoming shallow. I dug my fingers into the material of my jeans and closed my eyes. Where would I even start?

"I think I just had a panic attack…" I started, swallowing hard. "I came home and as soon as I pulled into the driveway I couldn't breathe, and my vision went blurry."

"Oh my gosh, Diana, are you ok? Do you need me to come over? Although that might not be possible at this exact moment—I'm on lockdown." Tess sounded worried on the other end.

"No, you don't need to come over, I'm ok. There's just one major problem…" I trailed off, biting my lip and turning my face towards the dark stormy sky.

"And what's that?"

"Well…all the glass in the living room broke. Shattered. Lightbulbs, the sliding door, everything. It's all destroyed. My mom is going to *kill* me when she sees it. There is a fire that magically appeared in the fireplace, and nobody is home. I could have *sworn* it wasn't there when I walked in, but maybe it was. I was trying to focus on *breathing.*"

I opened my eyes and could see that the storm above had started to dissipate in the distance. The warm raindrops were melting the layer of snow beneath to unveil small patches of grass in the field behind our house. The clouds turned from an angry black to a grey, and the thunder rolled off into the distance softly.

"How the heck did you do that?" Tess asked, confused.

"I don't know. I mean, I screamed. But I don't think I hit 'breaking glass' opera level octave screaming. I had all this pent-up energy I needed to just let out. Weird things are happening, Tess. I feel…different. I'm stressed, on edge. I've been having nightmares almost every night. I don't know how to explain it," I responded.

"I know what you mean," Tess started, "Something is off, I can feel it too."

I breathed a sigh of relief. Thank God Tess didn't think I was crazy. I wasn't alone in this, at least.

First, we see this giant wolf with human-like eyes. Then we hear that there was a wolf attack right in town. We have a new kid at school in the *middle* of the semester, Ms. Finch is acting entirely strange, and now I am breaking glass with my screams and having panic attacks out of nowhere. Not to mention I've been tired all the time, my dreams constantly plagued by these nightmares.

But I feel this weird pent-up energy inside me, too. I feel like I'm being tugged in two different directions. I'm dreaming of a place I've never been, with a white wolf that has a red sigil that I've never seen. And this *new kid* happens to draw this *exact* place during art class? Weird didn't even begin to cover it. Was any of this a coincidence?

"Listen, my mom isn't home yet. I am going to head to the library before I clean this mess up, can you meet me?" I asked.

"No can do, comrade. The parentals have me on strict lock down. I got a C- on my history paper and I will probably have to study for the next month straight to make up for it."

"Dammit."

I ran my nails up and down my jeans as I thought about what to do next. I had to do some research, there had to be something in the newspaper archives at the library that would give me some clues as to what was going on in this town. Maybe I had missed something when I had searched on my computer the other day. Maybe this was all a coincidence, and there was a perfectly reasonable explanation. I also wanted to do a background check on Nik, see if there was anything useful about him from his last school. It was awfully suspicious that everything turned crazy right after he came to town.

"I am going to head there anyway, I'll let you know what I find."

I stood up brushing off the back of my jeans and tossing the mess of auburn curls over my shoulder and out of my face.

"Ok, babe, let me know what you find. Everything's going to go back to normal, Diana," Tess reassured me.

"I hope so, Tess." I let out a humorless laugh.

"I know. Stay strong."

Tess hung up with a click.

The library was only about a ten-minute drive from home. I pulled onto Herring Street and parked in the first spot I could find out front. I made my way to the computer lab in the back room of the downstairs wing and settled myself into a computer chair.

I pulled up the newspaper archive directory and searched "wolf attack." When the results popped up, there were four matches. The first result was for a wolf attack back in the seventies from the Silver Oaks Local Newspaper where a woman was attacked near the town hall. It said that she was playing with her dogs in her backyard when a wolf attacked her, killing one of her dogs and wounding her. Her husband shot the wolf and upon later inspection it was determined the wolf had rabies. This one didn't fit the bill.

The next article was from the Clear Creek County Times from the nineties. A woman was riding her horse on a trail that led through the center of town when she crossed paths with a wolf. The wolf became aggressive, but the horse stood its ground, and the wolf ran off. That same wolf was later shot and killed while attacking a farm in Lawson.

The third story was from the Silver Oaks Academy School Newspaper. A man was attacked on Beacham Street while out for a walk. A witness claims to have seen an incredibly large wolf grab the man and drag him into the woods. His body was never found, and nobody was ever reported missing. A chill ran down my spine as I stared at the computer monitor. Beacham Street was right at the intersection of the long road that led to the mountain landing. It was only *minutes* away from my house.

The wolf was never found, and neither was the body. The article stated that the witness claimed the wolf was larger than a normal wolf, even bigger than a bear. The writer of the article made sure to point out witness testimony was not always reliable, likely trying to explain away the witness statement as an over exaggeration.

This could easily have been the same wolf that Tess and I had seen last weekend, the same wolf that had attacked Mrs. Madden in town. I checked the date of the article, and it was dated only a year ago. How had I never heard about this before? I didn't always read the school newspaper, but an attack happening this close to home would surely have been the talk of the town. Wouldn't this have been included in the local newspaper as well? Since the body was never found, was the investigation still open?

I hit the print button and folded the piece of paper, sliding it into the pocket of my coat. I checked the last article, which was from the Clear Creek County Times. This one was an attack right outside of Empire. No humans were hurt, and the wolf attacked a flock of sheep before being shot and killed by the farmer. Only four reports of wolf sightings in the surrounding towns in the last fifty or so years, and only one that fit the description of what Tess and I had seen in the woods.

I returned to the computer and opened a new window, searching 'giant wolf, human eyes.' The search returned no results of any worth, only fan art and poorly done Photoshop images.

Last, I opened a new tab and searched 'Nikolai Dragovya, Colorado.' No results returned. *No* results? Surely there had to be something on here, everybody left a digital footprint of some kind. He didn't have any social media? No records of him having been on a sports team at his old school? I tried typing only his name, and still no search results. No school records? Voting records? This was odd. I wish I knew what the name of the school was that he had attended before ours.

At least I had found one article of worth in the archives. Patting my jacket pocket to ensure it was safely tucked away, I shut off the computer with a tired sigh and made my way back to the Subaru.

By the time I got home, a blanket of darkness covered the town. The clouds were dark and thick, appearing as if they could swallow our little grey house whole. I had forgotten to turn the front lights on before I left, but every light inside was turned on now. I guess Mom had come home early and found out about the back door...

I parked the Subaru in the driveway and cautiously made my way to the front door. The light of the moon did little to guide me over the stone pathway. The thunderstorm had melted some of the snow but it had left behind a thick layer of black ice once the sun had set and temperatures had plummeted.

I paused at the front door, my hand on the knob. What was I going to say to her? How could I explain this? I didn't have an explanation. Even *I* didn't know what had actually happened.

I turned the knob, and the door groaned as it swung open. There, in the living room, stood my exceptionally angry mother with her arms folded. My brother lounged on the recliner with his feet up and a smug expression plastered across his face. She turned to me, her face a mask of fury.

"I was just telling Mom how I came home from lacrosse practice and found the sliding door shattered, along with every single light in the room. Did you throw a *party*?" He laughed clutching his stomach. "This place was trashed!"

"No, Jake," I started in an angry, clipped tone. "Who would have a party in the middle of the afternoon?" I turned from him to my mom whose expression was none too forgiving.

"Do you care to explain what happened here, Diana?" she asked, pushing her thick-rimmed glasses up the bridge of her nose.

What could I say? How on earth could I explain this with anything that sounded like a rational scenario? *Oh yeah, sorry, Mom. I came home and had a panic attack, screamed, and shattered all the glass in the room. Sorry about the mess. Oh yeah...I also saw a giant wolf when I ran off to have some alone time last weekend and he looked like he was human or something. I am definitely not losing my mind.*

I was guilty of leaving it without cleaning up...but I couldn't exactly drive to the hardware store and buy a new glass door, install it, and have time to make everyone dinner before she got home from work. I knew once she found the door, she would never let me leave the house again. I took the risk of sneaking off to check the library archives before she came home, knowing I would almost certainly be grounded.

"Listen...I can explain," I started, holding my hands up to stop Jake's objections.

What was I going to say? How could I possibly explain this?

"I was cleaning up the living room and found Jake's old soccer ball under the couch. I kicked it, and it flew into the glass door and shattered it," I said. I hoped it sounded remotely convincing, but Jake's smirk told me otherwise.

"...And the lights?" she asked, her arms still folded, her mouth set in a thin line.

"Well...once the back door was shattered a bird came flying in. I was chasing it around the living room...swatting at it..." I trailed off, trying to keep my face serious but I could feel a laugh bubbling up my throat. I never was any good at improvisation. Jake looked incredulous from the armchair.

"You couldn't come up with a better excuse than that?" Jake laughed, folding his arms behind his head, enjoying this all too much.

"This is none of your concern young man," my mom scolded. That was his dismissal. The only good thing about having a brother that was so much younger than me was that he was never included in the "adult" stuff. Jake got up without another word, his face still bursting with the effort of holding in his laughter, and went up to his room.

"How do you expect to pay for this?"

"*Pay* for this?" I asked. This day kept getting better and better. "I don't have a job, how could I pay for anything?"

"Maybe you will need to get one. I took the liberty of cleaning up *your* mess while you were gone, and Jake helped put up a screen so no more *birds* could get in." She narrowed her eyes. "Where did you run off to anyway leaving the house like this?"

"The library," I replied honestly. I could practically see the smoke coming out of her ears.

"I am too tired to discuss this any further. Eat some dinner and go to bed." She did look tired. Her normally perfectly quaffed hair was pulled back into a low ponytail and her shirt was disheveled and untucked. She had a hard enough time raising two teenagers alone and working crazy hours, I needed to do a better job looking after myself.

I felt a pang of guilt as I headed towards the stairs. I was old enough to be responsible, I would be going to college next year. I didn't know how to avoid a situation such as this, when I had no explanation for it in the first place. I was too tired to eat, and I hadn't had a good night's sleep since Friday. I could feel the exhaustion wearing on me.

My legs were heavy as I took each step. I changed into a T-shirt and a pair of old raggedy sweatpants. I brushed my teeth, washed my face, and pulled my hair back in a daze. I climbed into bed and closed my eyes.

What on earth was going on? I couldn't think clearly. My thoughts felt foggy and heavy, as if I was wading through quicksand to connect the dots. I felt Waffles join me and curl up beside me on top of the comforter. He snuggled in and began to purr. Despite my mind going back and forth, trying to reconcile what had happened today, I bundled myself into the covers, sleep quickly taking me for the first time in days.

Before I had gotten so much as two steps down the hallway of my English classroom, I heard my name called out and I turned, backtracking towards the school office.

"Diana Barnes, is that you?" the voice called in a thick southern accent.

I stepped over the threshold into the office, adjusting the strap on my backpack so that it wouldn't keep slipping down my shoulder.

"Yes?" I replied, searching for the voice.

"I thought that was you." Mrs. Pierce stood from behind the secretary desk. "I haven't seen you in so long. My, how you have grown into a beautiful young lady." Luckily, I hadn't had to spend much time in the front office since Freshmen year when we had first moved here. Mrs. Pierce probably remembered me as the short, awkward, student from back then. I had grown at least a few inches since, and while my hair was still frizzy at times, I had learned how to tame it into soft ringlets. When I had the time to battle it, that is.

"Thank you," I replied. "It's good to see you, Mrs. Pierce."

"I'm glad I ran into you," she said, shuffling through the papers on the desk in front of her. "Someone turned in a book with your name in it last week and I haven't had a chance to track you down…" She trailed off, checking her desk drawers.

"My Spanish book?" I asked, I had misplaced it a few weeks ago and couldn't remember where I had left it. Luckily, I shared Spanish period with Tess, so we had been sharing her book.

"Yes, dear. I must have left it in the counselor's office, give me a moment to grab it."

Mrs. Pierce shuffled off down the hallway towards the counselor's office and I turned back towards the door, hoping to catch Tess as she walked by. My next breath caught in my throat as I locked eyes with Nik sitting in one of the chairs that lined the wall by the door. His ankle was propped up on his knee, his hands clasped together in his lap, and he was staring straight at me. I quickly turned back towards the secretary desk, a blush creeping up my cheeks.

I brushed a piece of hair that had fallen into my face back over my shoulder, tapping my foot impatiently as I waited for Mrs. Pierce to return. What was taking her so long? The front office suddenly seemed especially small, and I couldn't wait to get out and head to first period.

I heard footsteps approaching from behind, but I didn't turn. On the counter before me were stacks of papers in bins, and a long, calloused hand reached over my shoulder and grabbed a paper out of the "Approved Absences" bin. Nik brushed my shoulder as he removed his hand, clearing his throat so close to me that I could feel his breath on my neck. This time I did turn, my hair falling over my shoulder again with the movement.

"Excuse me," I said, but he didn't move. He was the one who should have been saying excuse me, he was standing so close to me it would appear to be something entirely different to those walking by the open doorway.

He met my eyes before his lazy gaze traveled down, over my shoulders, my chest, hips, and eventually my feet before he raised his eyes back to mine slowly. His eyes focused on my lips before he took a step back, silently. He inclined his head ever so slightly before returning to the chair by the door, the permission slip in his hand. He crossed his legs again, his ankle resting on his knee, his eyes still on mine.

What the...

As I was about to say something to him Mrs. Pierce came down the hallway, my Spanish textbook in her hands.

"Here you go, my dear. I'm glad I was able to put my finger on it for you."

"Thank you, Mrs. Pierce, I appreciate it," I told her, grabbing the book from her and turning to leave. "Have a great day!" I called over my shoulder, not stopping to put the book in my backpack. I headed straight down the English hallway, a shiver running down my spine. Something about Nik was...unnerving.

When I walked into class Mr. Sampson eyed me as I entered the room, even though I was *sure* I wasn't late today. I had slept like a baby and woke up with plenty of time to get to first period for the first time in weeks, despite my little detour at the front office.

I took my regular seat near the back and settled into my desk while I waited. I hadn't seen my mom this morning and all I could think about was how disappointed she had been with me last night. I had no explanation for any of this, and I wasn't sure what I would say to her the next time I saw her.

I started to draw on the top of my notebook to distract myself, the guilt feeling heavy in my chest. At first, my sketch was a couple of stars intertwining, but it quickly became a moonlit sky with a large wooden door leading to a long, empty, black corridor. Huh. I hadn't even been consciously thinking about that nightmare from the other night.

"What's that?" a voice sounded from over my right shoulder. "Looks familiar, have you ever been there?" I turned to find the seat next to me occupied by none other than Nikolai Dragovya. His mouth was turned into a smirk, his eyes alight with some inside joke, I'm sure. His blond hair looked radiantly bright against the black of his leather jacket, I hadn't noticed when I had seen him earlier. Did he own anything that *wasn't* black?

"I meant to ask, is this seat taken?" His smile deepened as he leaned forwards across the desk towards me. Why was he talking to me? He hadn't even acknowledged me when I had quite literally grabbed onto him for dear life on the ice yesterday. Or when he had completely invaded my personal space in the office just now.

"I'll take that as a no..." He laughed at my lack of response. I continued to glare at him, confusion creasing my brow. He shucked his leather jacket off and hung it on the back of his chair, revealing yet another black shirt, a long-sleeved thermal that clung tightly to his body. He was tall, standing well over six feet and looked more like he was in his twenties than eighteen like the rest of us. His sharp jawline complimented his high cheekbones. He could have been cut straight out of a Calvin Klein advertisement. How annoying.

I swallowed and turned to face him.

"No," I responded in a crisp tone.

He cocked an eyebrow.

"No, this seat isn't taken, or no, you've never been there?" he said, pointing towards the worn-down door and endless dark corridor I had drawn on top of my notebook.

"No, I've never been there," I said curtly, turning back to face the front of the room. Class had to be starting any minute.

"Looks familiar to me," he responded with a shrug, tucking his pencil behind his ear.

"So, this seat *is* available? I'm surprised these other kids aren't busting down the door to sit right next to the prettiest girl in class," he said, his eyes still on me. No smirk, no sign of insincerity. I swallowed hard. I couldn't tell if he was being sarcastic or not, because there was no way anybody would think I was the prettiest girl in school. Not with Tess hanging around. Best to play it off.

"It's probably because I'm such an ice queen." I didn't turn towards him, my eyes still fixed on the chalkboard at the front of the room. "Since when are you in this class?" I asked.

"Transfer. You aren't the ice queen type. You're the soft, artistic type, aren't you? I bet you like photography, painting, and reading. That's your thing." Lucky guess. Why was he still talking to me? We sat across from each other in art yesterday and he hadn't so much as said a word. He was awfully chatty today.

"You wouldn't know anything about that would you? You're the overconfident, self-absorbed type, aren't you? I bet you like looking at yourself in the mirror, being a loner, and pretending you're too cool for school. That's your thing," I responded tersely.

"Yes, yes, and no. I don't pretend I'm too cool for school, I *am* too cool for school." He laughed. The smile on his face deepened, reaching his eyes. "That's one thing I never took you for…a firecracker," he said with a note of surprise in his tone. "You're easily set off, but I like that," he added with a wink.

"Shocking, someone I have never spoken to didn't know something about me?" I feigned surprise. "You're egotistical, and I *don't* like that," I said.

He burst into a fit of laughter and sat back in the desk resting an arm behind his head. "Definitely a live wire. Explosive. I like you, firecracker," he said as I met his eyes. He held my gaze and my breath caught in my throat. His eyes were *so damn* blue, and somehow, they were familiar. Was arrogant and blond my type? My mouth traveled to his lips which curved into a wicked smile. This is the type of boy that would ruin your life and expect you to say 'thank you.' I cleared my throat and blinked, bringing my thoughts back into focus.

He might be cocky, but he was also witty and sarcastic and some small part of me was thrilled his attention had fallen on me. I wasn't sure what I had done to deserve it. Compared to girls like Tess I was…plain, and quiet. I wasn't unattractive, but I wasn't a standout when compared to other girls at Silver Oaks. What interest could I have sparked in him? He could easily have any girl in this school, Tess included, even though she would like to pretend otherwise.

"Alright, alright, settle down now class," Mr. Sampson started as he called the class to attention. I faced forwards and pulled out a blank page in my notebook, feigning attentiveness as he began his lecture. I could feel Nik in the desk next to me as if there was a cord of electricity between us. It felt static, palpable and dangerous.

Nik crossed his arms and sat back, tilting his head against the back wall. I was overly aware of him, seeing his every movement out of the corner of my eye. I tried to engross myself in the lecture to take my mind off him. I couldn't afford this distraction. I needed to find out what the hell was going on with this wolf in town, clear the mountain landing for a safe return, and get through the rest of this school year with no more strange incidences.

No more broken glass, no more panic attacks, and no more talk of giant mutant wolves. He was the last thing I should be thinking about right now. I had the urge to overanalyze every word he had said to me and tell Tess every grueling detail later.

I pinched the bridge of my nose to try to stop myself, but my thoughts had a mind of their own. She would not be pleased that I was crushing on the bad boy with an attitude problem. The black corridor had looked familiar to him because it was the same one he had drawn in art class yesterday, did he not realize? The same ruins from my dream. But how could that be? How had we both seen it so clearly, but I had never been there? I made a mental note to ask him about it later. Nik didn't glance my way again for the remainder of class, and when the bell rang dismissing first period, he turned to me with a wink.

"See you later, firecracker."

I practically ran to third period Spanish, and to my surprise Tess was there before me, sitting in the back. I settled into my chair and took out my supplies before delving into the juicy stuff.

"Mrs. Madden is out of the hospital but still no details on the attack. She is going to have her husband running the coffee shop temporarily, which means I have to make it to my shift on time this afternoon. Do you mind dropping me off?" Tess asked.

"No problem." I smiled, she appeared to be in a good mood. This was good.

"So, what else is new besides Silver Oaks being turned *upside down?*" She laughed, crossing her legs and sitting back in her desk.

"I talked to Nik this morning," I blurted out.

"You *what*! Details, woman, details. When, where, why, how?" Tess' eyes looked as if they were about to pop out of her head. She was excited, not disappointed, another positive sign.

"This morning in English, he said he transferred into the class."

"...And...?" she prompted, clapping her hands excitedly on the desk.

"And he made a sarcastic remark about me being an artistic daydreamer and I insulted him by calling him self-absorbed."

"Well, you are an artistic daydreamer," she pointed out. "You are crushing, major, I can tell. Look at you blush!"

"I am not blushing!" I countered, even as I could feel the heat rushing to my cheeks to betray me. I had never noticed any other guy at Silver Oaks Academy. Why Nik? Why now, when my life was turning upside down?

Well, he did have model good looks and piercing blue eyes. *Piercing blue eyes. Human eyes. I had seen those eyes somewhere before. But where?* I felt a wave of recognition wash over me. Those were the same eyes that I had seen Sunday morning at the mountain landing. But those eyes, they belonged to a wolf...

It couldn't be. Things like this just didn't happen...they didn't exist. Now I was getting crazy. But...could it be? Could Nik be something...*other*? I would keep this factoid to myself for now. I could only imagine Tess' reaction at my latest theory.

"Diana, I know you. You are crushing on him. Oh boy...you're looking for trouble with this one." She whistled, rolling her eyes.

"What's that supposed to mean?" I asked.

"That he is a transfer from another school, we know zero about him, he's a weird loner with no friends here, and he's got an attitude. He could be a crazy maniac or something," she pointed out, "although...he would be a sexy maniac."

"I only think he's cute, that's all." I conceded, "Nothing wrong with that." I also thought he might be a were-wolf...pending further investigation.

"Imagine the beautiful, freckled, fair-haired children you would have." She laughed, resting her chin on her hand dreamily. I kneed her hard under the desk.

"Ow...you're no fun." She pouted, pretending to be hurt. Spanish class started, but I couldn't pay attention. The only thoughts that swam through my head were ancient ruins, long empty corridors, and piercing blue eyes with perfect blond hair.

Tess and I entered the lunchroom, putting our backpacks at our usual table and getting in line to grab food. When I returned to the table, I found Sloane and Tess already there, munching and chatting away.

"I'm only going to eat celery and chicken for lunch. I need to fit into this slinky black number by the time winter formal comes around," Tess told Sloane. Sloane pretended to nod thoughtfully, but I could tell her thoughts were elsewhere.

"If you lose any more weight, you might disappear," I told her with a meaningful glance.

"Wouldn't that be something." She laughed. The last thing I wanted to see was Tess fall back into the spiral she had been in last year, with all her rules and restrictions. Even Tess, who was seemingly perfect on the outside, could be insecure about herself. She would look amazing in that winter formal dress, no matter what.

"Where were you yesterday, Sloane, home sick?" I asked, changing the subject. Tess shot me a thankful glance from across the table. Tess wasn't open about her insecurities with anyone else, but we always had each other to lean on.

"Oh, um, yeah," she responded, taking a bite of a french fry. "I didn't feel so great..." she trailed off. That appeared to be an understatement. Her skin was pale and chalky, dark circles rimmed her eyes.

"Didn't I hear that you saw some giant wolf or something? That's what everyone's saying...you must have been hallucinating or something..." one of Tess' dance friends chimed in with a condescending air, rapping her manicured nails against the lunch table. Where had this news come from? And how had Tess not shared it with me? She was the center of gossip in this school. If this was a rumor, she had to have known.

"Oh um...I don't know. I don't want to talk about it," Sloane admitted, slumping into her seat.

"Sloane, what did you see?" I asked, turning towards her, her eyes meeting mine.

"I thought I saw a big black wolf. It was...the size of a horse or something. I was in the backyard playing with my sister and it came out from behind the trees. We both ran into the house, but by the time my mom came out, it was gone. It was probably nothing. As I said, I haven't been feeling too great." Tess and I met eyes across the table. Had she kept this from me, or had she not known?

The lunch table fell silent. I believed Sloane, and I'm sure Tess did too after what we saw last weekend, but we weren't about to admit that in front of everyone else. I would see if I could run into Sloane later and compare details about the wolf. This was something that needed to stay between us.

The rest of the lunch period passed painfully slow with the only topic of conversation being which style handbag was going to be on trend this coming spring. I couldn't imagine Tess buying another handbag. She would need to evict her parents and make their bedroom a floor to ceiling walk-in closet for all her shoes and accessories. I couldn't be less interested in talking about fashion trends, but I was thankful to Tess for changing the subject and taking the attention off Sloane. The last thing I wanted was for rumors to be spread around about her. She was my friend and Tess and I would protect her. She hadn't imagined what she'd seen, but there was nobody else that would believe that except for us.

I put my lunch tray away and quickly made my way down the hallway to art. I was anxious to see if I would get to talk to Nik again, or if he would ignore me as he did yesterday. I wondered if Tess' presence would make any difference in the matter.

Tess was close on my heels, still conversing about the do's and don'ts of fashion with someone from our lunch table. I threw my bag down onto the table closest to the door again and grabbed a chair. Tess curled her lip when she saw I was honoring the new seating arrangement and reluctantly pulled out the chair next to me.

"I forgot we switched seats so you could sit with your new *boyfriend.*" Tess laughed. I kicked her under the table and her eyes went wide.

"Hey! That's the second time today," she responded, giving me her best faux pout.

"Don't say it so loudly, someone could overhear," I whispered.

"Well, we certainly wouldn't want that," Tess said with a roll of her eyes.

"Did you know about the rumors? That people were making fun of Sloane for seeing a giant wolf?" I asked.

"No, I swear I didn't. Maybe I'm falling out of the gossip loop by spending so much time with you," she joked with a raise of her eyebrow.

"Hah, hah. I just don't want people to give her shit for it."

"I agree. Don't worry, I will talk Christine and the rest of the girls down," Tess assured me. Sloane made this the fourth wolf sighting, assuming that this was the same wolf that had attacked Mrs. Madden. It had to be the same wolf. What were the chances there was more than one giant black wolf that had wandered into Silver Oaks?

The bell rang and Nik was nowhere in sight. A substitute teacher walked in and put his briefcase down on Ms. Finch's desk.

"Ms. Finch is absent today, and I was told to have you work on your portfolios. Get to work," he said with a dismissive wave of his hand. He sat in the rolling chair at Ms. Finch's desk and propped his feet up, pulling his phone out.

"Something isn't right with Ms. Finch. She hasn't seemed right these past few days. She's been anxious and tired, and all we ever do is work on our portfolios. We haven't learned anything new," Tess commented. Something with Ms. Finch *did* appear off. She had gotten angry at Nik on Monday for being late, and she had been frazzled and disheveled all the time lately.

Tess and I collected our portfolios and returned to our table.

"Am I late?" Nik asked as he sauntered in, pausing by the door. He had his hands in his pockets, no backpack in sight. Did he not carry any books around? How did he plan on graduating in a few months if he didn't study?

The substitute merely waved a hand, motioning for him to sit. He pulled out the chair next to mine and sat, his knee bumping into mine. Our eyes met, and I quickly glanced away, but not before I saw the smirk plastered across his face. Suddenly, I felt nervous. Should I say something first? I didn't want to sit here in silence, awkwardly. I could say something first...what was the big deal? I swallowed my anxiety, determined to stop overanalyzing, and pulled a piece of art from my portfolio.

"Seeing as the bell rang a solid five minutes ago, I think it's safe to say the hallways are deserted and you know you're late," I pointed out without meeting his eyes. I uncapped a black ballpoint pen and began working on the Mandala art that I started, but never finished, a few weeks ago.

"I guess I'm lucky Ms. Finch is absent then, huh firecracker," he replied with another bump of his knee. He rested his arms on the table, leaning in towards me, and Tess coughed. I felt the urge to kick her under the table again. Hard.

"What are you working on there?" he asked, watching me intently.

"My portfolio," I answered after a long pause. "I presume you aren't interested in working on yours?" I asked, indicating the blank tabletop in front of him.

"Nah." He shook his head. "Not unless you plan on modeling for a portrait session," he laughed. So, he was just messing with me, then. He ran a long hand through his hair and met my eyes from under his thick lashes. That pang of familiarity hit me again, and I couldn't help but stare. His eyes were the precise shade of blue that I had seen on the wolf at the landing, and they were the same round, open shape. What were the chances?

Tess cleared her throat loudly and Nik broke eye contact first, giving her a look of disdain. I turned my attention towards Tess, who gave me a wide-eyed glare. I cleared my throat and drew my attention down to her portfolio piece. She had drawn the landscape at the mountain's landing. Even without much natural artistic talent, she had managed to capture the landing on a spring day; blue and purple flowers in full bloom. The scene reminded me of the wolf article that I had printed in the library and folded into my jacket pocket. I had almost forgotten about it.

I reached into the pocket of my jacket and grabbed it, unfolding it in front of me. I passed it to her without a word, and she let out a soft gasp when she saw the headline. Nik inclined his head, interested in what I had passed to her.

"You don't think..." Tess trailed off, meeting my eyes.

"I do think. This could be the same one," I told her. "We need to look into this."

Nik whipped his arm out and grabbed the article from Tess before either of us could stop him. He held the thin piece of paper in his long fingers, his eyes darkened when he saw the title.

"Where did you get this?" He turned to me, his tone serious.

"I printed it off the library computer. It's from the school newspaper. Why?" I asked.

His eyes were darting across the words, skimming the article quickly.

"You should stay away from this. I'm serious."

Why was he warning me to stay away from looking into the wolf attack? This wolf had invaded my favorite place to go, and likely attacked Mrs. Madden. I certainly wasn't going to let it go when this could be a lead into finding this thing and figuring out where it came from. And why it was here. If it's still on the loose, it could be a danger to everyone in town. Was I onto something here? Was he nervous that I would piece this all together, and did he not want me to? I could feel Tess' eyes on me as I returned to my artwork.

"What do you know about it?" I asked.

"Nothing, but this isn't the kind of stuff two young ladies such as yourselves should be searching after," he said. I glanced up and met his heavy gaze.

"Ok, dad." I replied, deadpan. Tess stifled a laugh with the back of her hand, but Nik's eyes were on me again, serious.

"Wouldn't want either of you getting hurt now, would we?"

There was a threatening tone that lingered in his words. He knew something about this. I could feel it, and I was going to get it out of him.

"I know how to be careful," I said with an exaggerated wink. Who was he to tell me what to do, anyway?

"You might not like what you find," he said, voice stern. "Be careful." His eyes turned dark again.

"I will," I replied.

He was practically a stranger—why did he care either way what happened to me or Tess? He slid the article back across the table to Tess, who grabbed it and folded it away. I was sure I would be hearing all about this later on our way to the coffee shop.

The rest of art passed in silence as we avoided conversation and worked on our portfolios. When the bell rang, Tess and I went to put our supplies away and by the time we returned to the table, Nik was gone.

When the last bell rang, I went to my locker to get my books before driving Tess to the coffee shop. I turned the knob and pulled, but it would not open. Frustrated, I mouthed the numbers as I entered them, again and again.

"Fifty-two, sixteen, seventy-nine, twenty." *Come on.* I've had this locker since sophomore year and it had never given me this much trouble before. It felt as if the world was cosmically against me this week. I tried again, and again, but it was stuck. Maybe it was jammed? I tried pushing it a few times, but nothing happened. I reached back to put my heavy bookbag on the floor behind me before trying again.

"Open, dammit," I whispered, bending down to unzip my bag. The red locker swung open with a squeak, smacking me in the back of the head.

What on earth? Did this locker just open...when I told it to? I grabbed my biology book from the locker and slammed it shut. Looking up and down the hallway to make sure nobody was watching, I tried it again.

"Open," I whispered, closing my eyes and concentrating. I heard the squeak of the door and opened my eyes to see the locker door swinging open and clanging against the wall. *I had to be imagining this.* This shit only happened in movies. I slammed the locker shut and rushed off to the parking lot to meet Tess.

I was going crazy; I *had* to be going crazy. That was the only explanation for any of this. Or was I dreaming? Had everything that happened since last weekend been a dream and I was about to wake up any minute? If this was real, if that actually happened...had that been me who had broken all the glass at home? Who had miraculously started the fire? I walked to the Subaru quickly, too anxious to be careful about slipping on the black ice in the parking lot.

"Woah, woah, woah, who peed in your cheerios?" Tess asked, leaning against the Subaru as I stormed towards her.

"Get in," I responded, hurrying over to the driver's side.

"Are you ok, Diana? You look seriously upset," Tess said.

"Get in," I repeated as I tossed my bag in the back seat and got in.

Without another word, I tore out of the parking lot towards The Daily Drip to drop Tess off. She buckled her seatbelt and held on, trying not to swing back and forth as I took each corner.

"Are you going to tell me what's wrong?" she asked in a small voice, "you took off from school like a bat out of hell."

I didn't respond. I had to get to the coffee shop first. I had to get away from school. I needed a minute to digest this and sit with my thoughts. Could I have...no. No. I couldn't even think it. But could I be something...supernatural? Could I be something...*other,* too? I had no explanation for opening the locker and no explanation for breaking the glass. There was no explanation, because this kind of stuff just *didn't* happen.

I turned onto Spring Street and pulled the Subaru into a spot on the street in front of the row of shops. I closed my eyes, taking a few deep breaths to center myself. I could feel Tess waiting nervously in the passenger's seat beside me.

"Tess, I opened the locker at school by...by telling it to. I said 'open,' and it did. I thought I was imagining it, so I tried it again...and it worked," I confessed.

"You *what?*" she asked, incredulous.

"It was jammed. I tried opening it a million times and all I did was whisper 'open,' and the damn thing did. And the broken glass, I think I did that too," I confessed, swallowing hard.

Tess was too stunned to speak at first. She looked down and I could see a million thoughts swirling behind her eyes.

"You mean...you think you might...have magic or something?" she asked, "like a witch?"

"Honestly, I don't know what it is. I don't know how to explain it. All I know is I am totally *freaked out*, and nothing makes sense anymore."

"Well, you know what we have to do, right?" she asked, meeting my eyes once more.

"Uhh…no. What do we have to do?" I asked, my grip on the steering wheel so tight my knuckles were turning white.

"We have to try to cast a spell," she replied simply, a small smile creasing the corner of her lips.

"You can't be serious…" I trailed off, shaking my head. But maybe…maybe she was right. Maybe the only way to tell what was going on with me was to *really* put it to the test.

"Yes, I am serious," she replied. "We absolutely need to see what you can do, or if this is all some kind of freaky coincidence that you're imagining. Tonight. Your place. I'll bring the candles."

"Candles?" I asked, throwing her a comical look.

"In the movies they always light some candles before they do spells. I don't make the rules." She shrugged. She started to gather her things to head into the coffee shop.

"Whatever is going on, Diana, we are going to get to the bottom of it." She gave my shoulder a reassuring squeeze before heading into The Daily Drip for her shift. Maybe she would get more information on the wolf attack from Mr. Madden that she could share with me later tonight.

I released a deep breath, realizing I could not keep this tension bottled up inside of me. I didn't want to believe any of this was real. I used to dream of the paranormal, and my friends and I used to pretend we saw ghosts and had magic when we were younger...but it was just that, pretend. None of it was real. Could there really be magic in the world? There was a piece of me that wanted to believe it, wanted it *so* badly. Could it really exist?

I felt my phone ding in my pocket, and I reached to grab it out of my jeans.

Have to work late...Jake is sleeping at a friend's. You are on your own for dinner. Love you xoxo Mom.

Perfect. That meant I wouldn't have to confront her about the glass incident from last night and face my own guilt for at least another day. That also meant that the house would be empty tonight, perfect for spell casting, if that's what we were really going to do.

Now, I just had three hours to kill.

I left the Subaru parked on the street in front of the row of shops and decided to hit up the new bakery in town to study and kill some time.

The downtown area had lots of new shops and restaurants, but still managed to stay quaint and cute without feeling overcrowded. The shops lined both sides of the street with pristine brick walkways and brand-new painted store fronts. There were tall lampposts decorated with fairy lights. It gave the whole downtown area a magical feel against the melting snow.

I walked past The Daily Drip, heading further down the street towards the bakery. *Buttercream* was decorated with a cute pink sign and a small Parisian style teal table set out front.

The inside of the bakery had a large case filled with all sorts of sweets, with seating tables on the right-hand side complete with matching decorative teal chairs. I swung the door open, and my nose filled with the sweet scent of cupcakes and cookies. It was quiet. There were only a few other patrons scattered at the tables enjoying their sweets. This would make a great study spot, and I made a mental note to tell Tess about it later.

I reached the counter and ordered a hot chocolate and a chocolate cupcake with Oreo buttercream frosting. I grabbed my treats and found a table by the big front window and settled in, taking out my biology notebook. A little self-care was exactly what I needed to take my mind off all the craziness that had been going on lately. A little alone time to re-charge and get some homework done, and some much-needed comfort food.

I took a sip of my hot chocolate, careful not to spill any on my notebook. It had a thick and rich flavor. Yup, this was going to be my new favorite place.

My first bite of the chocolate cupcake confirmed it; I was in heaven. I dove into the chapter I was behind on and took some notes, taking my time to ensure I was being neat and thorough. The cupcake was gone in no time, and so was half of my biology assignment.

I took another sip of hot chocolate, finishing the last page of the chapter, as I heard the bells on the door chime as someone entered.

I felt a bump on my knee as someone sat down in the teal chair across from me. I slowly dragged my eyes up from the page to see Nik sitting there, arms crossed, a smile plastered across his face that was becoming all too familiar. I glanced around the bakery to see that it was now completely empty save for the girl working at the counter. She sat in the corner, scrolling through her phone. I hadn't heard anyone else leave, but now we were alone.

"What are you doing here?" I asked, confused.

"I came to get a cupcake. What else would I be doing here?" he asked with a winning smile.

"I don't know. Maybe...following me?" I responded with a cocked eyebrow. "You don't seem like someone who eats cupcakes, or hangs out in a bakery," I added with a wave of my hand, indicating how out of place he looked sitting across from me.

He wore the same black leather jacket and ripped jeans he had on earlier today at school. He had black bracelets clasped at his wrists and when he leaned forwards to shuck his jacket off, I caught a glimpse of a tattoo on his upper chest. It reached up his neck and across the back of his shoulder. I hadn't noticed that he had tattoos before, but he was always wearing long-sleeves or jackets at school. He crossed his feet at the ankles and leaned back, crossing his arms again. I wondered how many other tattoos he had and where they might be. I shook my head, trying to clear that thought from my brain. I couldn't be thinking about that right now.

"Now, now, that is downright stereotypical. Just because I'm a bad boy, I can't enjoy a cupcake?" he asked, feigning offense. He clasped his chest with both his hands and gave me his best puppy dog eyes.

"So, you admit you're a bad boy?" I asked, putting down my pen in the spine of the book and closing it in front of me to hold my place.

"I admit nothing," he said with a smirk, tilting his head and sitting back again. "I was simply walking around downtown. I decided I would check this place out. It just so happened you were here too," he acknowledged with a wave of his long hand in my direction.

"Yeah…ok," I agreed skeptically. We seemed to be having a lot of perfectly calculated run-ins this week, for it only being a Wednesday.

"What are you doing here, firecracker? Studying?"

"Yes…typically people need to study in order to get good grades. Maybe you didn't get that memo seeing as I've never seen you with so much as a backpack," I pointed out with a raised eyebrow.

"You've been watching me, then." His smirk deepened.

I realized my mistake too late and felt a hot blush creep up my neck. Having a fair complexion and wearing my embarrassment plainly on my skin was going to be the absolute death of me.

"That's because I don't need to study," he continued, "I have it all up here," he tapped his forehead.

"Sure, you do…" I trailed off, opening the book again and starting to read where I had left off. I shouldn't be playing into this. I should be finishing this assignment.

"You can't possibly be this boring," he said, gesturing to the book in front of me.

"Who says I am boring?" I asked, feigning offense as he had earlier.

"Me. I say you are boring. And I am an authority on most things. What are you doing tonight, firecracker?" he asked with a smile.

Well...I did have plans tonight, but I couldn't exactly tell him that I was planning on casting spells in the living room with my BFF to see if I had some hidden magical powers.

"Nothing," I responded, biting my lip. I guess I did sound boring to an outsider. I never went out, skipped all the high school and college parties I was invited to, and mostly kept to myself and my hobbies.

His mouth fell open.

"How can you claim you aren't boring, and yet you have no plans?" he asked.

"I do have plans, actually. They just don't include you."

"Ouch, Diana. That hurt," he replied, holding his hand to his chest. How did he know my name? Had Tess said it in front of him? We had never been formally introduced before. "You should come down to Elixir tonight. A few of my friends and I are going."

Elixir. That's just perfect. Here I am, thinking maybe I have some hidden magical abilities, and the name of the new dance club in town is called *Elixir*. What were the chances?

"Elixir? On a Wednesday?" I asked.

"Why not?" He shrugged. "But don't bring Tess."

"And why not?" I asked, curiosity getting the better of me. I had no intentions of meeting him at Elixir...ever...but why did he want me alone?

"Because she's shallow, vapid, and annoying," he replied, deadpan.

"That's not very nice. She's my best friend. And you don't know her at all," I replied, internally seething. Who was he to say anything about Tess? He had never met her, let alone had a conversation with her. Why was he so *rude*?

"Which makes absolutely zero sense to me," he added with an eye roll, "what could you two possibly have in common?"

"You don't know me at all…" I pointed out, "and as I said, I already have plans tonight."

"Your loss," he replied with a shrug. I started to read my biology chapter again, but he didn't get up to leave. I could still feel his eyes on me as I read the same sentence over and over again. What was he thinking? What was his interest in me? If I was so *boring,* then why even bother? I heard the bells on the door chime again as someone else came into the bakery.

This newcomer was dressed just like Nik. He was tall, definitely over six feet, with a black leather jacket and matching black Henley shirt. He wore black jeans although his were not ripped, and his hair was gelled back to keep the curls out of his face. The stranger lingered at the door, glancing around the empty bakery until his eyes rested on us. Was this some type of bad boy uniform I didn't get the memo about? I knew almost every person in this small town, but this made for the second stranger I'd encountered this week.

"What are you doing here?" Nik asked, not taking his eyes off me. How could he see who had come in? His back was to the door…

"Oh, you know, just checking in. Making sure good ol' Kolya hasn't gotten into any trouble," he said, grabbing a teal chair and dragging it over to our table and sitting backwards on it. Kolya? Was that a nickname for Nikolai?

"You damn well know I'm always in trouble, Puck," Nik responded, giving the boy a clap on the back. These two were clearly friends. So, Nik did have friends in town after all, just none that Tess or I had ever seen before.

"Ain't that the truth," he responded with a wink. "Now where are my manners. The name's Puck, darling. You must be Diana," he said, holding his hand out to shake mine. I took it tentatively, giving it a shake. I was so confused. How did *he* know my name? My eyes slid to Nik, whose expression gave nothing away. Had they been talking about me?

"Yup, that's me," I responded slowly. "Do you go to school with us?" I asked. "I've never seen you before."

"No, love. I'm home-schooled. But I'm looking to transfer in for the end of my senior year. Trying to convince my parents I need to make more friends and add some extracurriculars to my resume, and all that." Another newcomer in only a few days. The last person our age that was new to town was...well, me. And that was almost four years ago.

"I see," I said with a smile. He also had the faint sign of tattoos peeking out beneath his jacket at his wrists. His eyes were green, these weren't the blue eyes from the mountain landing.

"Are you coming to Elixir tonight?" he asked with genuine interest, glancing between me and Nik. Had he known Nik was going to invite me?

"Sorry, I've got other plans," I replied. "I actually thought Nik was lying about having any friends to go with at all."

Puck slapped his knee as he laughed. "Oh, I like you already."

"Ha-Ha, hilarious," Nik responded as he pulled out his chair and stood. "We better get going, Puck."

"But I just got here," he responded, putting on an over-the-top pout. Nik simply blinked back at him in response.

"Well, it was nice meeting you, Diana," Puck said, giving my arm a nudge across the table. Had they been together before Nik came into the bakery? Or was Nik expecting to meet him here? Nik grabbed his jacket and headed for the door, Puck following him. He stopped with one hand on the knob before turning back.

"Let me know if you change your mind, firecracker," he said with a smirk. He and Puck disappeared down the street, leaving the doorbells ringing in their wake. He never did get a cupcake.

After finishing my biology chapter, I headed back home to make some dinner for me and Tess. I figured she would be starving after her shift, and it gave me even more to do to keep myself busy and take my mind off everything. Cooking was another creative outlet for me, and I loved losing myself in the process.

Not long after I fired up the stove, I heard the front door open, and the click of Tess' heeled boots in the foyer. Her dad must have been able to pick her up early. She came bursting into the kitchen with a duffel bag slung over her shoulder.

"I think I managed to bring all the essentials," she said as she heaved the bag onto the kitchen table and started taking out each item, one by one.

"Candles, check. Feathers, check. Lighter, check. It really is too bad we don't have a magic spell book, but thank God for google, am I right?" She laughed, throwing herself down into one of the chairs at the kitchen table.

"Well, I hope you're hungry because I can't cast any spells on an empty stomach." I laughed from the stove, giving the pot of pasta a stir.

"Always," she replied, kicking her feet up on the chair opposite from her. "So, how do we do this, anyway? You're the one who's seen all the witchy movies and stuff."

"You think I know?" I scoffed, "I was hoping you would have some ideas, seeing as this entire thing was *your* idea to begin with."

"I am as in the dark as you are," she replied.

"I have convinced myself I am losing my mind entirely and that this whole thing is one big dream that I am about to wake up from at any moment." I moved the pasta to the strainer and gave the sauce still simmering on the stove another stir.

"If you are losing your mind, then I am losing my mind too. And statistically, I just don't see that happening," she pointed out.

I gave her an exasperated look over the sink as I plated our pasta and sauce, making my way over to the table and setting the plates down. Tess kicked her feet off the chair with a sigh so I could sit down across from her.

"Your cooking is so good it *might* be enough to make me forget about all this craziness," she said around a mouth full of food. "You know how much I love fresh basil."

"No amount of pasta can make me forget about everything that's happened this week," I replied.

"Yeah…you're probably right," she conceded. "Want to hear the details I got about Mrs. Madden at work?" she asked.

"Obviously. I knew you were holding out on me," I accused as I brought another fork-full of pasta to my mouth.

"Mrs. Madden is ok, she only has some superficial wounds that needed stitching. She is back home and resting. She will return to the coffee shop next week."

"And the wolf?" I asked.

"She claims it was a big black wolf, big as a horse, with round blue eyes. Sound about right?" Sounds *exactly* right. This had to be the same wolf we had seen at the mountain landing, unless there were multiple blue-eyed, black, giant, wolves running around Silver Oaks.

"I knew it," I told Tess. "But what do we do now?"

"Your guess is as good as mine," she replied, wiping her mouth with a napkin. "Not much we can do."

"You're probably right." What did I think I was going to do with this information once we confirmed it was the same wolf? It's not as if I could go out and trap it or perform genetic experiments on it. I could ask Nik…he seemed to know more than he was letting on. I would have to ask him the next time I ran into him, which would probably be very soon if this week was any indication. Running into him when I least expected it was starting to feel like a pattern.

"What did you do to kill time while I was at The Daily Drip?"

"I checked out that new little bakery down the street from your work. It's super cute, we should go there some time," I replied, thinking of how in reality I had done *very little* studying due to an unwelcome visitor. "I also ran into Nik," I admitted as she took a large bite full of pasta.

"You waited until my mouth was full to spill those beans!" she accused, chewing furiously to try to get it down. "What! When? Where? Woman, we have talked about this. You can't just come out with something like that, I need the details!"

"I was studying at the bakery, and he came in. He sat at my table and we talked for a bit. Then his friend came in and they left," I took another bite of food to buy me some time.

"A *friend*? What did he look like? Was he cute? How old is he?" she asked excitedly as she slammed her hand on the table with each question.

"He looked like Nik. Same height, but with brown curly hair and green eyes," I told her. "He had the same bad boy thing going on, leather jacket and all. He also had a British accent."

"A *British accent*?! Oh, this is good. This is *really* good. One for you and one for me." She laughed, nudging me with her elbow.

"No...none for any of us. Nik is trouble, and so is his friend."

"What did you guys talk about, anyway? How long did he stay?" she asked, prying for more details.

"Only a few minutes until his friend showed up. He teased me about being a boring nerd, then invited me to the new dance club downtown, Elixir," I confessed.

"He *WHAT*? And you weren't going to tell me about this? Why are we not going *right now*," she asked, standing up and putting her dish in the sink excitedly.

"Because, we have more important things to attend to." I gave her a pointed look, motioning to the witchy materials she had laid out across the table. "I cannot be distracted by a cute boy right now."

"So, you admit it...*finally*. You think he's cute," she gave me a not-so-subtle wink.

"*Fine*, I admit it. I think he's cute. But that's *all*. I don't like him I just think he's cute. We don't even know anything about him, Tess. And when I went to the library, the other night to do research in the archives, I googled him. There was nothing. *Nothing*. Not a trace of a Nikolai Dragovya ever existing," I told her.

"That certainly is interesting. I would have expected an arrest record or something," she said with a laugh as she gathered her bag of magical items. "Are you done yet? I cannot wait another second before we find out if we are both absolutely losing it, or if there is something else going on here," she said as I took my last bite of pasta.

"Finished," I replied with a swallow, bringing my plate over to the sink. "I'm...nervous," I admitted.

"Don't be. Either we made it all up, or you are a witch. Either scenario would be hilarious if you ask me." I fixed her with a glare as I washed up our dishes and followed her into the living room.

"So, neither of us know what we are doing. Where do we start?" I asked, settling down on the floor across from her and crossing my legs.

"I say we start with something super simple. Like the opening spell you did on the locker," she replied, setting the candles down on the ground around us and lighting each one.

"You said you've felt as if you have pent-up energy you can't release. My theory is that it's your magic trying to work its way out," she finished lighting the candles and tossed the lighter back into her bag.

She placed the black feather between us and sat back, crossing her legs. The candles circled us on the carpet, illuminating our faces in the darkness of the living room. "Try to lift the feather," she suggested.

I closed my eyes and tried to focus on the feather and lifting it off the ground. I peeked an eye open to find the feather still sitting on the ground where Tess had laid it.

"Nothing happened," I said, peering up at Tess.

"Try harder," she insisted, placing her hands on her knees with her palms turned upwards. "Try it like this, this is how I meditate."

"And since when do you meditate?" I asked, shooting her a questioning glance.

"*Focus.*"

I mimicked her position and focused on the feather again. Instead of only thinking about the feather lifting off the ground, I imagined what it would look like floating in the air. I imagined it moving under my command, slowly drifting upwards. I peeked my eye open and checked the ground before meeting Tess' excited eyes. The feather was gone.

"Diana!" Tess exclaimed, slapping my knee and pointing upwards.

There, floating above us in the rafters of the vaulted ceiling, was the lone black feather.

"No. No way. Absolutely not," I exclaimed, rushing to stand. The feather slowly descended, floating down until it lay motionless at my feet.

"Nope." I shook my head in disbelief. "I don't believe it."

"Dude...I don't know what to tell you other than you *need* to try again. You did that!" Tess exclaimed pulling my arm down until I was seated across from her again. "You did that. Do it one more time," she pressed.

I brought my legs back underneath me and rested my palms face up. I would not close my eyes this time, I needed to see this clearly. I focused again on the feather and what it would look like floating in the air between us. Ever so slowly the feather softly lifted off the ground, stopping at our eye level. I focused on holding it there, thinking about how it looked suspended between us.

I caught Tess' eyes across from me, wide with anticipation. As I glanced away and my concentration broke the feather went up in flames, falling back to the carpet with a sizzle. Tess yelped and jumped up to get out of the way, the feather still on fire on the padded carpet between us. I jumped up to stomp on it, hoping that would suffice and put the fire out. The feather lay in a charred pile, leaving behind a rather large soot stain.

"Uh…" I started, "I don't think that was supposed to happen."

"No babe, I don't think so." Tess grabbed my arm and pulled me close, hugging me tight. "But this proves *everything* that's been happening. You. Are. Magic. You are a witch, and that means that the wolf was something *other* too." She held me tight for another minute before letting go, a look of sympathy in her eyes as she gave my arm a gentle squeeze.

I could feel a single hot tear rolling down my cheek and I moved to swipe it away. I wasn't crazy. I wasn't making it up. I wasn't imagining it. *I was magic.*

How had I not known? Why was this only manifesting now? Did it have something to do with the wolf, or with Nik coming to town? I had so many unanswered questions, and nobody to turn to for answers.

"I'm not crazy." I sighed, throwing my head back and wiping my face with relief.

"You're not crazy," Tess repeated as she rubbed my back in small circles.

"But I have no control over any of it, look what I just did to that poor feather," I pointed out. "And what I did to the glass…this could be dangerous."

"I know," Tess admitted, casting her eyes towards the floor where the burned remains of the feather lay. "Maybe with a bit of practice…"

"Yeah, maybe," I acknowledged. "Maybe I just need to practice. Somewhere without carpets, preferably," I said with a soft laugh.

"You have to admit, even though you lit that feather on fire without meaning to, it's still pretty cool." Tess grinned.

"Yeah, maybe a little," I conceded, nudging her in the side.

"Maybe we practice the easy stuff?" she offered. "You had no problem opening things, right?"

"You're right." I cast my eyes towards the front door. "Open," I whispered, picturing the door opening under my command. A second passed, and the door opened, suddenly slamming against the opposite wall with a bang. It was much more forceful than I had intended.

"See, easy." I laughed, realizing it had likely scratched the drywall or left a hole where the door handle had hit the wall. Tess and I couldn't stop laughing, bursting into a fit and collapsing onto the couch. If I ruined the house every time I tried to practice this magic, my mom would surely kill me. Or kick me out.

"Your mom is going to kill you when she sees this stain on the carpet," Tess wheezed, still clutching her stomach.

"She sure is." I grinned. "Apparently, my magic is good for one thing at least. Destroying things."

"Now can you close the door? It's freaking cold outside," Tess said, sitting back up on the couch and rubbing her hands together against the chill in the night air.

I turned my eyes back towards the door and as I was about to close it, I could see the dark silhouette of a hunched figure outside the doorway.

"What is *that*?" I asked, pointing a shaky finger.

Tess leaned forwards to get a better look, and her mouth fell open as she saw what it was that I had seen in the open doorway. I could hear the wet snapping sounds of snarling and licking as my hand dropped back to my side, my skin growing cold.

Just outside the open doorway were three enormous black wolves.

"Close the damn door!" Tess yelled, jumping up to stand on the couch. "Close it *now*!"

"*Close!*" I yelled as I pointed towards the door and leaped up from the couch, ready to slam the door shut with my body weight if necessary. The door began to swing shut under my command, but before it caught the latch it burst back open, slamming into the wall again with a thunderous crack.

On the threshold, the first wolf was attempting to squeeze its massive body through the door frame. The wolf snapped its jaws, saliva flying from its curled back lips. It was so tall and wide I wasn't sure it would even fit through the door, and for that I was thankful.

"What do we do?" I screamed, turning back to Tess in a panic. "We *cannot* let that thing get inside!"

"We need to close the door!" she yelled from her spot on the couch.

"It's not a mouse, Tess, it can still get you from up there," I pointed out as I ran towards the front entrance. I grabbed the door, narrowly avoiding the wolf's snapping teeth, and forced my body against it as hard as I could.

"I need a little help over here!"

Tess hesitated for a moment before jumping down from the couch and joining me, pushing as hard as she could against the door. We made some progress, but still couldn't get the door to close all the way. The wolf's massive head was still stuck between the door and the frame.

"Push harder!" I yelled, using my shoulder to try to get more leverage.

"I'm trying!" she exclaimed.

We pushed and pushed, but the wolf had its head firmly lodged in the door. I could hear the snarling and snapping of the other wolves, and if they joined in, we would not be able to hold the door much longer. *How on earth* were there more of them? I hadn't seen the blue-eyed wolf among these. That meant there were four giant wolves that had found their way into Silver Oaks.

"What do we do?" I panicked. "We can't hold this door forever."

Tess worried her bottom lip with her teeth but said nothing. She was thinking the same thing I was, if those other wolves pushed on the door, we were toast. Why were they outside my house? Why were they trying so hard to get in? What did they want?

My arms started to burn from the effort of pushing and I felt my grip begin to weaken. As I was about to lose my grip entirely, we heard a yelp from outside, and the door slammed shut with a final bang. Tess and I exchanged a surprised glance and together we peered through the window. What just happened? Were the wolves retreating?

Through the windowpane I could see the three wolves turning to face a figure that had come up behind them. I couldn't quite make out who it was in the dark. The silhouette was distinctly human.

"There's somebody out there!" I exclaimed. "We have to help them!"

"And what, exactly, would you like us to do? Stab the wolves to death with your three-inch pocketknife?" Tess pointed out. "We don't have any way of defending ourselves."

My head was swimming and I couldn't think. Was there anything in the house that we could use as a weapon against them? Had Mom kept Dad's old gun that he'd had before he passed away? I couldn't let that innocent person get torn apart out there by these wolves while we hid inside.

Another loud bang drew my attention back to the window. Through the glass I could see that there were now *four* wolves outside the door, the lone figure was gone. Where had they gone? Had they gotten away?

The fourth wolf leaped towards the lead wolf that had been trying to get into the house. His enormous jaw latched around the other wolf's neck, clamping down with razor-sharp teeth. The fourth wolf was the biggest of them all, and as it turned, shaking the other wolf in its grip, I caught sight of its piercing blue eyes. This must be the wolf we had seen on the mountain landing. But why were they attacking each other? What was going on? The other two wolves stood back, not wanting to get involved in the ongoing struggle, letting their leader take the brunt of the attack.

"What are they doing?" Tess asked, her eyes darting back and forth between the window and me.

"I don't know," I admitted. "It looks like that fourth wolf is attacking the leader."

"And the person?" she asked.

"I don't see him anymore..." I bit my lip.

The lead wolf yelped and fell to the ground under the weight of the larger one, pinned beneath his large paws, his jaw snapping close to his face. The other two wolves exchanged a nervous glance before taking off, running off into the nearby wooded area without looking back.

"The other two left. It's only the leader and the big one now," I said, grabbing onto Tess' arm. She rested her head against the door and closed her eyes, unable to watch.

The lead wolf struggled and snapped its teeth but wasn't able to get out from under the weight of the larger wolf. They were yipping and growling at each other, the larger wolf having firmly pinned the other one down. I took a deep breath and swallowed, glancing over at Tess who remained slumped against the door. When I brought my eyes back to the window, I couldn't believe what I was seeing.

"What the..." I trailed off in confusion, my brow furrowed.

"What?" Tess asked. "What's happening now?"

"The wolves are...gone," I replied uncertainly, "I only see two people..."

"*What* is going on in this God forsaken town?" Tess asked as she picked her head up from the door.

I gently pushed Tess aside and grabbed the door handle, flinging it open and running into the yard. I was about to get some answers, one way or another.

On the front lawn lay a slender, but muscular man who appeared to be in his mid-twenties with a scruffy beard and tanned skin. He was struggling under the other man who had him pinned to the ground with his arms. He glanced up, meeting my eyes, and I sucked in a breath through gritted teeth. The man pinning the other one to the ground was Nik, his eyes moved from me to Tess, then back again.

"What the hell is going on out here?" I asked, crossing my arms over my chest.

Nik looked up once more, his brow furrowed as if deciding something, then gave the guy a hard shove and pushed to his feet.

"Diana, get back in the house." His voice was cool against the night air as he turned back to the man who still lay half sprawled across the snow, his hands on his hips.

My mouth thinned into a hard line. "You do not tell me what to do." His eyes hardened before he closed them, taking a deep breath and letting it out through his nose. "What are you doing outside my house? And who is this guy? And where the hell did the wolves go?"

"What wolves?" he asked with a sweeping hand, glancing around and indicating there was nothing but darkness around us.

"Don't play with me. I want answers, now. There were four wolves out here, then two, and now there are only two *people*. Who the hell are you, and what is going on?" My voice was hard, and Nik's jaw tensed under the light of the moon. "Enough games. Who is this?" I asked, pointing to the man who had gotten up and now stood beside him.

"This is…an old friend of mine. He was just *leaving*," Nik replied through clenched teeth. He gave the stranger a shove, and the man gave him a hard look before walking off without a word.

"That didn't look very *friendly* to me," I pointed out. "Why are you here? Why is *he* here?"

"He was…lost. He's been around town looking for me," Nik answered.

"Bullshit. How were there giant wolves out here one minute, and then they were gone the next?" I could hear Tess scoff from behind me.

"Maybe we should go inside and talk," he offered, moving towards the front steps. I stepped into his path.

"I want answers, and I want them now. I don't want you to lie to me, I know what I saw." I turned towards the front door and let both Tess and Nik pass before closing and locking it behind me.

"Talk. Now." I pointed towards the couch and watched as Nik settled onto it, kicking his heels up on the ottoman.

"I should be the one asking questions. What were you two doing in here? Hosting a séance?" he asked with a raised brow, sweeping his arm to indicate the charred feather and lit candles spread in a circle around the living room. I could feel the blood paint my face red, embarrassed that he could see the leftover materials from our little spell casting session.

"I asked you first," I insisted, crossing my arms over my chest and blocking the doorway in case he tried to leave. His cold and hard demeanor from earlier was gone, replaced with his usual, witty, arrogant self.

"You two are exhausting," Tess groaned, bouncing into the armchair by the fireplace.

"I'll make you a deal." Nik smirked. "You tell me what you two were doing in here, and I will tell you what really happened outside."

As embarrassed as I was about this whole ordeal, that was a bargain I was willing to make. I couldn't wait one more day not knowing what was going on in this town, and how far this newly discovered magic reached.

"You first," he offered.

"Fine," I grumbled.

"Tess and I were…" I paused, worrying my bottom lip with my teeth. "We were casting spells." I don't know what I expected from him, some sort of comical reaction, or a laugh at the very least, but Nik became preternaturally still on the couch. He didn't so much as blink.

"Your turn," I pushed, moving into the room and taking the armchair across from Tess.

Nik tracked me across the room silently as he watched me settle in, pulling my knees up to my chin and curling my arms around my shins.

"Well, are you going to say something?" Tess huffed leaning forwards and moving her hand back and forth across his face as if he was in a trance.

"You were...casting spells?" he asked.

"Yes, as a matter of fact, we were," I replied defensively.

"And what would make you think that you could, or should, be casting spells?" he asked, finally coming out of his daze.

"That wasn't part of the deal, you said you would tell us what happened outside if we told you what happened in here," I pressed.

"New deal, why would you do something this stupid?" he asked, an edge creeping into his voice.

"What's stupid about it? I figured you would laugh at us and call us crazy." I shrugged.

"It is crazy, but not for the reason you're thinking. Spells are dangerous, you have no idea what you are doing." He ran a hand through his silky blond hair, which somehow still looked perfect despite the fight that had gone down outside.

"So...you believe in spells? In magic?" I asked.

"We have a lot more to discuss than I thought, it seems," he declared, running a hand down his face. "I need a drink."

"Let's jump right in, shall we? Because you obviously know a hell of a lot more than we do," Tess added.

"That's right," I tacked on, nodding my head.

"Well. Two against one." Nik smirked. "My favorite."

"Ew..." I said at the same time Tess said, "Gross."

"Let's start with why you two had the *insane* idea to do this"—he pointed at the charred feather that still rest on the carpet—"and then we will get into my half of things. Scouts honor."

"Fine," I agreed. "Tess, would you like to do the honors?"

"Hell no, this is your deal," she replied. I shot her a cold glare that had her squirming in her seat. "But I have your back, girl," she tacked on.

"Gee, thanks for the support." I rolled my eyes, stopping to gather my thoughts. Where should I start? "When I was at school earlier today, I was having a hard time opening my locker, and I felt this energy and frustration building inside of me. I said 'open' to the locker and, well, it...did," I finished. Nik gestured for me to continue.

"I tried it again, to make sure it wasn't a fluke," I added.

"You're leaving out a big part of this story," Tess said, polishing her nails off on her shirt. "Like...big."

"Thank you for the commentary, Ms. Fowler," I deadpanned with a glare. "That's why I said you should tell it."

"What are you leaving out?" Nik asked, genuine curiosity in his voice.

"Earlier this week I had an...incident," I started hesitantly. "I drove home from school and felt like I was having a panic attack. I came into the house, and I felt this pressure on my chest, I couldn't breathe. It built and built until I screamed and it sort of...exploded out of me." I could see a muscle tick in Nik's jaw as he leaned forwards, clasping his hands together as he rested his elbows on his knees.

"I shattered the glass slider and all the lights in this room, hence the make-shift door." I indicated the back wall where my mom must have called a handy-man to install a mis-matched slider to keep the room closed off until we could order a new one. "And a fire started in the fireplace that I could have *sworn* was not there when I walked in."

I sat back and let out a deep breath, relieved to have told someone else what was happening with me, besides Tess.

"Oh, and it started thundering and lightning, there was this huge storm off in the distance," I finished. "Strange for winter."

Nik remained silent, his electric blue eyes never leaving mine. Did he know what was going on with me? Did he have answers to all the questions I'd had since he came to town?

"And your wolf buddies out there," Tess started, pointing at the front door, "we saw one of them on Sunday. At Diana's mountain landing that she likes to visit for alone time."

"You make me sound so...weird," I interjected.

"Sorry babe, it is what it is," Tess offered with a shrug.

"That wasn't one of my 'wolf buddies' that you saw on Sunday," Nik replied with air quotes.

"Then who was it?" I asked, "because it was a giant black wolf that looked exactly like the ones we saw outside. It was huge, with piercing blue eyes."

Nik paused, rubbing his chin, thinking about how he wanted to answer. His eyes met mine with an almost sad expression in them, and he let out a sigh as if he knew this moment was inevitable.

"It wasn't one of those other wolves that you saw on the mountain landing. It was me." A heavy silence hung between us as none of us said anything for a long moment. Nik's eyes held mine.

"Sorry…one more time for those of us in the back…" Tess started, raising her hand up in question as if she were in class. She shot me an unbelieving glance.

"That wolf that you saw in the clearing at the mountain-top. That was me."

"What are you saying?" I asked skeptically.

"I am saying…that I am a shapeshifter," he breathed, "but not just any kind of shapeshifter. I am a…Nightshade. I am a witch."

I couldn't even formulate the words that were on the tip of my tongue. Ever since Nik arrived, everything had started to *change* and go haywire. I thought I was going insane, but everything that had happened tonight proved that I wasn't. I hadn't been imagining things, all of this was real. I had thought for a moment he might be a werewolf, but this was equally as hard to wrap my head around. I found out that I have magic tonight, did that mean that Nik was a witch just like me? Could I shapeshift too?

"I'm going to need some details…" Tess interrupted my thoughts. "I'm big on the details."

"I'm not even sure where to start," Nik replied, slowly shaking his head.

"Did you know?" I asked, my voice sounding thin and tinny in my own ears. "Did you know that I was a witch, too?"

"Yes," he answered honestly, meeting my eyes again, sympathy clear in his expression.

"Why didn't you say anything?" I knew I sounded weak and small, but I felt a sting of pain at him having kept this from me. I couldn't believe he had known…from that first time we had met. And these past few days, I had struggled to piece it all together.

"Magic doesn't develop this late…when you have magic it usually develops around eleven or twelve. When we first met, I thought maybe you might be one of the rare witches who has had magic most of their lives but cannot draw from it themselves," he mused, "but that is obviously not the case."

"I didn't have a lick of magic until I met you," I accused.

"Sometimes that can awaken it, being around another magic user," he explained with a nod of his head as if this explanation made the most sense. "Especially a powerful one."

"So, you're a powerful witch then?" I asked with a sheepish laugh.

"Very," his eyes sparked, and a smile played on his lips.

"Why didn't you tell me?" I questioned, "I think that's something I would have liked to know."

"Would you have believed me?" he asked. "If I told you that you were a witch, and that you had magic without letting you find out on your own, would you have believed me?"

I bit my bottom lip realizing he was right, I would have thought he was mad, and I would have avoided him and written him off.

"No," I admitted, "I just wish I had known. I have been completely unhinged these last few days. I could have hurt someone..."

"Magic can be extremely hard to control, especially if you don't know anything about it. I wouldn't be surprised if someone put a concealment or silencing spell on you, so that you wouldn't know, and you wouldn't find out. You are the only one with magic in your family, to your knowledge?" he asked.

"As far as I know." I shrugged. Would my mom have told me if she did? Would Jake? My father had never said anything, and there was no indication that I could remember that he might have been a magic wielder before he passed.

Nik covered his mouth with his hand, deep in thought.

"Can we go back to the wolf thing for a second? Are you telling me that Diana can turn herself into a giant wolf?" Tess asked, glancing from me to Nik.

"No, Diana can't turn into a wolf," Nik laughed. "She isn't a shape shifter like me. She isn't a Nightshade. She's a different type of witch."

"Care to elaborate?" she asked, eyes wide.

"Can't, I'm late to meet Puck at Elixir," he replied as he stood up and stretched his long arms over his head. The movement revealed a patch of toned skin just above his belt.

"You are not going anywhere. We had a deal, and I want answers." I stood as well, moving to block his way to the door.

"I did give you answers," he pointed out as he pulled his shirt back down with a saccharine smile.

"Not enough. I need more details, pal, I am totally in the dark here. I need you to explain to me what is going on." I poked him in the chest with an accusatory finger. He slowly looked down to where my finger still rested on his chest and rose his eyebrows.

"Did you just call me pal?"

"Listen, I will quite literally hold you captive until I am satisfied with the information you have given me," I replied tersely, removing my finger from his chest.

"That doesn't sound all that bad, firecracker." He winked.

"I am being serious," I insisted.

"Me too." He smirked. "Come to Elixir and I'll give you the rest of your answers."

"I already told you, I can't tonight." I shook my head.

"Yeah…" he started, glancing around at the still lit candles, the charred spot on the carpet, and the crack in the drywall where the door had slammed open. "You guys look *really* busy."

"Really busy *cleaning up*." Tess laughed from the corner chair, slapping her knee. *It wasn't that funny.*

Nik took a step closer, my hand clenching into a fist at my side. He tilted his head to the side, bringing his hand up to rest on my shoulder.

"Please come to Elixir, and I promise I will give you the rest of your answers." His voice was a soft caress. I swallowed hard against the warm look in his eyes.

"You already promised that I would get my answers if we told you what we were doing in here," I pointed out.

"Has anyone ever told you that you are entirely exhausting?" He breathed. I could smell the faint scent of cinnamon on his breath and felt a warmth pool in my stomach.

"Every. Damn. Day," Tess chimed in with another laugh.

"If I'm being honest, I cannot handle any more excitement today." I sighed. "And it's a school night."

Nik dropped his hand from my shoulder with a laugh and brushed by me, starting for the door. "And you say you aren't boring." He laughed softly. I shot daggers at his back as he grabbed the door handle.

"I'll see you tomorrow, firecracker," he said with a smile in his voice.

"And Tess," I tacked on.

"And Tess," he conceded with a sigh. Tess waved from the corner chair but didn't bother to get up.

"And you'll answer more of my questions?" I asked.

"We'll see." He grinned as he quickly slipped out the door and into the night. I turned back towards Tess, my shoulders heavy under the weight of all of this new information.

"One, I cannot believe both you and Nik are witches. Two, you are crazy for not going to Elixir with him"—Tess ticked off on her fingers—"and three, we have to clean up this mess before your mom gets home, or you will be grounded until the end of time."

"I agree with you on two of those points," I replied, blowing out the candles on the floor and moving them to the coffee table.

"And who's to say I didn't want to go?" she asked innocently. "You didn't even ask me."

"*You* just want to meet his cute friend," I accused.

"So?" She laughed, tossing her hair back. "That's not a crime."

I rolled my eyes and finished cleaning up the feather, scrubbing the carpet as best as I could with a cleaning solution. Most of the stain was gone, but I positioned the ottoman just right so that it would take weeks for Mom to find what was left of it. By then, I could blame it on Jake.

"Do you want to stay over tonight?" I asked, "It's getting late."

"Let me call the rents, I'm not sure if I'm still on lockdown from that bad grade or not."

I made my way to the kitchen to put the cleaning supplies away. By the time I made it back Tess had gotten permission from her parents to stay, and we headed up to my room to unpack everything that had happened tonight.

We changed into pajamas and got into bed, turning the lights out as I heard my mom come home downstairs, the front door shutting. I hoped she would be too tired to notice the crack in the drywall, maybe I could patch it tomorrow and she would be none the wiser.

"I can't believe you were right." Tess sighed, turning to face me in bed, grabbing a pillow to hold in her arms.

"Me neither." I laughed in the darkness, barely able to make out her face in the dim light. "I still have so many questions. What kinds of witches are there, other than shape shifters? Why was Nik on the mountain that day? What was with his bearded *friend* on the lawn? Why were they both here to begin with?"

"We have to corner him during art class tomorrow," Tess replied resolutely.

"He's in my first period now," I teased.

"You can't get these answers without me!" she pleaded, grabbing my arm. "I might not be the one with magic, but I still want to know what's going on with my best friend and her oh-so-delicious crush."

I gave her a nudge under the blankets and she laughed, squeezing my arm.

"You know I would never leave you out," I assured her. "But we won't get any more answers tonight, let's get some sleep."

The next morning Tess and I dressed in a whirlwind, having overslept *again.* We raced to school, the excitement of seeing Nik again pumping through my veins as if I'd had three cups of coffee. Tess and I parted ways for first period, and I took my regular seat in Mr. Sampson's class at the back. I waited and waited, but Nik never showed.

The day slid by as if I wading through quicksand, impossibly slow and somewhat painful. I couldn't wait to get to art class to see if Nik would show up, then. Maybe he had overslept this morning and was running late? It couldn't be a coincidence that he was absent right after everything that had happened last night.

I could barely eat my lunch and when the final bell rang I practically sprinted down the hallway to the art room, trying to keep my excitement at bay. I had so many questions I needed to ask him, so many loose ends left untied. When class came to a start and Nik was still nowhere in sight, I could feel myself deflate. Was he avoiding us after last night? I could see the same question plastered all over Tess' face.

I wished I had his number and I could text him. Where was he? My last hope was that he would show up at school tomorrow because I could *not* go the whole weekend without knowing more about being a witch, and what this meant for me.

I was too nervous to try any new magic after what had happened with the feather catching fire, so I stuck to opening and closing my locker when nobody was looking. I reveled in the feeling of energy swelling up inside me like a tidal wave and then releasing in a rush as the magic left me. That feeling of bottled-up emotions had to have been my magic trying to get out, just as Tess had said. How many others were there like us? How could I learn to control this magic, and what were its limits?

The entire drive home from school and the remainder of the afternoon was spent lost in my own thoughts. I was day-dreaming of what it might be like to move things from one place to another, or starting a fire without a match. What else could I do? There were practical uses to this magic like turning the TV on without having to get up, but what other spells was I capable of casting? Nik had said this magic could be dangerous, is that what he meant? That there was a side to this magic that I didn't even know about?

I busied myself with making dinner and cleaning up, heading up to my room early, unable to focus on any homework.

This news had turned my entire world upside down and I felt both elated and exhausted at the same time. How many times had I pretended to be a witch with my friends when I was younger, and wished that I had magic? I couldn't even count.

Were Jake and my mom like this, too? Did it run in the family? And why had it taken so long for my magic to manifest? Nik had said that being around another magic wielder could awaken my abilities, did that mean that Mom and Jake both didn't have magic? If that was the case...where did this magic come from? Had I inherited this from my dad? He had been so serious and practical, I couldn't imagine that he had been hiding a secret like this that I hadn't known about.

I was able to calm my thoughts enough to drift off, my eyes heavy. Waffles curled up on the duvet next to me, purring softly. I was moments from sleep, my thoughts filled with magic and wolves, when I heard a faint scratch on my windowsill that sent chills down my spine.

What on earth was that?

I lay flat, completely motionless, afraid I had imagined the scratching outside my window. Moments passed in silence until I heard it again, a faint scratching against the back windowsill.

Was someone out there? Or was it a tree branch moving in the wind? When I heard the noise a third time I quietly peeled back the flannel covers and padded to the window on my tiptoes. I tried my hardest not to creak any of the worn, wooden, floorboards. I carefully peeled back the curtain to peer outside.

At first I couldn't see anything except the glare of the moonlight against the window, but as I pulled the curtain back further, I could see someone crouched on the narrow piece of roof that hung over the deck. I startled, moving back from the window and letting the curtain fall back into place.

"*What are you doing?*" I hissed softly, "Are you insane? You scared the living daylights out of me."

"Are you not going to let me in?" the voice that was becoming all too familiar replied. I let out a frustrated breath before pulling the curtain aside again, Nik's face now in full view outside the window.

"How did you even know this was my room?" I pointed out in a whisper.

"Lucky guess? Open the window," Nik urged.

After a long moment of debating why this was a horrible idea I unlocked the window, sliding it open and stepping aside to allow him room to come in. This was *definitely* a horrible idea, and if my mom heard us, I would never hear the end of it. I could kiss the possibility of ever leaving the house again before graduation goodbye.

"What are you doing here?" I asked as he climbed through, his boots hitting the hardwood with a sound that made me cringe. He turned to close the window softly behind him.

"I wanted to talk to you." He shrugged, as if crawling through my window in the middle of the night was a complete-ly normal thing to do.

"And it couldn't wait until tomorrow?" I asked rubbing my eyes and shaking my head, I had been *this close* to finally quieting my restless mind and falling asleep.

"I felt bad about leaving you high and dry at school today, I know you were looking forward to seeing me." He nudged me in the side as he made his way towards the bed. The house was quiet, and his whisper rolled over my skin like silk. Somehow, it felt more intimate in the cast of the moonlight shining through the window, his face dipped in shadow. His skin felt smooth against mine as he moved past me, his jacket sleeves rolled up past his elbows.

"You have to be quiet, my mom is down the hall." I motioned with my finger over my lips. "If we wake her up, I will never see the light of day again."

"She's still mad about the whole glass incident?" He laughed softly. "How did she take the destruction of her carpet?"

"She doesn't know about that yet," I whispered, folding my arms across my chest. I had gone to sleep in an oversized shirt and shorts, only now realizing I wasn't wearing a bra. I immediately felt a wave of embarrassment roll over me, but Nik wouldn't be able to see the blush rising to my cheeks in the darkness. He walked past me and sat at the edge of my bed, taking his jacket off and making himself comfortable.

"You're not staying..." I started. His eyes roved over me, noting my T-shirt that was just long enough to cover my sleep shorts. It must have looked like I wasn't wearing pants at all. He raised an eyebrow at me in the dark.

"Just a little while, there are a few things we need to talk about." He lay back against the bed, propping himself up on his elbows and patting the bed beside him. "Come sit."

I quietly walked back to the bed and sat on the opposite end, grabbing a pillow to hold over my chest. "What was so important that you needed to crawl through my window in the middle of the night?" I asked, rubbing the sleep from my eyes again.

"I thought you wanted some answers, firecracker," he teased.

"I do. I guess I'll take what I can get," I sighed. "So, let's talk."

"There's so much you don't know. Some things would be easier if I showed you, rather than told you. It will all start to make sense eventually." He ran a hand through his silky blond hair. "I'll start at the beginning." I nodded, and he continued.

"There has always been magic in this world, as long as the histories go back. But witches don't normally live in this mortal realm."

"There's another *realm*?" I whispered.

"The witch realm, Istmere. There are three cities in Istmere, torn apart by war. Most witches fled to the mortal realm to avoid being caught in the crossfire. It was not too long ago that things in Istmere were incredibly different."

"Who were the witches fighting? Other witches?" I asked, "How long ago was this?"

"The War at Siraleth was only about fifteen years ago, but this hate, this has been brewing for far longer. The shape shifter witches, the Nightshades, were fighting the witches with storm magic, because they were extremely powerful. More powerful than the shape shifting witches could ever hope to be. And they were abusing that power. The witches without specialties, the shades, were getting caught in the crosshairs and didn't want to pick sides. Many escaped back to this realm, to avoid fighting."

"What happened to them?" I asked, "the shape shifting witches and the storm witches?"

"The shape shifting witches still live in the other realm," he replied. "You can access it from certain points across this realm. The shape shifters eventually won the war against the storm witches, and have taken the throne in Istmere."

"And the storm witches?" I pushed, already knowing what he would say before he spoke again.

"They are dead. Many fled to this realm, and many stayed to fight. It was an all-out slaughter. Those that fled to this realm were hunted down by the queen."

"And you are a shape shifting witch," I confirmed, biting my lip and casting my eyes down to my hands that were clasped tightly around the pillow in my lap, picking away at the fingernail on my thumb.

"Yes," Nik nodded, "a Nightshade."

"And you are very powerful?" I asked, bringing my eyes back up to his.

"Yes." He nodded, a soft smile on his lips. "I can also wield shadows and illusions, not something every Nightshade has the ability to do."

"What am I?" I asked, my voice small. Nik's eyes traveled to my hands where I continued to anxiously pick away at my nail, but he said nothing about it.

"Once I realized you could tap into your own magic, I thought you were one of the shades, the unspecialized witches. But now, I'm not so sure." His eyes held mine in the dark.

"What makes you not sure?" I asked, "I definitely can't shapeshift if that's what you mean."

"No, that's not what I was thinking. You are most certainly not a Nightshade. I was thinking that maybe...maybe you have...storm magic." His eyes shone brightly even in the dim lighting, and I found myself leaning towards him across the bed.

"You think that storm the other day...that when my energy kept building and needed to get out, that I...that I... did that?" I asked, confusion threatening to swallow me whole. If I was a storm witch, what did that mean for me?

"I do." He nodded somberly. "That feeling where you're about to burst from the magic filling you up...I don't feel that. I don't know any other witch who feels that. *We* control the magic, the magic doesn't control us. Stormshades have *always* had a harder time grappling with that."

"But you said all the Stormshades fled and were hunted by the queen or killed in the war. How could I be a Stormshade if that's the case?"

"Some must have slipped through the cracks," Nik replied, and a cold chill ran over my body, goosebumps breaking out across my skin. I leaned away from him, the realization suddenly weighing down on me.

"So...I'm one of the villains in this story. You aren't here to kill me, are you?" I could hear the crack in my voice as I held his gaze, unable to read his expression.

"Of course not, firecracker." He smiled, but it never reached his eyes. Under the weight of this new revelation, I wasn't sure it was genuine. "And you aren't one of the bad guys. Being a Stormshade doesn't make you inherently evil. You just need to learn to control your magic, before it controls you." He made it sound so simple, when I had only found out I had magic at all a few days ago. I felt a kernel of relief at knowing we weren't at odds, him being a Nightshade and me possibly being a Stormshade.

"But without another storm witch, how will I be able to learn to use or control this magic?" I asked.

"I may not be a storm witch, but I can help you," Nik offered.

"You would do that?" I swallowed hard. "You don't even know me…" I replied, my eyes downcast. I could feel the nail on my thumb begin to bleed and I tried my hardest to stop picking at it.

"From what I do know about you, I like you, firecracker. If it stops you from breaking glass and setting things on fire, I'm happy to help." He grinned, giving me a playful nudge, his hand warm against my cool skin.

"I appreciate that," I answered sincerely. "Where do we even start?"

"Simple magic. Looks like you've got opening and closing all set for the most part, we need to work on other things similar to that. Locking and unlocking. Moving things…but maybe we will stay away from feathers," he laughed softly.

"Did you grow up in Istmere?" I asked. I couldn't imagine what the other realm might look like, but I wanted to find out desperately. I wondered if that would ever be an option for me, given what I was.

"Yes, I grew up in Istmere. In a city called Akra, fondly referred to as The Stone City."

"Why is it called that?" I asked.

"The entire city is built into the side of a mountain, all the houses and walkways made of the same tanned stone. The only way in or out are the winding roads that lead up the mountain to the castle, then back down again."

I wondered if I would ever get to see The Stone City someday. My thoughts traveled to the other unanswered question I had, about Nik and the mountain landing the other day. "Why were you in the woods the other day, when I first saw you in your wolf form?"

"I was patrolling. Occasionally, there will be a witch in the mortal realm who wants to stir up trouble. Some other witches I know got a lead, and we were checking things out."

"In the woods?" I asked, suspicious. What trouble could a witch stir up in the middle of nowhere?

"As I said...we were patrolling. And the witches that came here last night, they won't be bothering you again. I took care of that."

"What did you do to them?"

"I took care of it," he repeated, his mouth hard. "They probably smelled your scent and came to investigate. Since you've started using magic, your scent has...changed."

"You can smell me?" I asked, sniffing the hair at my shoulder inconspicuously.

"In my wolf form, yes." He smiled. "And you smell just fine, firecracker."

"That doesn't sound like a rave review," I pointed out, but Nik only rolled his eyes and leaned back again, propping himself up on an elbow.

"So, when do we start practicing?" I couldn't wait to have someone show me how to use my magic and control it, to test the limits and find out what I could do.

"This weekend?" He offered with a shrug. "No time like the present. Plus, if you don't get a handle on it soon your mom might need an entirely new house." He laughed.

"Who else do you know here that is a witch?" I asked.

"Other than Puck, nobody. Just acquaintances, Puck is my only friend in this realm," he responded.

"Puck is a witch?" I hadn't imagined he was wrapped up in all of this, too.

"A shade." Nik nodded in confirmation. "Not a Nightshade or a Stormshade, but still pretty damn powerful if you ask me."

"This is...a lot to take in. My head is spinning." Only yesterday I thought I was living a perfectly normal life. Perfectly ordinary, possibly a touch delusional. Now I found out that not only was the new guy at school a witch, but I was too, and there was another realm with cities full of witches which I had possibly descended from.

"Is my family the same as me?" I asked.

"That's the thing," Nik mused, "one parent has to be a witch in order to pass the magic on, but it isn't something we typically hide. We are *proud* to be magic wielders, if one of your parents was a witch, I would think they would have told you. And if you were around another magic wielder all your life, your powers would likely have awakened much earlier. Unless they were a storm witch, and they were hiding who they were themselves. If you or the witch in your family was spellbound and unable to access their powers, that could explain why you didn't manifest until I came to town."

"My mom and I weren't close until my dad passed. Maybe it was my dad. He was always busy working, I can't picture it." I sighed. Was one of my parents spellbound? Which one of them was hiding this big of a secret?

"As I said, it usually manifests much earlier. I think someone spelled you, and I'd really like to know who."

"Yeah, you and me both," I huffed, laying back against the pillows. My eyes were starting to feel heavy again.

"Can I ever visit the other realm?" I asked, a little sleepily.

"I don't see why not." He shrugged. "The capitol city is in ruin, it's been destroyed and deserted since the war. Then there's Prins, it's a small city, that's the best place to go. Best ale you'll ever have. I'm from Akra where the queen resides, maybe we avoid that city altogether for now."

"Does she still hate Stormshades?" I asked, closing my eyes.

"Yes, and she's the most powerful Nightshade I've ever seen."

"I'd love to see one of the cities someday," I replied wistfully, picturing it behind my closed eyelids.

"Then someday I'll take you." Nik had a smile in his voice. The bed moved as he quietly got up and pulled his leather jacket back on, my eyes popping back open.

"Where are you going?" I asked, "I have more questions."

"I'm sure you do, but for now you need to get some sleep."

"How do you expect me to sleep after all this?" I waved my hand in the air. "My whole world has been turned upside down in a matter of one day."

"It's a lot to take in, but you'll adjust. You already are, whether you know it or not. When my magic first manifested, I was certainly *not* able to close a door on the head of a giant wolf," he laughed.

"Yeah...that was pretty epic." I smiled.

"I'll see you this weekend for magic training, firecracker." He gave my leg a squeeze before heading towards the window.

"You won't be in school tomorrow?" I asked. I could hear the disappointment in my own voice and wanted to smack myself. I hoped he hadn't heard it too.

"No, I've got a few things I need to take care of," he replied. He gently pulled the window open and stepped out onto the roof, turning back to face me.

"Don't miss me too much." He winked.

"You are an incorrigible flirt," I told him, rising from the bed to close the window after him.

"Only for you, firecracker," he whispered before turning and jumping off the rooftop.

I grabbed the windowsill with a gasp, leaning out to see where he had landed. The yard was dark with only a sliver of moonlight to see by. When I squinted, I could just make out the silhouette of an enormous black wolf retreating into the woods.

When my alarm went off on Saturday morning I had already been lying in bed awake. Thoughts of what it would be like to learn more about my magic were swimming through my head.

Friday had slipped by in a blur, and as promised Nik wasn't in class again. My grades would seriously start slipping if I wasn't able to regain focus. This entire week I had been distracted. I had barely done any of my homework, and I could feel myself starting to truly fall behind in my studies for the first time.

In third period I had told Tess all about Nik's late-night visit and how he had snuck through my window. I told her about the witch realm, and how Nik thought that I might be a Stormshade. Tess insisted on coming with us this weekend to train with my magic, but I feared it was too dangerous, having proven I had little control over it. I had promised her that I was all hers Saturday night, I even conceded to checking out Elixir with her for battle of the bands.

I spent the morning ensuring all of my chores were done; my clothes were folded, the bathroom was clean, and all the dishes were done. The last thing I wanted was for my mom to stop me from my weekend plans because there were things she needed me to do around the house. I had told her I was going to Tess' house for the afternoon, but where Nik and I were truly going remained a mystery to me.

I took an extra-long time getting ready, crafting my curls into perfect ringlets down my back, and even putting on a bit of makeup. Would he be taking me to the mountain landing? It seemed as good a place as any to practice magic, nobody else knew about it besides him and Tess.

As I finished coating my lips in a pink gloss, I heard my phone chime from across the room.

I'm outside the text read from an unknown number. I peeled back the bedroom curtain to see a black BMW parked on the street with dark tinted windows, idling at the curb. I hurried to grab my blue velvet coat and scarf. The last thing I needed was for my mom to see the car outside and for my cover to be blown.

I rushed downstairs and sprinted out into the melting snow. The sun was warm in the sky, and I loved the feeling of it against my fair skin. It was a beautiful day, everything covered in a thin layer of the thawing snow.

I opened the car door and hopped in, anxious to put some distance between me and the house. I had texted Tess the plan so that she knew to cover for me if needed. Nik had one hand on the steering wheel, the other resting on the center console. He was dressed in his usual dark jeans and black leather jacket, but he had added a more weather appropriate pair of winter boots.

"How do you have such a nice car?" I asked, turning towards him.

"Good morning to you too." He smirked. "I have my ways."

He shifted the car into gear, and we took off down the street, safely away from the prying eyes of Mom and Jake.

"Of course, you do," I laughed. "How did you get my phone number?"

"Tess," he replied with a shrug.

Tess? How could she give him my number and not tell me? *When*? She sure was slick, we would be having words when we met up for battle of the bands later tonight.

"Are you going to tell me where we are going?" I asked as I buckled myself in. Nik didn't appear to care about the speed limit in this residential part of town.

"It's a surprise," he replied, turning left towards the downtown business district. He wasn't taking me to the mountain landing, then. That was the opposite direction. I hadn't been back there since last weekend, but now that I knew the wolf and Nik were one and the same, I had no reason to fear anymore. Except...if one of his other wolf friends showed up, that is. They didn't seem nearly as friendly, but he had said that he 'took care of it.' Whatever that meant.

We drove past the row of shops and continued on down the road towards the other side of town. It had been a long time since I had been down this way, and I didn't remember there ever being anything on this side of town. It was mostly deserted.

I turned to Nik with a raised eyebrow, but he kept his eyes on the road. We drove for another five minutes in silence while I looked out the window, snow dusted pine trees lining the road as we sped by. We were headed towards the base of another, smaller, mountain. Just as I thought we were going to drive up the dirt mountain road Nik took a sharp right, parking the car at the end of the street where the paved road met the dirt.

"We go on foot from here," he announced, jumping out of the car.

"Is it far?" I asked.

"No, it isn't far," he replied, coming around and opening my door for me. A tingle of surprise ran through me, he was being awfully gentlemanly today. There was a narrow-beaten path that twisted between the mountain and the pine trees and we started down it, the snow crunching beneath our boots. Nik's hair looked shockingly bright in the reflection of the sun off the snow. As if he could sense my eyes on him, he ran a hand through it restlessly. Was he nervous?

Several minutes passed before I could spot a clearing ahead, a small frozen pond off to the left side. The view was beautiful, the snowy mountain in the backg023round with blue spruces reaching towards the sky. In the summer I bet this meadow would be filled with beautiful wildflowers. Nik came to a stop in the middle of the clearing, spreading his arms wide.

"Here we are," he said with an incline of his head.

"What is this place?" I asked, stuffing my cold hands into my jacket pockets.

"This is one of the places where you can access Istmere, the witch realm," he replied. "There are lots of portals in different spots across the country, but this is one of them."

"Where is the portal?" I asked, glancing around and seeing nothing but the mountain, the trees, and the melting snow.

"It isn't a physical thing," he explained. "There is a spell that accesses the portal to the other realm. There are specific places where the spell will work, usually spots with lots of residual magical energy."

"And this is one of those spots?" I asked.

"Yes," he confirmed. "I figured this would be a good place to practice. It can be easier to call on your magic in places that already have lingering magical energy."

"Will it also be easier to control, then?" I bit my lower lip as he nodded. I was more worried about being able to control my magic than anything else. I was fairly confident it would respond as soon as I called on it. I didn't want to experience that same feeling that I had the other day, where the magic built up inside of me to the point where it burst out chaotically, shattering everything around me. "Will we be going to the witch realm?" I asked.

"No," he replied, shaking his head. "I do not recommend an unpracticed witch simply waltz into Istmere. You'll need to be able to protect yourself if you're ever going to go there."

"Protect myself with magic?" I questioned.

"Yes, or with a sword or dagger." He laughed as my eyes went wide.

"A *sword* or *dagger*?"

Nik nodded. "Istmere is like the Old World. There are no cars or technology, everything is run by magic. Gunpowder and ash prevent magic from working. You can't cast a spell with gunpowder residue on your hands. And if you wanted to trap a witch without access to their powers, an ash circle or cage is a good way to do it."

I couldn't imagine a place like that. Did they know the mortal realm existed? How big was the other realm, anyway? Did they train in magic from a young age? My head was spinning with a million unanswered questions.

"You grew up there, right? Why did you come here?" I asked.

"My family came here a few years back, but I had initially stayed back in Akra. It wasn't my decision," he replied softly. It was clear he hadn't wanted to leave Akra and follow his family to this realm.

"Let's get started. I can tell you have a million more questions, but if we answer them now, the sun will set before I've even had a chance to teach you anything. We'll have more time for questions later."

He shucked off his leather jacket and threw it down onto the snow, leaving him in only a plain black T-shirt. I could see the swirling designs of the tattoos peeking out at his neck and biceps. What were they designs of? I thought about what it would feel like to run my finger down along them, my hands running under his shirt and exploring the hard muscles there.

A spark lit his eyes as if he could tell the direction my thoughts had taken.

I cleared my throat and my eyes snapped back to his. "Aren't you cold?" I asked, gesturing to his overall lack of winter clothing.

"No," he replied, a wicked gleam lighting his eyes. He lifted his hand, and moments later a ball of flame rested within his palm. My jaw dropped as I watched the orange flames lick against his skin, never touching it. Never burning him. It was as if the flames were hovering right above the surface.

"How did you do that?" I asked, astonished. I hadn't even known this type of magic was possible.

"All witches have *some* control over the elements. Earth, water, air, and fire. Nightshades have lesser abilities than a Stormshade would, but we can still do things like this." He nodded towards the flames. "It keeps me warm."

"I don't think I can do that." I shook my head.

"You already have," he replied, extinguishing the flames by closing his hand. "You started a fire when your magic detonated, and you set that poor little feather on fire too. You may not have meant to do it, but you've already done it. You've used your fire magic, now we just need to *control* it."

He was right. I didn't mean to use fire either time, but I had. But could I control it the way he did, in the palm of his hand? Wouldn't it burn me?

"I thought you said we would start with simple magic?" I asked, nervous.

"This is simple magic," he explained. "Moving things from one place to another, unlocking things, starting fires. They don't require actual spells."

"Actual spells?" I asked, confused.

"Yes, spoken spells. Something more complicated such as accessing the portal to Istmere, for instance, requires a spoken spell."

"Where do those spells come from?" I asked.

"From other witches who have taught you. Or from grimoires, a family's book of shadows. It's passed down from generation to generation. I learned from my mother, who learned from her mother."

"Do I have a grimoire?" I couldn't imagine anyone in my family having written down their more complex spells to pass on.

"You must." He shrugged. "Every family does. The question is, who in your family is the witch?" he grinned.

"Who, indeed," I mused. "I can't exactly come out and ask my mother..." Was it hidden in my house somewhere? Had I ever come across a book I wasn't allowed to read, or a book that had been buried deep in the attic? If other witches learned from their grimoires, how was I supposed to learn when I didn't have one? I could feel my face fall, my eyes dropping to the snow. Would I ever be able to use *and* control this energy stirring inside of me?

"As a Stormshade, you'll be able to do a hell of a lot more than this. I'll teach you." His voice pulled me from my thoughts. If Nik taught me, would I be able to catch up? Would I ever have enough control to visit Istmere?

"Let's try this," he started, taking a step closer to me and opening his palm to reveal a ball of flame again. "You're going to focus on the palm of your hand, and the feeling of something in it. Picture what it would look like and feel like to have the flames against your skin. They won't burn you if you don't let them. Imagine they hover right above the surface. Simply *wanting* the ball of flame won't conjure it, you have to actually picture it, *feel it*." He took a deep breath. "Imagine that the flame belongs to you, that you control it. You decide how big it is, how hot it burns. Feel the energy deep in your core and channel it into your palm. Remember to breathe deeply."

I opened my hand before me tentatively, feeling the cold chill in the air against my bare skin. Nik looked so warm and confident across from me, conviction in his eyes as I took a deep breath and focused on the palm of my hand.

I did as he said, imagining the flame and the feeling of its heat. Imagining it was under my complete control. Several moments passed and nothing happened.

"Keep trying," he encouraged. "Imagine the well of energy deep in your stomach. Channel that energy to do your bidding." I nodded before turning back to my hand to try again.

I could feel the energy just outside my grasp. I focused first on drawing that energy out of my core, out to my fingertips, and I could feel the magic as it moved inside of me. The energy passed from my core up through my chest, down my arm and towards my fingers. As I opened my eyes a small ball of flame lit in the center of my palm, red flames licking at the tips of my fingers. I pictured the flame burning bigger, hotter, lapping against my skin and warming me from the inside out. My eyes snapped up to Nik's, and he was watching me with a deep intensity, a seductive smile on his lips.

"That's it," he encouraged in a low voice.

I had done it. *I had really done it.* I had a ball of flame in the palm of my hand, and it was *mine*. I controlled it, not the other way around. I could feel the well of energy as it spilled into my fingers and then back into my core as if it were on an endless loop. All I needed to do was focus and keep my concentration, not letting my emotions control me. The lingering magical energy of the meadow didn't hurt either.

"Now throw it at me," he said from his spot across the meadow.

"Throw it at you?" I muttered back, confused.

"Yes, throw it at me," he insisted.

I pictured the ball of flame leaving my palm and rushing towards him. Just as I could feel the added burst of energy pull from my core, the flame shot out across the space between us and he caught it in the palm of his hand. The flame was gone from my fingers, but I could still feel the warmth it had left behind.

"Very good," he praised. "You make an excellent student, firecracker."

A smile split across my face. I had actually done it, I had created fire and *controlled* it. "I must have a very good teacher," I teased, watching as Nik extinguished my flame in the palm of his hand.

"A good teacher?" He mused, "There are several things I'd like to teach you."

"About magic?" I asked, my breath catching in my throat.

"And other things," he breathed, his gaze heated.

Once again, I found myself imagining what it would feel like to have my hands on his skin. He took a few steps towards me. He was so close to me now that I could feel the heat rolling off his body. My eyes met his as he took another step, closing the final distance between us. His hand came up to cup my cheek, my skin hot under his touch.

"That blush is intoxicating," he murmured, brushing a lock of curls behind my ear, "especially when it's for me."

My eyes locked with his as I felt the faint touch of his fingers tracing my jaw, and when they stopped, he ran his thumb across my bottom lip. Was he about to kiss me? Did I want him to?

His gaze was smoldering, threatening to melt me right where I stood. My eyes moved to his full lips, and I swallowed hard, feeling the nervous tension pressing against my chest. He cocked his head to the side with a wicked grin.

Just as I was about to lean in my phone rang, startling me.

"Seven devils," Nik swore under his breath, dropping his hand back to his side.

I hastily fished my phone out of my back pocket and answered, turning away. The moment had passed, *what terrible timing.*

"Hello?" I answered, a note of exasperation in my voice.

"Girl, I have texted you like six times, where have you been?" Tess asked on the other end.

"I'm with Nik," I replied, "not that you didn't already know that."

"It's getting late," she said, "I didn't think you'd still be together. I wanted you to ask your little boy toy and his friend to come with us to battle of the bands tonight."

"I thought you wanted me all to yourself tonight?"

"I decided I wouldn't mind meeting this mysterious and handsome friend of Nik's," she laughed. "Are you going to ask him, or not?"

"Sure Tess," I conceded, "I will ask."

"Good," I could hear her smile through the phone. "You better get your butt back here to get ready, it's almost dark out."

I hadn't realized the time but Tess was right, we had been practicing magic the entire day but it had felt as if only moments had passed. The sun was about to set over the mountaintops and dusk had enveloped the base of the mountain.

"Got it, can I come there to get ready? My mom thinks I'm at your house, remember."

"Of course, girl, I got you. See you soon," Tess replied before hanging up.

"Getting ready?" Nik asked with a raised eyebrow. "Special plans?"

"Tess and I are going to battle of the bands tonight at Elixir." I kept my eyes on my boots. "Do you and Puck want to come?"

"Battle of the bands," he mused, taking a long time to answer. My eyes raised to his when I was sure he was about to laugh at me. "Sure."

"Can you drop me off at Tess'?" I asked, relief flooding me. That was easier than I thought.

"Sure, let's get out of here, firecracker. You did really well today."

"Will I be able to control my magic like this outside of this place? You had said the magical tether here made it easier, but I'm worried about using my magic away from here."

"It will be easier, now that you know how it should feel when the energy comes forth and releases. It should be much simpler to replicate," he assured me as we started our walk back towards the car.

I couldn't wait to tell Tess what had happened today, about how I had created fire and controlled it. How I was able to throw it like a weapon, and how Nik and I had almost kissed before she had so rudely interrupted.

The walk back to the car was mostly silent. I could still feel the electricity buzzing between us and the heat from our hands nearly touching as we walked side by side. By the time we made it to the car the sun had completely set and the only light in the sky was the faint glow of moonlight against the snow. As I buckled myself in and we started off towards Tess' place, I caught a dark silhouette out of the corner of my eye. I could see the glow of three pairs of bright eyes in the darkness, watching us.

Nik hadn't noticed the pairs of eyes as they watched us pull out and head back onto the road, he had only asked for directions to Tess' house. We made our way back through downtown and over to the residential district. What were those eyes I had seen? Were those the wolves from my house the other night, the ones who had smelled my magic on me? What were they doing watching us? Nik dropped me off in Tess' driveway, planning to go pick up Puck and meet us at Elixir in an hour.

I had never been to a nightclub before and I was nervous, not knowing what to expect. I was going to rely on Tess to dress me for the experience since I didn't have any outfits that would suit the occasion. I would have to borrow something of Tess' anyway since I couldn't go home beforehand. The last thing I wanted was for my mom to tell me I had been out with Tess all day and had to stay in tonight to work on the homework that I had been neglecting.

Tess' dad answered the door and let me in, and I sprinted up the flight of stairs to the second story and down the long hallway to her bedroom. Her door was closed, and I opened it without knocking, slipping inside excitedly.

"About time!" she exclaimed from the bed, throwing her laptop down and scooting to the edge. "I need you to tell me *everything.*"

"I will, but I promised Nik we would meet him in an hour."

"And Puck?" she asked.

"He will be there," I assured her. "I have no idea what to wear, I'm going to need your help."

"My area of expertise." She smirked, hopping off the bed and moving over to the makeup vanity. "Sit," she instructed as she started pulling out makeup palettes and placing them on the vanity.

As she did my makeup, I told her all about how I had controlled my magic today and hadn't felt out of control. I told her about the portal to Istmere, and how the meadow Nik had taken me to acts as a magical tether. When I told her about how Nik and I had almost kissed, she just about fainted.

"I'm sorry girl, I definitely would not have called and interrupted if I had known you two were *busy.*" She laughed, applying blush to the high point of my cheekbones. What had that moment been? Had it only been the magic between us, the buzzing residual energy? Had he wanted to kiss me? I couldn't deny it, I had wanted to kiss him.

"If you don't stop blushing, I won't know where to stop with this," Tess laughed, indicating the pink blush she held in her hands. I sighed and closed my eyes, letting her finish my mini makeover.

Nik had said if we could replicate what I did today with my elemental magic, we could try some storm magic next. Then we could find out if I was truly a Stormshade or not. Storm magic was harder to control according to Nik, and I was nervous to try. Tess finished with a flick of her makeup brush and I turned to the mirror to admire her work.

My auburn ringlets remained loose around my face and cascaded down my back. Tess had applied a purple metallic shadow and black kohl around my eyes with a dramatic black mascara. My cheeks were contoured, and my lips were a neutral shade of mauve.

"You are a magician," I told her, admiring her work. "You don't think it's a little…much?"

"Girl, this is battle of the bands. I promise you, it is not too much," she said, putting some of the items back into the drawer. Tess was already set to go with a full face of makeup…she was always done up and ready for any occasion. Even if she had no plans and was sitting around the house, that was just Tess.

She moved to her closet and started to rummage through, trying to find the perfect outfits for us. She came back to the bed with an array of jackets, dresses, and tops. "Dress or Jeans?" she asked, turning to me.

"Do you even have to ask?" I replied, "Jeans."

"Ok, but then you have to wear heels…" she determined, biting her bottom lip and turning back to her closet for shoes.

"Small ones," I conceded, and although her back was to me, I could feel her roll her eyes. Tess decided on a slinky blue dress and black heels for herself and a pair of dark ripped jeans with a strappy black top for me.

"Uh…won't we be cold?" I pointed out.

"Good point," she replied, running back to her closet and pulling out two black leather jackets. She threw them down on the bed along with a pair of black suede wedges for me. They weren't small, but they were wedges. I could compromise.

We dressed in a hurry, watching the clock and realizing it was almost nine already. My car was still at home since Nik had picked me up, so we had to have Tess' parents drop us off. Tess insisted they park down the street so nobody would see us getting out of the car. As we started to walk towards the club, I could hear the bumping music blaring in the distance and I focused on not twisting an ankle in Tess' borrowed wedges. They were definitely taller than I had originally thought, and I felt like a skyscraper just waiting to break an ankle.

I felt a little self-conscious in Tess' outfit. The jeans were stretchy…so that wasn't a problem, but the low-cut strappy top was more revealing than I was used to wearing. Not to mention hardly anybody at school had ever seen me with makeup on. Tess had assured me that I looked good, but I still felt somewhat unrecognizable.

We gave the bouncer at the door our IDs and were promptly handed bright wristbands indicating we were under twenty-one years old. We passed through the doors and a wave of alcohol and sweat hit me as I adjusted my eyes to the dim lighting.

The bar was long and ran the length of the back wall of the club. To the left was a stage where one of the bands was setting up their instruments, to the right was a large, packed, dance floor. They were bumping the latest hits while waiting for the bands to start, and people of all ages were grinding together on the dance floor under the green lights.

"Want to get a drink?" Tess asked over the music, scanning the room for the boys. I nodded in response, and we made our way through the crowd of people to the bar.

"Two root beers," Tess ordered with a wink to the bartender. All that earned her was a roll of his eyes as he turned to grab our drinks. I wouldn't put it past Tess to try to get us fake IDs, and I was surprised when she hadn't even brought it up beforehand. I scanned the crowd, but didn't see Nik or Puck anywhere. It wasn't long before we were approached by boys from the lacrosse team wanting to flirt with Tess.

"Hey, Diana," Zach said sidling up next to me at the bar. "You look great tonight."

I could feel his eyes on me, running from my head all the way down to my toes. Zach was on the swim team and normally flirted with Tess, and acted as if I was her completely invisible sidekick. Was it the outfit that made him want to acknowledge me tonight?

"Hey, Zach." I nodded, giving him a tight smile. He was cute, with short, cropped hair, and a lean swimmer's body. Tess shot me a set of wide eyes behind Zach's back before turning back to the boy she was talking to. Seth, I think his name was.

"It's too bad you aren't in any of my classes this semester," Zach said with a stretch that revealed the thin stretch of skin below his T-shirt. "You must be in all AP classes."

"Not all," I replied with a laugh, sipping on my Root Beer. Little did he know I wasn't particularly good at school.

"Smart and sexy. You've got it all don't you?" he asked with a wide smile.

I had to slap my chest with the back of my closed fist to stop myself from choking or spitting out my Root Beer. *Was he flirting with me*? Zach Walsh, who had literally never even acknowledged that I existed on the same planet as him, had called me smart and sexy.

"Do you want to dance?" he asked, nodding towards the packed dance floor. Before I had a moment to object or catch my breath, he grabbed my arm and pulled me onto the dance floor behind him. I felt my inner self starting to panic. The only time I had ever danced was with Tess in my bedroom. I had never danced with a boy before, let alone been to a club that played this type of music. I had absolutely no idea what I was doing.

I followed Zach's lead and moved back and forth to the beat. He moved one hand to my hip and followed my movements, leaning close to whisper in my ear, "You know, I've always wanted to dance with you."

"You have?" I asked in surprise, I was sure he had never noticed me before. I thought Tess was more his type. I could feel him nod against me and move closer, our legs intertwining as we moved. His hand moved from my hip to my lower back, pulling me closer ever so slightly. Over his shoulder I caught a flash of pale hair at the bar next to Tess and felt a knot forming in my stomach. Were Nik and Puck here? We turned with the music and my back was now to Tess, but I could still feel eyes on me. Over my shoulder I could hear someone clear their throat and Zach immediately straightened.

"I suggest you remove your hand…" a deep voice purred at my ear.

Zach swallowed and dropped his hand from my lower back. "You have a boyfriend?" Zach asked, taking a step back from me. Before I could answer, Nik stepped up behind me and slid his arm around my waist, pulling be back against him. The movement sent a warm, tingling, feeling down to my toes as I felt his chest pressing into my back, his arm tight around me.

"Run along." He nodded towards the bar where the rest of Zach's friends were, a dark gleam in his eyes. Zach didn't so much as meet my eyes again before he took off through the crowd of packed bodies. Was Nik jealous? He sure *looked* jealous.

Nik said nothing as he released me and took Zach's spot, and we began moving to the music once more. I followed his lead, he had more practice than Zach at this, that much was evident. He brought both his hands to my hips, pulling me in closer. I could feel his breath at my ear and the smell of cloves and cinnamon as I closed my eyes. We swayed back and forth, Nik holding me close, and he slid a leg between mine as we rocked to the music.

"Who was that?" he asked.

"Just a guy from school..." I trailed off, losing myself in the music. I had never pictured Nik as a dancer at all, but he was damn good at it.

"Do you know him well?" he asked at my ear.

"No, actually. I had never spoken to him before tonight," I replied honestly.

I could feel the smirk that spread across Nik's mouth, even if I couldn't see it with my head buried in the crook of his neck. My arm was draped over his shoulder, my other hand resting on his at my hip.

"You do look particularly captivating tonight...but I wanted to be the first one to point that out," he breathed, wrapping one of those arms around my waist.

"Oh, really?" I whispered back, a little breathless being pressed this close to him. I could feel his thigh between mine as we rocked back and forth, and a shot of warmth pooled low in my stomach.

"Yes...really," he answered, placing a light kiss against my shoulder. I shivered, the feeling of his lips against my skin sending a shock through me. They were softer than I'd imagined.

"This top..." he started, running the hand not currently wrapped around my waist against the shoulder straps of my top underneath my leather jacket.

"These jeans..." He pulled back slightly so I could see his eyes traveling down the length of me. I felt as if I was on fire under his gaze, his eyes still such a bright blue under the green lights of the club. Tess was so much smaller than me, and it was a struggle to fit myself into these jeans, even with them being so stretchy. They were practically painted on.

"These heels…" he finished with a smirk, bringing his eyes back up to meet mine. "Intoxicating." He had said the same thing earlier at the meadow, when I thought he had been about to kiss me. I could sense the tension between us as if it were a tangible thing, taught and electric. It was as if his body was connected to mine by a thick rope of static energy, waiting to explode.

My magic responded to him from deep in my core, pressing on my skin from the inside, begging to come out. Our bodies were pressed together, his lips at my neck again, my arm wrapped around him when the strobe lights died down and the house lights came on.

"Welcome…to Battle of the Bands!" The emcee announced from the loudspeaker before introducing the first band, Oblivion. I blinked, the haze of tension clearing. Nik was still focused on me with a dangerous smirk, and I could feel Tess' presence at our side now. Nik dropped his arm from my waist and turned towards the stage.

"Sorry to interrupt…" Tess said sheepishly, moving forwards to whisper in my ear, "again."

"This time it wasn't you," I assured her with a whisper. She cleared her throat and gave my arm a squeeze, my other arm still brushing lightly against Nik's side. Nik nodded towards the bar and waved Puck over. Puck made his way through the crowd as the first band began to play.

"Puck, Tess. Tess, Puck," Nik yelled over the rock music, introducing the two. I could already see the stars in Tess' eyes as she gave my arm a firmer squeeze and turned towards the band.

We listened to the first three sets, swaying along to the music and cheering on some of our classmates before we made our way back to the bar, thirsty and sweaty. I could feel my curls plastering to the back of my neck as I ditched my leather jacket on a barstool and ordered another drink. Tess downed her water in a few gulps and turned to me, her eyes wide. She and Puck had been dancing, and I was glad she was having a good time tonight. She wiggled her eyebrows at me conspiratorially before turning back to Puck.

"I think your boyfriend is mad at me," Nik said, pulling out the barstool where I had thrown my jacket down and taking a seat.

"My boyfriend?" I asked, wiping the sweat from my forehead with the back of my hand, careful not to ruin the foundation Tess had carefully applied.

Nik nodded towards the other end of the bar where I could see Zach and a few of his other swim buddies, huddled together and staring in our direction.

"He's not my boyfriend," I replied, finishing my drink. "As I said, I've never talked to him before. And I'm pretty sure he was under the impression *you* were my boyfriend with the way you introduced yourself," I pointed out.

Nik was about to open his mouth to reply with some witty retort when Tess turned to us, her hand on my back.

"Come to the bathroom with me?" It was a rhetorical question, she all but physically pulled me along with her and closed and locked the door behind us.

"Dude. Puck is *cute*. Like...really cute. And British. Why did you not tell me how cute he is?" she exclaimed, grabbing my shoulders, and shaking me.

"I'm pretty sure I did tell you he was cute," I pointed out as she bounced to the sink and wet a paper towel, pressing it against her forehead to cool herself off.

"And you and Nik..." she started with big eyes, "I saw you two getting hot and heavy out there on the dance floor." I hoped I wasn't a terrible dancer, but I had nothing to compare the experience to. It had felt easy dancing with Nik, following his lead. I would be dreaming about the feeling of his lips at my neck tonight, that's for sure.

Did he like me? Did I like him? I couldn't deny I was attracted to him. I had never felt this way about a boy before. Sure, there were cute guys at school, but none of them had grabbed my attention in this way. But we still didn't know anything about him, and something in my gut told me he might be bad news.

"Can we ask them to give us a ride home?" she asked, smirking at herself in the bathroom mirror.

"Sure." I shrugged, it would be better than having Tess' dad come pick us up anyway, we wouldn't have to walk back down all those blocks in these ridiculous heels. My feet were already starting to hurt, and I had half a mind to ditch them if the floor weren't so sticky.

"And was that Zach Walsh I saw dancing up on you, too? You are on fire tonight."

"I don't like Zach," I replied, watching her pat herself down with the paper towel.

"Yeah, that's because you're all about Nikkkkk," she laughed. "I never thought I'd see the day, my Diana, totally smitten over a boy."

I rolled my eyes and joined her at the sink, checking to make sure my makeup hadn't smeared at all during all the dancing and sweating.

We made our way back to the bar, a line now forming outside the girl's bathroom. The fourth band had just started to play, and the crowd was more packed than ever. As we approached, I could see Nik still sitting on the barstool where I had thrown my jacket, but he was no longer alone. Lacey, one of Tess' dance friends, was settled between his open legs, a hand on his shoulder as she threw her head back and laughed at whatever he had said. Of course, someone would already be hitting on him. Lacey was perfect, the same long tanned legs as Tess, but with a head of voluminous wavy blonde hair.

Nik peered back at her through hooded eyes, not appearing interested, taking a long sip of what appeared to be a beer. Neither he nor Puck had the fluorescent underage wristbands that Tess and I had been stuck with.

"Girl, you better go get your man," Tess said at my ear.

"He's not my man…" I started, but she had taken off already to go find Puck. I thought about turning back to find Tess, but from what I could see I didn't think Nik was all that interested in Lacey. I circled around the bar and came around Nik from the back, wrapping my arm around his neck and sliding it down his chest as I faced Lacey with a smile.

Her face immediately fell, and she lost track of whatever it was that she had been saying. "Hello, Diana," she said stiffly. I glanced down at Nik, who now wore a devious grin. She looked as if she was hoping Nik would tell me off and I would simply disappear.

"Hello, Lacey. What were you saying?" I asked as she took a step back, out of the circle of Nik's legs.

"Oh…umm…" Her gaze traveled from my arm around Nik's neck, then to Nik's face before letting out a huff. "Never mind." Lacey turned on her four-inch heels and left, fuming.

"Jealousy looks good on you, firecracker," Nik teased, spinning his bar stool towards me so that it was now me who stood in the circle of his open legs.

"Jealousy?" I played dumb, "I have no idea what you're talking about."

"It didn't bother you? Seeing Lacey's hands on me?" he asked with a raised eyebrow. Oh, it bothered me alright, but I wasn't about to admit that to him.

"Oh, you and Lacey are on a first name basis now, are you?" I asked, resting my hands on his thighs possessively as I inched closer.

"She's in my biology class…" he replied, glancing down at my hands on his legs.

"And does she like you?" I asked.

"Yes," he replied with a smirk, turning his face up towards mine.

"And?"

"And…what? I don't like her back," he answered, sliding a finger into the loop on my jeans and pulling me closer. I moved my hands from his thighs to his shoulders as he glanced up at me.

"Who *do* you like?" I asked, I felt hot all over being this close to him again. I don't know where this burst of confidence came from. Was it the makeup? The outfit? Or was I feeling bold under the dark lights of the club?

"Wouldn't you like to know." He smiled, a dimple creasing his cheek.

I could feel someone approach us over my shoulder, and Nik's smile turned to a grimace as he stood and pushed me behind him protectively.

"What are you doing here?" he ground out.

"Checking in on you, *Kolya*. Making sure you stay on task." *On task*? Who was this guy, and what was he talking about? I peered around Nik's shoulder to see that the man standing before him was none other than the wolf from the other night, the one that had come to my house. Were the two men flanking him on either side the other wolves that had also been there, the ones that had run off?

"You need to mind your own business, Fletcher. I can take care of it." Take care of *what*? What were they talking about? Was this the reason Nik had been missing school this last week, whatever business it was he was supposed to be taking care of with this Fletcher? "I don't want to see you around here again," Nik said, steel in his voice. "It's bad enough you and your pack attacked that poor coffee shop owner to get my attention and to let me know you were in town. I get the message loud and clear." It was Fletcher or one of his cronies that had attacked Mrs. Madden? Was she a witch too, or had she simply been in the wrong place at the wrong time? A casualty of Fletcher's cruelness?

"You have your orders, and I have mine. We wouldn't want to involve Zion, now, would we?" *Who was Zion? What was he talking about?*

"I'm serious, Fletcher. Take your little rat pack and get out of town."

"Kolya, you seriously think I came here with only *two* witches in tow? I came here to see it *done*," he spat.

"And you will," Nik replied, his eyes blazing. "Now leave."

Fletcher locked eyes with Nik for a long moment and I could feel the tension building between them. What was it that Nik was supposed to do? I thought Nik said he had handled the other wolves, and they wouldn't be coming back? That clearly wasn't the case...

"Puck says they can drive us home," Tess announced, parting the crowd and coming to stand by my side, attempting to defuse the tension.

"You two love birds ready to go?" Puck asked, slinging an arm across Tess' shoulders and staring back at Fletcher and his pack.

"The same goes for you, Puck. Get it done, or I *will* call Zion. Or *maybe* I will have to do it myself," he chuckled. "Oh, how I would enjoy that."

Puck tensed next to us but didn't satisfy Fletcher with a reply. Fletcher turned on his heel and stalked off through the crowd, his witches following closely behind.

"Nik, what was he talking about?" I asked, a crease of worry between my brows. "He attacked Mrs. Madden?"

"It's nothing," he replied, grabbing my jacket off the barstool and draping it over my shoulders. "He wanted to make a statement, let me know I wasn't the only wolf in town."

"Is Mrs. Madden a shade too?" I asked.

"No." Nik shook his head softly. "She was unfortunately a random victim of his. Fletcher has never been particularly discerning when it comes to his victims or the lives of humans. As I said, it's nothing…and I will handle it."

"It sure didn't sound like nothing…" I replied. "What did he mean? Is this the business that kept you out of school this week?"

"Yes," he answered tightly, a hand on my back. "But it's nothing you or Tess need to worry yourselves about." He swallowed hard before meeting my eyes. Why was Fletcher in town, and why had he *really* shown up at my house the other night? Had it been because he had smelled my magic, or had it been something else?

Nik guided me through the packed crowd of bodies on the dance floor with his hand on my back. We made our way out to the parking lot behind the club. I sat shotgun next to Nik, Tess sat in the back with Puck. We made our way to drop Tess off first, and the tension in the car was palpable. What were they not telling us?

When Nik dropped Tess off, she gave Puck a kiss on the cheek, promising to text me first thing in the morning. I was hoping that Nik would drop Puck off next so I could talk to him alone, but we quickly made our way over to my side of town. We pulled up to the curb and I could see the lights still on in the kitchen, Mom must still be up. I got out of the car quickly, not wanting her to see Nik's car through the window.

"See you Monday?" I asked, unsure if he would be showing up to school or not. Whatever this business was with Fletcher, it seemed serious. He had missed school last week to handle it, and Fletcher was still here, in town.

"See you Monday," he repeated with a tight smile as Puck got into the passenger seat. As I reached the front door, I turned back and could just make out Nik and Puck having what appeared to be a heated argument as they sped off down the street.

I could hear my mom doing the dishes in the kitchen, so I made my way down the hallway to see her. I kept my leather jacket on for fear that she would have a heart attack if she saw me in Tess' low-cut top.

"How was Tess'?" she asked as I came around the corner. "You were out late."

"It was good," I told her, grabbing an apple out of the fruit bowl and pulling out a barstool at the island.

"We studied a bit, watched a movie, then a few of her dance friends came over to hang out for a bit," I lied as I took a bite.

"That sounds fun." She sighed, clearly exhausted. She hadn't even noticed the makeup or the outfit. Or she had, and she was simply too tired to get into it with me.

"Did you get called in again today?" I asked, taking a bite of the apple.

"Unfortunately," she responded, finishing the last dish, and throwing the drying towel across the front of the apron sink. "If they don't hire another anchor soon, I don't know what I'll do. These hours are running me ragged, I'm drained."

"I'm sorry, Mom." She had been working so much these last few weeks, I could see it was really starting to take a toll on her. I couldn't imagine how hard it was for her to raise me and Jake on her own, without Dad. I was almost off to college, but Jake was only eleven. She managed to do it all on her own, the least I could do was help her out. I tried to cook and clean when I could, but I knew this last week I had been slacking. I had been completely wrapped up in my own drama.

"I look forward to sleeping in tomorrow," she said, picking her glasses up from their place by the sink. "I love you, honey. Get some sleep."

She gave me a kiss on the forehead before sauntering up to bed. I sat in the kitchen alone, finishing my apple. Could I confide in my mom about everything that had been happening, or would it stress her out more? She always called me her little daydreamer, I'm not sure she would believe me if I told her. Even if I showed her, I think she would still have her doubts. I wish I had the type of relationship with her where I could be honest and she didn't immediately jump to the conclusion that I was nuts, or making it up. But could I blame her? Even *I* had thought I had made it all up this time.

I finished the apple, throwing the core in the trash, and returned to the bar stool at the counter. I opened the palm of my hand and focused on the fire. Could I create fire and control it, as I had practiced in the meadow? I didn't want to rely on the magical tether to keep my magic under control.

I focused on the feeling of energy in my core. As I had in the meadow, I imagined it traveling up my arm and to my palm, creating a small flame there. When I opened my eyes, my fingertips were alight with a small sphere of fire, smaller than I had conjured at the meadow, but it was still there. I closed my palm with the thought of releasing all that taught energy, and the flame extinguished. Nik was right, I could control the flames now. All I had to do was practice.

I made my way upstairs and washed all the makeup off in the bathroom sink, tying my hair in a high ponytail. I changed into my loosest pajamas and crawled into bed with Waffles, moving him off my pillow to cuddle against my side.

I had so much fun tonight, a text pinged in from Tess.

Me too, so much to talk about, I replied.

Tell me about it! Thanks for coming, Love you. Goodnight xoxo.

Love you too, Tess. Goodnight.

I plugged my phone into the charger and closed my eyes. I couldn't wait to practice my magic again, and to try my hand at storm magic. But most of all, I couldn't wait to see Nikolai again. He had ignored *Lacey freaking Peterson,* in favor of me. I couldn't believe it.

It still bothered me that I didn't know what Fletcher wanted, but I would have to trust that Nik was right...it didn't have anything to do with us. They would handle it. I could feel how tired my body was from dipping into all of that unused energy today. I turned the light off and fell asleep with the hope that

I would hear someone scratching at my window, but it never came.

I shouldn't have been surprised when Monday's first period rolled around, and Nik was a no-show. I hadn't heard from him since Saturday night and I had busied myself catching up on homework and house chores that I'd been neglecting. I spent Sunday night cuddled up on the couch watching movies and eating popcorn with Mom and Jake. When I skulked into third period, Tess could tell by the set of my shoulders, and my obvious frown, that something was wrong.

"No lover boy today?" she asked as I settled into my seat beside her, throwing my bookbag onto the ground between us.

"He isn't my lover boy," I huffed, pulling out my notebook.

"Whatever." She rolled her eyes. "You didn't hear from him yesterday?"

"No," I replied, resting my chin on my hand. "Have you heard from Puck?"

"Puck and I have been texting all weekend," Tess answered excitedly, her eyes brightening. A stab of jealously hit me in the gut. I was excited for Tess, that she had found somebody she liked, but somewhat envious that I hadn't heard from Nikolai all weekend. Things had gone well at the club and with my magic practice, why hadn't I heard from him? Was he busy tending to the "business" he had with Fletcher and his gang of nasty witches?

I was anxious to practice more complicated magic. I had played with my fire magic on Sunday and felt confident that I had a handle on the basics of it. I was eager to find out if I was a Stormshade, but too nervous to test it without Nik or Puck nearby. They were much more experienced than I was, having always known they were witches from early on. Even if they weren't Stormshades themselves, they knew more about this magic than I did. I needed to keep myself busy, I decided. I would dedicate this week to practicing the magic I already felt comfortable with and helping my mom around the house as much as possible.

"I'm sure he's just busy with the whole Fletcher thing," Tess said, seeing the direction my thoughts were taking plastered plainly on my face.

"Yeah, and Puck isn't? Remember what Fletcher said, whatever it is they've gotten themselves into…they're in it together."

Tess gave me a sympathetic smile and reached over the desk to grab my hand. "We are not the kind of girls to wait around for a boy," she started, sympathy in her eyes. "You and I are going to practice some of this tricky magic on our own. Screw them."

Tess was right. I was definitely *not* the kind of girl to be sulking, all because I hadn't heard from a boy.

"Deal." I smiled. "Tomorrow?"

"Perfect! I have a shift at The Daily Drip tonight. Mrs. Madden is back to work, and we are having a little 'get better' soiree in her honor. You're welcome to stop by and support your bestie at work if you want." She nudged me gently.

"Pass, but thanks for the invite," I laughed. "I have to catch up on my biology homework or I will *definitely* be failing that exam on Friday." Class came to a start, and I tried my hardest to focus on the lecture, letting the rest of the classes before art slip by in a daze.

Tess and I ate lunch with Sloane and her dance friends, Lacey Peterson nowhere to be seen. I wasn't sure I wanted to face her after I'd embarrassed her on Saturday, and I was thankful she was either absent or making herself scarce.

When we walked down towards the art room, the desk where Ms. Finch normally would be found rifling through her papers was empty. What was going on with her? Was she absent again? Tess was right; she had been acting incredibly strange lately. Tess and I gathered our materials and sat at the table near the door, despite the fact that Nik probably wouldn't be joining us today. The bell rang and to nobody's surprise…Nik hadn't shown. Tess and I started working on our portfolios, and when the second bell finally rang, a substitute teacher filed in.

"Hello, class. I am going to be your substitute teacher for the foreseeable future as Ms. Finch is out on medical leave. My name is Mr. Price." *That voice sounded so familiar.* I glanced up from my portfolio to see Fletcher standing at the front of the class wearing pressed black slacks and a collared shirt. He placed his briefcase on the desk and opened it, pulling out a lesson plan.

My mouth fell open, and I shot Tess a look of surprise as she nudged my leg under the table. *What was he doing here?* He swept his eyes around the room before finally resting on me and Tess, a menacing gleam in his eyes. He had shaved his face and gelled his hair back since I had last seen him, and he looked every part the young aspiring teacher.

"For today, we will continue to work on your senior portfolios. Tomorrow, we will jump into the new lesson plan that I have prepared," he announced, pulling out Ms. Finch's chair and sitting down.

"What is he doing here?" Tess turned to me, her mouth a thin line.

"You think I know?" I sighed, turning back to face her. I could tell from the smirk on Fletcher's face that he knew he had rattled us. First, he turns out to be one of the wolves outside of my house trying to *attack* us and break in. Then, he shows up at the nightclub and threatens Nik and Puck in front of us. Now, he shows up at school and is pretending to be a substitute teacher. Or—was he actually a substitute teacher? There was no way this was a coincidence. What was he playing at? To what end? To keep an eye on Nik? Puck didn't even go to this school, it couldn't be because of him.

"This is trouble…I don't like this one bit. Whatever it is those boys have gotten themselves into, I don't want any part of it." Tess bit her nail anxiously, swinging her gaze back and forth between me and Fletcher.

"Agreed. Stop looking at him," I said as I slapped her hand away from her mouth. "Too bad Nik decided to skip school today or else he would have to handle whatever this mess is that he's created for himself."

"Shouldn't we tell them?" Tess asked, pretending to work on her portfolio, but in reality, she was moving the charcoal around the paper and creating a jumble of smudges. I folded my arms across my chest and set my jaw.

"Let them deal with it. I haven't heard from him since we went to Elixir, and I am *not* texting him first."

Tess whipped her head around in surprise. "Good for you. I love that attitude. Let him come to you."

"Exactly," I nodded. As Tess and I sketched in silence, I could hear Fletcher's footsteps approaching, his fancy loafers tapping against the polished tile floor.

"Hello, ladies." He smiled, pausing at the edge of our table. "No Nikolai today?"

I paused to glance at the empty chair across from me, then back to Fletcher, my expression neutral. "Appears not."

Fletcher paused to scratch his stubble and leaned down, placing one hand on the table before me, the other hand on the back of my chair.

"Will you give him a message for me?" he asked, his voice uncomfortably close to my ear. I could smell the faint scent of clove cigarettes and whiskey on his breath. Was he *drunk*? Who had he fooled to get a substitute position here? They were hiring just about anybody these days, it seemed.

"Why don't you tell him yourself?" I replied. "He does go to school here..."

"Not for long," he countered in a clipped tone. What was that supposed to mean? Tess and I exchanged a worried glance, both of us equally confused.

"Just let him know, if he doesn't do as he's been told, there will be collateral damage." Fletcher leaned across me and with his other hand, he tucked a stray lock of curls behind my ear. A chill ran down my spine all the way to my toes as I scanned the classroom to see if anybody had seen. Was he talking about me? Would I be the collateral damage? I didn't have anything to do with this, and I didn't want to. Why was he threatening me?

"It's their business, not ours. Leave us out of it," Tess replied, seeing how uncomfortable I was under Fletcher's gaze.

"On the contrary," Fletcher replied, "you *are* involved. And tell your boyfriends that it better be done by week's end."

He straightened and returned to the desk, rifling through the mound of paperwork Ms. Finch had left behind. I glanced around the room, but it appeared our entire exchange had gone unnoticed by the rest of the class.

"What was that about?" Tess asked worriedly.

"I have no idea. I don't know how we could be involved when we don't even know what he's talking about, for crying out loud. I guess we will have to talk to the boys after all..."

I pulled out my phone and pulled up a text message to Nik.

Need to talk, it's important. Are you free later?

So much for standing my ground and not texting him first. Tess and I returned to pretending to work on our portfolios while I waited for my phone to chime. If I was going to get dragged into whatever business this was, I needed to learn how to use some of my magic defensively, and fast.

When a text finally sounded on my phone, I all but leaped at it, anxious to find out what Fletcher thought we were involved in.

Buttercream at 4. Bring Tess.

"He asked us to meet him after school," I told Tess, tucking my phone back into my bag. "Do you have time before your shift?"

"Of course." Tess nodded.

When the bell rang, Tess and I made our way to our final periods, but all I could think about was Fletcher. Was there another reason he had shown up at my house and tried to attack us? Could it be because I was a Stormshade? But I hadn't even confirmed that with Nik yet, how would Fletcher know?

As I walked out of biology and made my way to my car, my head was swimming with theories. I knew one thing for sure: Nik and Puck would need to come clean or handle this situation on their own. If Fletcher had shown up at school pretending to be a substitute, what else would he do to get what he wanted?

Tess and I made the drive through town as it started to snow, big thick snowflakes hitting the windshield and turning to slush. Tess changed into her barista uniform in the car so she could walk straight to her shift at The Daily Drip from the bakery. I parked the car right in front of the bakery as the snow started to stick to the road. Just what we needed…more snow.

We hopped out and quickly scurried inside, anxious to be out of the blistering cold and wind. The weather hadn't called for a snowstorm today, and I hoped it was a passing squall. The bell chimed as we opened the door and scanned the bakery. Nik and Puck weren't here yet.

"You were right Diana, this place is adorable," Tess admired as I grabbed a table by the back wall. Tess got us hot chocolates at the counter and joined me, passing me the warm mug. As Tess reached her hand out to the back of her chair to pull it out from the table, the chair quickly scooted backwards and slammed into her hand of its own accord. Tess' eyes snapped up to mine.

"Did you do that?" she asked, her brow creased.

"No, I didn't." I shook my head. "Did…you?"

"I—I don't know," she admitted, pulling the chair back and sitting down. Tess stared into the hot chocolate mug with a confused expression as I took a long sip of mine and watched her thoughtfully. Did Tess have magic? Or had that been my magic reaching out and I hadn't even known it?

Tess shook her head as if to clear her thoughts and settled back into her chair. The snow was falling in thick, heavy clusters, obscuring our view of the street from the storefront window. It was quickly turning into a blizzard outside, the wind whipping the flags on the lampposts back and forth angrily. If I didn't head home soon, I might get stuck here. My car was reliable, but it didn't do well once the snow had entirely covered the roads and became a slippery nightmare.

The bells chimed as the door opened and I lifted my head to see Nik and Puck walking towards us.

"Nice of you to join us," Tess said in a clipped tone.

Nik pulled out the chair next to me and sat on it backwards. Puck grabbed the chair next to Tess. "Always a pleasure," Nik responded, giving Tess a deadpan stare. What was his problem with her, anyway?

"Now, what's the emergency, love?" Puck asked, wrapping his arm around the back of Tess' chair.

"While you were off skipping school, we had ourselves a little visitor in art class today," I told them, crossing my arms defensively.

"A visitor?" Nik asked with an arched brow. "It's a bit late for Santa Claus, don't you think?"

"I'm being serious," I replied, giving his big black boot a swift kick under the table.

"Ok, ok," he replied, palms out, "who was this mysterious visitor?"

"Fletcher," I spit out, sitting back in my chair.

Nik's eyes shot to Puck's quickly before he focused back on me. "You're telling me that Fletcher was in art class?" he asked, a note of suspicion in his voice.

"I am telling you that Mr. Fletcher Price is our new sub-stitute teacher for the foreseeable future. Ms. Finch is out on leave." He exchanged a knowing glance with Puck, as if they were having a silent conversation with only their eyes. "Why would he be coming to our school?" I asked.

"Probably to keep an eye on me." Nik shrugged. "Puck and I already worked it out, and it's almost handled."

"*Almost* isn't quite good enough. He said that if whatever it is the two of you have gotten yourselves into isn't handled by the end of the week...there will be collateral damage." I rubbed a hand down my face. "He threatened me."

Nik's eyes were dark as he glanced down, his teeth grinding together.

"He should never have threatened you, and I promise you it will not happen again."

"How can you promise me that? You weren't even in school today." My voice cracked, betraying me. My whole world had already turned upside down when I found out about the exis-tence of magic. Now I was being dragged into whatever beef these two had with Fletcher—who was a shapeshifter with a pack of witches behind him. Nik might be an incredibly strong witch, but Fletcher had a bunch of witches loyal to him alone. Nik only had Puck.

"Firecracker, did you miss me?" He nudged my knee with his, a sinful smirk across his lips. "You did, didn't you? You don't have to answer...I know you did," he teased, trying to lighten the mood. Puck laughed across from us while Tess held onto her stern expression. I *had* missed him today, but that was beside the point. I didn't want to see Fletcher without Nik there; I wasn't strong enough to protect myself yet. I needed more time. I needed more practice with my magic.

"I'll be there, he won't touch you," Nik assured me.

"Too bad he already did…" Tess murmured under her breath, casting her eyes down at the table. I thought only I had heard her.

"What was that?" Nik stiffened beside me.

Tess swallowed hard before meeting his eyes. "He was super creepy. He leaned in and pushed her hair back…" Tess admitted, thinking about how uncomfortable the situation had been.

Nik's eyes shot back to mine, his expression murderous. His eyes traveled over my hair, as if to make sure not a strand was out of place before he reached over and grabbed a lock between his own fingertips.

"He will *never* do that again." His voice was almost a whisper as he tucked the lock he had between his fingertips behind my ear, sending a shiver down my spine for an entirely different reason. All I could do was nod.

"Are you going to tell us what this 'business' is, now that we're involved in it?" I asked.

"No," Nik and Puck replied in tandem.

"We will handle it," Nik replied resolutely. He kept saying that. He had said that the night Fletcher had come to my house, but then we saw him again at the club. And now we would have to see him at school every day if he was going to be our permanent substitute. Tess and I exchanged a glance across the table as they pushed their chairs back and stood.

"I mean it. I'll see you tomorrow," Nik said, squeezing my shoulder and heading towards the door.

"Text you," Puck told Tess with a wink as he followed Nik out into the building snowstorm.

The snow had started to fall harder while we had been in the bakery. I took my hot chocolate with me and drove Tess down the street to her shift, so she didn't have to walk in the frigid whiteout.

As I made my way out of the town center and towards my house, the snow only deepened, covering the roads in a thick powder. How Tess planned to get home after her shift was beyond me. Hopefully her dad had four-wheel drive and a set of chains. I parked my car in the driveway as a plow went by, doing its best to salt the streets before the storm took a turn for the worse.

I shook the snow out of my hair in the foyer, kicking my boots off and moving to warm my hands by the fire. I could smell my mom's famous lasagna from all the way out here. Had she gotten out of work early today?

"Is that you, honey?" I heard her call from the kitchen.

"Coming!" I called back, moving towards the scents of fresh basil and oregano.

"What's the special occasion?" I asked, pulling out a barstool and taking a seat at the counter. My mom turned to me with a smile, her hair pulled back into a tight bun, a dish towel thrown over her shoulder.

"Not only did we hire another anchor today, but they gave me a promotion!"

"That's amazing, Mom! Congratulations. After all the hard work and over-time you've been putting in, I'm glad they are showing how much they appreciate all that you do."

"This means no more crazy hours." She smiled, cutting up slices of warm French bread.

"I'm sorry I haven't been helping out around the house as much. I've been a little distracted," I apologized, the guilt settling in my stomach heavy as a brick.

"You know, if there is anything you want to talk about, you can always come to me." She peered at me over the rim of her glasses. I grabbed a piece of the fresh bread, dipping a piece into the dish of olive oil before me and popping it in my mouth to buy me a moment.

"I know." I smiled around the mouthful of food. There was a lot I could talk to my mom about, but I didn't think this was one of them. Would she even try to understand? Would she immediately think I was crazy? If she saw with her own two eyes what I could do...maybe it would be different. Everything was so fresh and new, I was still trying to figure everything out about my magic. I needed more time to process, then maybe I could talk to her about it. The thought of broaching that conversation with her made me feel nervous all over. I wanted her to understand me, and to believe me.

"Where's Jake?" I asked, dipping another piece of bread into the oil.

"Study group, as always," she laughed. "You know him, always the overachiever." I rolled my eyes. Jake and I couldn't be more opposite. While I didn't have bad grades by any means, I could never put in the type of work Jake did. He may only be eleven, but he already had his sights set on medical school, at the least.

Mom and I had a quiet dinner alone, catching up on all the details of her new position at work and telling her all about my classes. It was nice to catch up with her like this. We almost never had one-on-one time together. The lasagna was exactly how I always remembered. I picked all the crusty parts around the edges for myself.

We washed the dishes together, then curled up by the fire, me with my history book and her with a novella and a glass of red wine. I loved nights like these. There was nothing better than curling up with my mom under the blanket and spending time together, not talking.

After a few hours of studying, I could feel my eyes getting tired. As soon as I lay down and my head hit the pillow, I was pulled down into a dark and familiar dream. A dream with a long dark corridor and a cracked wooden door.

I pressed my hand to the wooden door, and it opened under my touch, creaking loudly, revealing a long, dark corridor. I glanced back, but there was nothing, no indication of where I had just come from. There was nothing but suffocating darkness in every direction.

The only way out was onward, down into the dark passageway. I tentatively stepped over the stone threshold into the corridor, the door slamming shut behind me of its own accord. I started down the windowless passage and I could see the faint glow of torchlight that lit the path further down. I needed to get down there, get down to the light, then I could see. I ran my hand along the stone wall to guide me, the only noise the soft sound of my shoes against the uneven rocks.

When I reached the part of the hallway that was lit by torchlight, I picked up my pace. Where did this corridor go? Where did it end?

I walked on for several minutes, and when I turned back, I could no longer see the door that had led me here. Did this corridor ever end at all, or was it infinite?

Just when I thought I might be stuck in this eternal tunnel, I could see something in the distance. Another door. This door was also wooden, but was adorned with a stained-glass window and a large iron handle. It wasn't nearly as old or as worn as the door that had led me here. This door appeared well maintained, not aged by the weather of time. Where did it lead? I grabbed the handle and pushed, bracing myself for what might lie beyond.

When the door swung open, it revealed a long spiraling staircase made of stone, lit by the same sparse torchlight. I gripped the iron railing and started down, down, down, into the infinite darkness.

After many long minutes of descent, the staircase came to an end on a shallow landing, with only one way forwards, another door. This door was made of stone and appeared as if it had been built into the walls itself. It seemed as if it was meant to be hidden and not easily discovered, blending into the adjacent masonry seamlessly. When I grabbed the large iron handle, it didn't budge. I tried pushing with all my strength, but still the door did not move. Would I be stuck here, in this endless maze, forever? What lay beyond this door? Was it stuck, or was it locked?

I could feel a surge of energy deep in my core, begging to get out, begging to be released. I pressed my hand to the door again, closing my eyes in concentration. I pictured that energy traveling up my body, through my arms and out my fingertips, seeping into the cold granite stone.

"Open," I commanded, snapping my eyes open. The door did as I commanded, swinging open to reveal what appeared to be an old

laboratory of sorts. The windowless room had a large wooden table running the length of it, covered in books and beakers, herbs, and liquids. The back wall shelves were filled to the brim with bottles of different Elixirs and concoctions, ripped out pages of a spell book tacked to the wall. I ran my hand along the table as I walked the length of the room.

Had someone just been here? A potion bubbled in a beaker with a lit flame beneath a hot cauldron beside it. A book lay open before me to a complicated spell in both English and Latin. I cast my eyes to the heading. Awakening.

I reached out, touching the tattered page softly. The book recoiled, slamming shut with a fierce snap. I pulled my hand back just in time as the leather binding wrapped around the book, sealing it shut. It was an old brown book, no bigger than a journal, but thick with worn and yellowed pages. The leather coverlet had started to tear in a few places, and at the center of the book, beneath the leather cords fastening it shut, was a bright crescent amethyst.

Why did this book look so...familiar? I felt the energy of the book as if it was reaching out to me, calling to me. But it was just a book after all. It wasn't sentient. Or...was it? I reached out to touch the crescent amethyst gem and as my fingers grazed it, a series of visions flashed behind my open eyelids.

A dark king sitting on his throne of shadows. A woman with pale strawberry hair fleeing a stone palace, a bundle pressed tightly to her chest. A woman with blue and white hair, raising a sword high above her head in victory, she turned, and her eyes were endless black pits. A war, witches slaughtering witches, fire burning down an empire. The blue-haired woman sitting on the throne of shadows, a pack of black wolves at her side. A city in ruin, stone buildings reduced to rubble as smoke rises from the ashes.

I blinked, and the images were gone. I was back in the same windowless room. The book had responded to my touch, but what were those visions? What did they mean? Somehow, deep in my gut, I knew this book was mine. This was my book of shadows, my family's grimoire. I had found it. I reached out to the grimoire again, trying to open the leather straps that bound it shut, but they did not budge.

"Open," I whispered, laying my palm flat against the leather jacket. Still, the bindings did not move. This wasn't just any grimoire, that much I could tell. It had shown me visions, visions from the past. It had protected itself when I had tried to read from it. The grimoire was spelled against intruders, so how could I open it? A long-forgotten memory began to surface, and I tried my hardest to grip it before it slipped away. In my mind, it sounded like a spell...but I didn't know any spells. Or did I? Had I been spelled to forget? I repeated the unfamiliar words over and over again in my head. Where had they come from?

I closed my eyes and focused, wetting my lips before reciting, "Aperi reginam tuam, aperi mihi." I pressed my palm to the book one last time, reciting the words that had popped loose in my mind.

"Aperi reginam tuam, aperi mihi," I said with more conviction.

The bindings slowly unfurled beneath my touch, the grimoire breaking open to the same page it had first been open to, awakening. As I started to read, the room around me became undone. The spell was a mixture of English and Latin words, and despite never having studied Latin, I understood it intrinsically. As the words fell from my lips, it was as if a twister had let loose in the small laboratory, swallowing everything in its path. The vortex began pulling the books and herbs into a whirling column, spinning faster and faster, leaving nothing in its wake. I quickly grabbed the grimoire and pressed it to my chest before it could be swept up in the wind.

"I'm waking up," I whispered, feeling a new surge of raw energy deep in my belly. I felt more alive, more awake than I ever had before. It was as if everything was coming into clear focus for the first time, as if I could finally, now, see clearly. The wind continued down the length of the room, collecting all the bits of paper and scattered bottles in its wake. I suddenly had the feeling that the tornado belonged to me. That this was my doing, that I had created it. Within that tornado, I could feel an endless well of energy, waiting to be tapped into. Could I siphon that energy?

"I'm waking up." The words left my mouth again, as if pulled from somewhere deep inside me. The storm magic inside me was waking up like an hourglass filling with grains of sand, little by little. I gripped the grimoire tightly, afraid that it would get swept up in the storm if I let it go. I could feel the magic swelling within me, filling me with more energy than I had ever felt before.

"I'm waking up." I bit down on my lip to stop from screaming out, the energy filling me to the brim, to the point where it was almost painful. I fell to my knees, the book of shadows still tight within my grip. When I felt as if I couldn't handle one more ounce of energy inside of me, that I was ready to crack under the weight of it, I opened my mouth and let it flood out of me on a deep, guttural scream.

The room became infinitely still. All the loose materials suspended in the air for one long moment before they fell to the stone floor with a clatter.

*I was a Stormshade, and I was **powerful**.*

I felt an entirely other source of magic within me now, waiting to be called upon. It was as if it had always been there inside of me, familiar, but out of reach. Hidden away. I could access it now, and I felt alive. I felt hungry.

"Diana, wake up." I could hear a voice off in the distance, but I glanced around the room and all I could see was the mess that I had created. Books and papers were scattered about, bottles of liquid had broken open and seeped into puddles across the floor. The laboratory was utterly ruined.

I couldn't bring myself to care. All I could think about was the new flame in my core, as if a new ember of energy now flickered deep within my soul. I had awoken something powerful inside of me.

"Diana! Wake. Up." The voice came again, and my vision started to blur, the room before me spinning out of focus. I could feel something pushing on my chest, but I couldn't see the invisible force.

"Wake Up!" the voice sounded, over and over. I had woken up. The room drifted away, and I was plunged into darkness once again.

When my eyes fluttered open, the brightness that welcomed me was blinding. I lifted a hand across my face to shield my eyes.

"*Finally,*" the voice said, and after a moment of adjusting, I peeled my eyes open to find Jake bouncing up and down on my bed with excitement. "We have a *snow day,*" he exclaimed, jumping down beside me on his knees. "Can you believe it? An actual snow day!"

"Then why are you waking me up early?" I grumbled, tossing the arm back across my face. Jake had opened the blinds on the windows and peeled the duvet back, leaving me with only the thin sheet covering me. I felt a shiver roll over me as I tried to pull the comforter back, but Jake grabbed it with his little hands.

"Early?" Jake laughed. "It's not early, silly. Mom turned off your alarm so you could sleep in. It's almost noon!"

I turned towards the nightstand and sure enough, the numbers on the alarm clock read 11:47 a.m. How had I slept that long? And *what* was that dream?

"Mom's making pancakes," Jake announced. "Let's go! Last one to the table is a rotten egg!" He leaped off the bed and fled from the room, satisfied that I was awake enough that I wouldn't roll over and go back to sleep.

I let out a groan and rolled over, reluctantly tossing the sheets off me. We hadn't had a snow day in…forever. It always snowed in Silver Oaks; it was no big deal. They never bothered to close the roads since everybody was capable of driving in it. How bad had the unexpected storm gotten last night?

I glanced out the window to see that the snowfall had stacked on the roof of the deck high enough that it obscured half of my view to the backyard. Digging my car out later would be super fun.

With a groan, I pulled on a knit sweater over my pajamas and some slippers, tossing the sheets back over the bed. I could still feel the residual ember of energy in my core from the dream I'd had last night. But that was impossible…wasn't it? It was just a dream. But somehow, I felt…different. More in control. More awake. I could feel the well of energy as I had yesterday, but it somehow felt easier to access. Easier to dip into.

I had dreamed of that same dark corridor again, but this time it had taken me somewhere. It had taken me to my book of shadows. But where was that place? I had never been there before, but I thought maybe Nik had since he had sketched it, too. Did it actually exist, or did it only exist in my dreams? I was sure I had seen that book before; it had felt *so* familiar. But where had I ever seen it?

I picked up my pillow and fluffed it, tossing it back down on top of the covers. I grabbed the second pillow and lifted it, stifling a yawn. When I went to toss it back onto the bed, a soft gasp escaped my lips. There, beneath the pillow, lay the leather-bound grimoire with the amethyst crescent. My book of shadows. My grimoire. Somehow, against all reason, I had taken it out of the dream with me.

No...it couldn't be. It wasn't possible. It had only been a dream, hadn't it? I rubbed my eyes and opened them, sure that I was hallucinating. But no, the grimoire was still there, laying among the pillows. Where had it come from? I had been holding it in my dream...but then I had woken up. When I reached out to grab it, I could feel it respond to me, a surge of energy running up my arm like electricity.

"Let's go, Diana!" I could hear Jake yell from the bottom of the stairs.

I needed to hide this and deal with it later, but where could I put it that neither Jake nor my mom would find it? I crossed the room to my dresser and opened my underwear drawer, tucking it beneath the stack of fabric. That would have to do for now, at least until I had more time to figure out what had happened and what I planned to do with the grimoire now that I had it. If this truly was my family's book of shadows, I had to protect it, at all costs. In the hands of the wrong witch, it could be dangerous. It likely contained long-forgotten spells.

I hurried downstairs before Jake came back up looking for me, crossing the living room and following the rich smell of pancakes. Mom had the works set up. The countertop was filled with all sorts of toppings in little bowls. Chocolate chips, blueberries, strawberries, whipped cream, even sprinkles. It wasn't a proper snow day without pancakes. I pulled a seat up next to Jake and we filled our plates with short stacks while Mom turned back to the stove and continued cooking, a smile across her lips. Jake poured a heavy mound of maple syrup atop his before digging in, while I covered mine in chocolate chips.

After digging my car out from last night's snow, I'd have plenty of time to catch up on homework and study for Friday's biology exam. I would *also* have plenty of time to investigate that mysterious book of shadows I had hidden up in my room. Thank God for snow days. How had it just *appeared* beneath my pillow like that? Had I actually *pulled* it out of the dream with me? I didn't think such a thing was possible, but there was so much about this magic that I didn't know yet.

I couldn't wait to call Tess and tell her about it. I wondered around a mouthful of chocolaty pancakes if the roads would be plowed enough for her to still come over later and practice magic with me. I felt a new sense of control and confidence with my magic. I wasn't as nervous to tap into it as I had been. Would I be able to try my hand at some storm magic soon?

Mom joined us at the counter and served herself a stack of warm pancakes. The three of us ate breakfast together, laughing and smiling for the first time in what felt like forever.

I warmed myself by the fire and focused on my homework, anxious to call Tess later and investigate the mysterious appearance of the grimoire. I hadn't touched it since this morning. After a few hours spent studying by the fire, I made my way out to shovel the snow around my car and take care of the driveway. By the time I had successfully shoveled the nearly three feet of snow away, the sun was almost setting. I shook out my snow boots and jacket in the foyer before sprinting up to my room to text Tess.

Plow has already been by here a bunch of times and the roads are clear. Just finished the driveway. You still coming over? I texted.

My phone pinged, and I checked the message.

You got it, see you soon.

I couldn't wait to show Tess the grimoire firsthand. A piece of me thought that when I went to fish it back out of the drawer it wouldn't be there, and the whole thing had been an elaborate dream. I hopped in the shower, letting the hot water loosen the tension in my muscles from being out in the cold for so long. I brushed my hair out and pulled it into a bun at the top of my head before returning to my bedroom and searching for the grimoire in my underwear drawer. Sure enough, there it was, right where I had left it.

I sat cross-legged on the carpet before my dresser, the grimoire in my lap. It looked and felt exactly how it had in my dream. The cover was composed of tattered and worn leather, the leather string bindings fastening it shut in a knot at the front around the amethyst crescent moon. I moved to open it, but the bindings would not budge. In my dream I had needed to say a spell to open it. What is it that I had said?

"Aperi reginam tuam, aperi mihi." The words came to me as they had before. As if I had always known them and was pulling them from the deep well of my memory. As I said the words, the leather bindings began unfastening on their own, falling to the side and allowing me to open the grimoire. When Nik had said he was sure my family had a book of shadows, I never imagined I would find it. The dream had felt so real, but it *was* just a dream, wasn't it? Had the grimoire come to me, knowing I had been searching for it? Could a grimoire do such a thing?

I could hear the front door open downstairs and Tess bounded up the staircase, throwing my door open in a huff and tugging her jacket off excitedly.

"Puck asked me on a proper date, can you believe it? We are going to dinner tomorrow and I am beyond excited." She paused when she saw me sitting on the floor, the grimoire in my lap. "*What. Is. that.*"

"I think it's my family's grimoire, my book of shadows," I replied, stroking the leather-bound book with a delicate finger.

"Your—what?" Tess finished throwing the jacket down on the bed and joined me on the floor.

"My book of shadows. Nik said that every family has a book of shadows, or a grimoire. Since we aren't sure which of my parents is the witch, I wasn't sure where to even begin searching for mine."

"So where did you find it?" she asked excitedly.

"I found it in a dream. Last night I dreamed of this long dark corridor. I've dreamed of it before, but never like this. In the dream...I followed the corridor. I went down this spooky spiral staircase, and in the room at the bottom was this book. It wouldn't open at first, not until I said a spell. I think it's spelled to only open for me, or those of my bloodline at least," I told her.

"Let me see!" Tess grabbed for the book and as soon as her fingers touched the tattered pages, the book snapped shut, fastening its bindings. Exactly as it had for me when I had originally touched it in the laboratory. "Woah."

"I know, right?" I laughed. "Let me put this theory to the test," I handed Tess the grimoire, and she held it firmly in her lap.

"Repeat the spell and see if it opens for you. Maybe it's the spell that opens the grimoire."

Tess repeated the words, but the grimoire did not budge. She tried to pry it open with her fingers, but it was firmly fastened shut. She handed it back to me and I held it in my lap, repeating the spell. The book popped open once again and Tess and my eyes met.

"So, it only opens for you, then," Tess said.

"Looks like it." I shrugged. That confirmed it, then. It must be that because it was *my* family's grimoire, it would only open for someone in my bloodline, even with the opening spell.

"Since when do you speak Latin?" Tess asked, confused.

"Since…never. I have no idea. I never studied Latin before, but the spell came to me when I needed it. Maybe I always knew it, but was spelled to forget it. I don't know…" I trailed off, turning to the page for awakening. I moved so that Tess could see the book over my shoulder.

"When I read this page, I felt something wake up inside me. As if there was this magic that was locked down and I couldn't fully reach it before. I felt a new ember of energy that I could pull on, but I haven't done any magic since this morning to test it out," I told her.

"You think maybe you were spelled, too? To not be able to access your full powers?" Tess asked.

"I'm not sure. All I know is that I feel that well of magic much easier now than I did before, as if it's right at the tips of my fingers. It feels like it's an extension of me, I wouldn't even have to try that hard to control it anymore." Her eyes were transfixed on the page open in my lap. "In the dream, I also created a vortex. I'm not positive, but I think I *am* a Stormshade. I'm not sure what that means for me, if the Stormshades were hunted into extinction…"

"Have you told Nik any of this yet?" Tess asked.

"No, I wanted to tell you first." I smiled, nudging her with my shoulder.

"I am honored," Tess replied, holding a hand to her chest and wiping away fake tears. "There's one thing I still don't get...if you found the book in a dream, how is it here, *now*?"

"That's a good question." I bit my lip, deep in thought. "My dreams have always felt real, but I've never taken anything with me out of a dream before. I didn't feel like I had control of the dream, it felt as if the dream had control of me, if that makes sense. All I know is that when Jake woke me up this morning, I had been holding the book in my dream. Then there it was, buried beneath my pillow."

"That's incredible. Have you looked at any of the other spells?" she asked.

"No, not yet. The way Nik explained it is that simple spells don't require you to *speak* them, it's the special spells, the ones that are more powerful, that require that. Those are the spells found in the grimoire. Every family's book is different, containing different spells passed down from their family and the generations before. Who knows what this book might contain that maybe Nik hasn't even seen before," I answered.

"Well, let's take a look!" Tess squeezed in closer to me so she could look over my shoulder without the book snapping shut again, resting her chin on my shoulder. She was sure to keep both her hands firmly planted on the floor.

I opened to the first page, and it appeared to be instructions on creating a potion, it wasn't clear what that potion might be. A picture of a sparrow and a sprig of thyme were sketched into the narrow margin, little notes and scribbles covering the page.

The next page appeared to be some type of love spell, but this one was written entirely in Latin. The spells were a combination of English and Latin, some I understood, others I didn't. As we flipped through, more and more spells appeared to be written in Latin, and we weren't able to decipher what they meant.

Each page contained handwritten notes scribbled across them from my ancestors, and I wondered who in my family had this book in their possession before me. Who had written these notes? Where was that room located in the real world? Or was it not in our world at all...but in the witch realm, Istmere?

Tess and I flipped through the grimoire, eager to see if there were any other spells we might be able to understand. The grimoire was thick and had to be a few hundred pages long. When we reached the end Tess turned to me, our heads spinning.

"So, now you just have to learn Latin?" Tess asked on a breathless laugh.

"I guess so," I mused, "but I don't remember knowing the spell to open the book before, it slipped into my head on its own. As if it was a deeply buried memory. I wonder if the same thing would happen the longer I try to decipher these spells."

"Well, what are we waiting for, let's see what you can do!" Tess put some space between us and looked at me expectantly. She wanted me to show her what I'd learned since we last tried magic together, and I'd burned the carpet and broken the sheetrock.

I dipped into the well of magic in my core, and much easier than before I conjured a ball of flame in the palm of my hand. The flames licked at my skin without ever touching it. Tess stared with wide eyes as I threw the ball of flame from one hand to the other, juggling it effortlessly.

"Dude. That is so cool."

"Nik says every witch has some basic control over the elements because our magic is tied to the earth. What makes a Nightshade special is that they can also shapeshift. A Stormshade is unique because they can control the elements a step further, *creating* storms. In the dream, I swear the vortex I created became a well of energy all its own. That I was able to pull on that energy, too, not only the magic that I have intrinsically."

"Maybe that's why everyone thinks the Stormshades are dangerous? Because if they can pull energy from the storms they've created...they would be endlessly powerful. They wouldn't tire, and their magic wouldn't need to be replenished before they tapped into it again. Sounds like a recipe for a crazy powerful witch to me."

My eyes snapped up to Tess. "I think you're a genius."

"It's not every day I get *that* compliment." Tess laughed, throwing her pin straight brown hair over her shoulder.

That is *exactly* what it felt like in my dream. As if the vortex I had created had also created a separate energy for me to use as fuel. Was that why the Nightshades were pitted against the Stormshades? Were they jealous of their power, eager to steal it for themselves? Nightshades were powerful, but at some point, their magic would deplete and need to be replenished.

Were the Stormshades abusing their power, or was there more to the story than Nik was letting on?

"This is all I've tried," I told Tess as I extinguished the flame in my palm.

"What about another element? Can you hold anything else in the palm of your hand?" she asked. I hadn't tried yet, but I imagine it would be the same principle as conjuring the flame. The other elements seemed less dangerous than fire in comparison.

I opened my palm again, face up, and focused instead on the cool trickle of water instead of the sizzling heat of flame. I pictured that the water would sit in the palm of my hand, never touching my skin or getting me wet. As easily as I had summoned flame, a spherical ball of water now hovered against my palm. I pictured it breaking off into two, then three, then four, and watched as the spheres multiplied. They formed a line of whirling water spheres, lined up in the palm of my hand.

"That looked easy enough." Tess laughed with a shrug. When I had tried any new magic before, I had to focus much harder to use my energy to do my bidding. This felt as easy as breathing.

Had the awakening spell truly unlocked something inside me? I focused on the water and imagined it suddenly getting cold, and turning to ice. As soon as I dipped into that well of magic in my core the spheres of water stopped rotating and froze in place. They became four glistening icicles hovering in the air.

"Ok...I wish I could do that."

I laughed as I pulled the magic back and the icicles disappeared into thin air. I swept my hand to the right and imagined the pages of the grimoire flipping open at my will, and sure enough the pages began to turn rapidly.

"What about some storm magic?" Tess asked conspiratorially.

"First of all, we are inside. Second of all, storm magic can be dangerous from what I've heard. I'd rather try it with another magic user nearby in case something goes...wrong."

Tess nodded in understanding, "I can't wait to see what you can do with that type of magic. It's going to be incredible."

"I hope so. It feels as if it's right there for me to grab, like it'll be easy now." I scanned the room until my eyes fell on the cinnamon scented candle across the room on top of my nightstand. I focused my energy, snapped my fingers, and just like that the candle wick lit.

"Jealous." Tess laughed, pushing me over and dissolving into a fit of giggles. "You'll never have to get up to get the remote ever again."

"Yeah, because that's the coolest thing about this magic." I rolled my eyes, sitting back up and pulling Waffles into my lap as he sauntered by. He grumbled in refusal, but eventually settled into a neat little ball of fluff within the circle of my legs.

I wish I had known about this magic all my life. How would my life have been different if I had always known? If I was spellbound like we suspected, would I ever have been able to tap into my magic if I had never encountered another powerful magic user? I had so many unanswered questions spinning through my head. Just as I got some answers, I immediately had new questions. It felt like an endless loop, getting to know this new world of magic.

"Did you say that Puck asked you out on a real date?" I asked, suddenly remembering how Tess had initially announced it when she had walked in on me with the book of shadows.

"Yes!" she squealed, throwing herself onto her stomach and resting her head on her elbows.

"Details, woman. Details," I repeated Tess' famous words with a laugh.

"So...we have been texting back and forth, and he asked if I would want to go on an official date with him, to dinner. We are going to this cute little Italian bistro over in Fraser, and he is paying."

"That's amazing Tess, I'm so happy for you. Does this mean you're a taken woman?" I teased.

"Let's not get ahead of ourselves here," she laughed. "I know Puck doesn't have a specialty like you or Nik, but his magic is still pretty cool. He's sexy, and he has that bad boy thing going on...not as much as Nik, I'll admit. But maybe that means he will come *without* the side order of trouble."

"Here's hoping," I joked, crossing my fingers. I closed the grimoire and tucked it safely back into my underwear drawer. If nobody else could open it besides me, I didn't have anything to worry about, did I? I needed to find a better, and more discreet, place for it. This would have to do for now.

"Do you know if the grimoire belonged to your mom or your dad?" Tess asked, moving from the floor to throw herself down on the bed.

"I don't know, and I'm scared to ask. My mom has always thought I was a crazy little daydreamer, but what if she was pushing all that stuff down because it was a part of her past? Or what if it was Dad, and my mom never knew before..." I trailed off. If it *had* been my dad, we might never know, now that he was gone. He hadn't seemed like the type to hide this heavy of a secret, but neither did my mom. I didn't know who I could trust anymore.

"Do you and lover boy have plans to test out this storm magic of yours?" Tess asked as I threw myself down on the bed next to her.

"Saturday. He's taking me back to the meadow to work with our magic again." I told her. Could that be considered a date?

Tess wiggled her eyebrows comically, "Oooh lala!"

"Oh, please." I bumped her in the shoulder and we both laughed. "He's not my lover boy."

"Whatever you say, witch."

Nik picked me up after lunch on Saturday and we were driving towards the hidden meadow with the windows rolled down, the winter day unseasonably warm. School had been tense the remainder of the week with Fletcher watching over our shoulders at every moment. Nik had successfully avoided a public confrontation with him, but we hadn't had a minute to ourselves. I hadn't told Nik about the grimoire or the dream yet.

Tess had spilled all the details about her date with Puck. They had gone to the little Italian bistro, then gone for ice cream after. He dropped her off at home and had been ever the gentleman. He hadn't kissed her goodnight which she was slightly upset about, but knowing Tess that probably made her even more attracted to him. Having to work for it. Most of the boys at school threw themselves at her, she didn't have to put in any effort whatsoever. That made dating at Silver Oaks Academy predictable, not that I would know anything about that.

We pulled up to the mountain that we had parked at the base of the week before, getting out of the car and ditching our winter coats. The sun beating down on my face felt so nice, leaving my skin tingling from the warmth. Nik moved around to the back of the car and popped the trunk, revealing two long swords that left my mouth hanging open.

"What the hell are those?" I asked, raising a brow.

He looked from the trunk to me, then back to the trunk. "Swords."

"Yes, thank you. And what on earth do we need swords for?" I asked, crossing my arms.

"As I told you, you need to learn to defend yourself. Magic is one way of defending yourself, but what if you find yourself in an ash circle? Or an iron cage? We could start with daggers if you prefer, but I think the footwork will be easier to learn with these," he nodded towards the gleaming steel.

"That's…that's not exactly what I thought you meant when you said I had to learn to defend myself. Why would I ever be in an iron cage?"

"What did you think I meant?" he asked, his lips twisting into a smirk. "And I don't think anyone *expects* to ever be held in an iron cage, hence the preparation."

"I'm not exactly sure, but this wasn't it. I've never held a sword before."

"Obviously. That's why I'm going to teach you. Are you nervous, little firecracker?"

"I mean...yeah. Yes. Wouldn't anyone be nervous to *sword fight* for the first time? This isn't exactly common in this realm. Not to mention you have a significant amount of height and weight on me," I gestured to his form with my hand and his grin deepened.

"True. I'll go easy on you," he said with a wink. "It is common in the other realm. If you ever want to go there, you'll have to learn." He grabbed the lighter, smaller, of the two swords and flipped it by the handle, tossing it to me. I hadn't been expecting it, and it clattered to the dirt at our feet as my arms remained crossed.

"Seriously?" he asked, a laugh in his voice. "I have my work cut out for me." He grabbed his sword, placing it in a scabbard across his back, gesturing for me to do the same with mine. The sword felt awkward between my shoulder blades, but it wasn't as heavy as I'd first imagined. I still thought I would prefer a dagger. Since I knew nothing about hand-to-hand combat, I would let Nik make the decisions, for now.

As we walked towards the meadow clearing Nik walked close enough to me that his hand kept brushing against mine, sending a rush of heat to my core. I shot him a sideways glance, but he didn't meet my eyes. A playful smile across his lips told me he knew exactly what he was doing. His pale hair was radiant in the glow of the sunlight, his T-shirt showing off his tanned skin and tattoos. I thought, not for the first time, about where those tattoos might start and where they might end.

When the clearing came into view I went running ahead, my head thrown back towards the sun and my arms spread wide. A laugh bubbled up from my lips as I spun, I couldn't believe how much it felt like a clear spring day. The meadow was free of all snow and the grass was surprisingly dry. To think it had snowed a few feet this past week, but it had warmed up enough to melt it all away. Spring was on its way, and it couldn't come soon enough.

"I take it you hate the spring," Nik teased, joining me at the center of the meadow, his heavy boots crunching against the dry grass.

"Loathe it," I teased back with a smile, squinting against the bright sun.

"Where should we start, firecracker?"

"I guess we should start with these swords?" I offered, motioning towards my back where the light broadsword was resting between my shoulder blades.

"Let's do it," Nik replied, grabbing the handle of his sword and pulling it free from his scabbard. I tried doing the same, but was not nearly as graceful as he had been.

A laugh bubbled to his lips as he stepped forwards. "You are going to hold it like this, your grip should be firm, but loose. You don't want to white knuckle it and grip it to death."

I nodded, holding the sword as he had instructed and lifting it to waist height.

"Very good. Now when I swing my sword forwards, you will parry. I want to focus on defense for the moment."

Nik stepped forwards again, swinging his sword towards me in slow motion. I did as he said, and the sword sent a reverberating shock up my arm as they clanked together. If this was slow motion, I couldn't even imagine what that would feel like in a real battle when the sword was swung at full strength.

Nik taught me a combination of defensive moves and instructed me to use my height and my size to my advantage. While I was short and not especially muscular, I was fast. I needed to take advantage of that and not come at someone with brute strength.

By the end of our short training session I was sweating, my breathing heavy, and my arms sore. The broadsword may have appeared light at first, but swinging it around for the last hour was surely going to leave me sore tomorrow.

"For your first time with a sword, I have to say I'm impressed," Nik said as he returned his sword to his scabbard and used the hem of his shirt to wipe the sweat from his forehead. My eyes immediately traveled to the skin of his abdomen that had been exposed before I caught myself and glanced away. Nik's eyes met mine with a heated gaze, and I wiped my own forehead with the back of my hand. "You'll be a pro in no time," he broke the silence as I met his eyes again.

"Let's hope I never have to use these skills."

"Agreed." A muscle ticked in his jaw and his eyes were serious. "If you ever visit Istmere, I want you to be able to protect yourself. Using a sword and dagger will be a useful skill."

"Can we use a dagger next time?" I asked excitedly with a raised brow.

"You're enjoying this, aren't you?" he asked.

"A little," I admitted. I had never been much good at sports, but I felt strong with the broadsword in my hands. Powerful. This is something I might actually excel at.

"We can definitely train with a dagger next time. That will likely be the best weapon for you, it will pair well with your speed and agility." I had never imagined someone would use the words *speed* and *agility* when referencing me before.

I was hoping the dagger wouldn't leave me as sore as I was sure the broadsword would. I could feel the muscles in my back aching already, and I made a mental note to take some ibuprofen as soon as I got home. I slid the sword back into the scabbard at my back.

"All this sword fighting had me distracted. I just remembered I never told you what happened to me the other night," I responded, relaxing my arms back to my sides and meeting his gaze.

"What happened to you?" He took a step forwards, a note of concern in his voice.

"Nothing bad," I assured him with my hands out, "I only wanted to tell you about my dream."

"Your dream?"

"Yes, my dream." I took a deep breath to steel myself. I jumped into the story and told Nik all about how I had dreamed of the long dark corridor again. The same one I had been sketching on my notebook in class. The same one he had drawn that day in art class. I told him about how when I followed that long dark corridor it wasn't endless as I had initially thought, but rather it led to a long spiral staircase that wound down to a room, a laboratory of sorts. His brow furrowed as he listened.

"The odd thing is, when I reached the room, I found a book inside. A book that snapped shut at my touch. A book that required a special spell to open it. A spell that I spoke without *ever* remembering the words before." Nik took a step closer.

"When I did open the book, I realized it was my family's grimoire. My book of shadows."

"You dreamed of your family's grimoire? Do you remember ever having seen it before, maybe when you were younger?" he asked.

"No." I shook my head. "It felt familiar, somehow. But I didn't recognize it. Not until I felt its energy. It was open to a spell of awakening, and when I said the words aloud, I felt...different. As if something had been unlocked inside of me. As if the storm that I then created right there in that room had an energy all its own." Nik's lips parted slightly, his eyes darkening.

"Who else did you tell about this?" he asked, taking another step closer and closing the distance between us, his hand on my shoulder.

"Just Tess." I met his intense gaze. "Why?"

"Listen to me carefully, Diana. You cannot tell anyone else about that awakening spell. Do you understand?" His eyes were serious, his grip on my shoulder tight.

"I understand." I nodded, biting my lip. His eyes traveled down to that lip before slowly traveling back up to meet my eyes again. "What's the big deal about that spell?"

"That isn't just any spell." He shook his head. "*That* spell awakens a witch's dormant storm magic. It proves what I already thought...that you *are* a Stormshade. And a dangerous one, at that. Dangerous enough for someone to spellbind you when you were too young to remember."

"Dangerous?" I recoiled, his hand falling from my shoulder as I took a step back. How could I be dangerous when the worst thing I'd done thus far was break some glass and burn a carpet. And that was *before* my storm magic had awakened. Would I even have been able to access my storm magic before I had performed the awakening spell?

"You don't realize how rare the power is that you have." Nik shook his head. "You can't let anyone know, or they will want it for themselves. Do you understand? You need to keep this between us. I wish you hadn't told Tess."

"Tess is my best friend, I tell Tess everything. She won't say anything, I promise," I replied defensively.

"Good." He nodded. "You need to be protected. If Fletcher ever found out..." He trailed off, his eyes on his feet.

"He won't," I assured him. He nodded again, deep in thought.

"Not just any witch can create a storm and then pull energy from it. The witches who were thought to be able to do that...well...they were killed a long time ago."

"You think I'm in danger?" I asked, a clear edge of panic in my voice.

"Yes, I do. If anyone were to find out," he replied. "This is serious. Your magic has awakened now, you can't tell *anyone*. You have to keep this hidden. *That* magic is what makes you dangerous. With that type of magic, you will never run out of power." He confirmed what I had already suspected, that the Stormshades might have been hunted for an entirely different reason than we originally thought. That others coveted that endless power for themselves.

"We didn't even get to the best part of the story," I teased.

"And what might that be?" A soft smile reached his lips, but it never reached his eyes. Did he honestly think that other witches would be after me if they found out? With this new-found magic, wouldn't I be able to keep myself safe? Protect myself?

"After the awakening spell, I woke up. When I lifted my pillow, the grimoire was right there, as if I had it in my possession the whole time."

"You have the grimoire?" he asked, his eyes widening. I nodded in confirmation. "You took it from the dream?"

"I mean, I didn't *take* it. Not on purpose, anyway. It was just...there. When I woke up."

"Where is it now?" he asked, taking a step towards me again.

"My room," I replied simply as he took another step forwards. I could smell the scent of coffee and cinnamon on his breath.

"Do you know what this means?" he asked, breathless.

"Obviously not..." I quipped.

"Diana, you are a dream walker." He ran a hand through his mess of hair.

"A dream walker?" I repeated.

"Yes, a dream walker. When you walk in dreams, you have the ability to take things with you, to *touch* things as if they were real. To visit places as if you were *actually* there." He shook his head in astonishment.

"Is that...rare?" I asked.

"Rare?" He laughed. "You could say that. The last person that had that ability, that I know of, was the Dark King. He has been dead for more than a decade."

"The Dark King?" I asked, the words sparking a memory within me from that night I encountered the grimoire for the first time. The vision I had in that dream, the vision the grimoire sent me.

A dark king sitting on his throne of shadows. A woman with pale strawberry hair fleeing a stone palace, a bundle pressed tightly to her chest. A woman with blue and white hair, raising a sword high above her head in victory. She turned, and her eyes were endless black pits. A war, witches slaughtering witches, fire burning down an empire. The blue-haired woman sitting on the throne of shadows, a pack of black wolves at her side. A city in ruin, stone buildings reduced to rubble as smoke rises from the ashes.

I had a vision. Whether it was real or not, I wasn't sure. But I had a vision. One that involved a dark king.

"Is it possible to—to see things from the past? To have visions?" I asked, trying to pin down those memories and make sense of them. They had flashed before my eyes so quickly and were gone just as fast.

"Yes," he replied, cocking his head to the side. "The grimoire sent you a vision, didn't it?" he presumed. I nodded in response.

"That isn't entirely uncommon for such a powerful magical object. What did it show you? What did you see?"

I explained that I had seen a dark king, about the woman with the blue hair, the empire burning. As I spoke the pallor of Nik's skin turned ashy and white, from the set of his jaw I could tell he knew *exactly* what I was talking about. When I finished, he was quiet for a while. His eyes looked everywhere except to meet mine.

"I can tell that you know what I saw. Tell me," I insisted, shoving my hands into my jean pockets.

"Are you sure you want to know, firecracker? It isn't a fairy-tale." He shook his head with a grim smile.

"I'm sure. Tell me." Nik sighed deeply, glancing to the sky as if to find his resolve. He swept his hand, palm out, and a set of chairs appeared before us out of nowhere. I quirked a brow but said nothing. Was that something I could do, too?

"Shapeshifter, remember?" He smirked, taking a seat in the chair across from me and gesturing for me to do the same.

"You can shapeshift things other than yourself?" I asked, sitting across from him.

"Of course." He shrugged, leaning back and crossing his legs at the ankles. So, not something I could do as well, then. I still didn't understand how any of this magic worked, and I was anxious to learn all I could.

"What you saw, what the grimoire showed you, it must have been the War of Siraleth," he told me.

"I want to know everything. I want to know what happened to them."

Nik took a deep breath and let it out slowly before he began.

"A long time ago, a war started between the Nightshades and the Stormshades." I nodded, remembering how he had told me this part the night he had snuck into my room through the window. "The Nightshades wanted to put a stop to the Stormshades, because they were more powerful than them, thus more dangerous. This war between shades has been going on for a hundred years, but it came to a boiling point at the War For All Times. The war was led by the Dark King, Osiris, who had lived for hundreds and hundreds of years."

"That's possible?" I asked.

"It shouldn't be, witches are not innately immortal. Osiris used black magic to make himself eternal, or so we all thought. After the War For All Times, Nightshades made a truce with Stormshades, but they were no longer allowed in the palace or the capitol city. Many years passed and Stormshades were thought to be eradicated entirely from Akra, The Stone City. That is, until the Dark King Osiris fell in love with one." This was starting to sound suspiciously like a fairytale, but I kept my mouth shut and waited for the other shoe to drop.

"This woman hid her true nature from him for many years, but when he found out what she truly was, he cast her out of The Stone City. Osiris was changed, he had softened and became weaker because of it. Years later, a general in his arm thirsted for his power, and plotted to overthrow him. The general formed an army for themselves and stormed the city of Siraleth, killing Osiris and taking the throne. The new ruler of Istmere made it their mission to eradicate Stormshades for good, and to take down any witch who stood in their way. That new ruler is named Donika." *A woman.* It must have been the woman from my vision, the one with blue and white hair and endless black pits for eyes.

"What we didn't know at the time, was that Donika was the daughter of the long-lost love that Osiris cast out of the palace. She was born before their love affair, to a different man that raised her in her mother's absence. Many think she killed Osiris as revenge for her mother, few know the truth."

"And what is the truth?" I asked, riveted.

"The truth is that Donika was born dark. She played with black magic from a young age, but she would have killed the king, regardless. Many call her the Black Heart. She's known as the Shadow Queen. The truth is, her mother died by Donika's own hand, simply for being a Stormshade." Donika sounded truly awful. Who could kill their own mother? Simply because of what they were? This must be the woman I saw raise her sword in victory, having killed her mother *and* the Dark King. All for power. How twisted. Now she sits on the throne, corrupt, killing all who move against her.

"What happened to the other Stormshades?" I asked. "If she vowed to have them all hunted and killed?"

"That's the thing..." Nik started, shaking his head. "There are none. They either fled to the mortal realm where they were hunted down, or they were killed in the War at Sir-aleth."

"But...I'm a Stormshade," I whispered.

"Exactly." Nik leaned forwards, grabbing my hands between his. "Which is why you *cannot* tell anyone about your awakening. Not your mom, not Jake. *Nobody*." I nodded in understanding. My life could be in danger simply because of what I was. Because there were no more Stormshades, or so everybody thought.

"And you need to hide that grimoire. Don't let anybody see it. A Stormshade's grimoire contains spells that could easily be manipulated if they were to get into the wrong hands." I nodded again, swallowing hard.

"There's something I want to show you." He stood, dragging me with him.

"What is it?" I asked, the chairs disappearing behind us with the wave of Nik's hand.

"It's a secret," Nik teased, pulling me towards the pond that was no longer frozen over as it had been the last time we had visited the meadow. We stopped a short distance away, Nik raising his hands towards the water, palms out.

"*Suscipe me ubi opus est ire,*" Nik recited under his breath, his eyes closed.

"Wait!" I tugged on the sleeve of Nik's T-shirt as he repeated the words, the ground before him starting to shimmer. He turned to me, his face creased in concentration.

"We can't go to Istmere, I'm a *Stormshade* for crying out loud. They will kill me!"

"Not where we are going," he replied, turning back to the opening portal. "Where we are going, there is no one. It's deserted, I can promise you that much."

The water before Nik turned to a shimmering clear blue, the areas to his left and right blurring into obscurity. I imagined the portal as a doorway that we would walk through, but beyond the shimmering gloss on the water all I could see was the stillness of the pond beyond.

"Take my hand." He turned to me with his arm extended and I grabbed it without hesitation. "Stay with me." Together we stepped onto the shimmering water as if it was solid ground, and we fell into nothingness.

For a while it felt as if I was stuck in the 'in between.' There was nothing around me, no light, no taste, no smell. It felt as if I were trapped in a dark dream, one that I would wake up from and not remember. My eyes were open, but I saw nothing before me. That unending darkness came to a crashing halt as I felt myself falling with no way to catch myself. My stomach dropped, and before I knew it I was standing on the other side of the portal, wherever that was. I could feel my hand still in Nik's as my vision came back into focus.

I turned, and the portal behind us was nothing but a patch of shimmering grass before it evaporated altogether. Wherever Nik had portaled us, it was breathtakingly beautiful.

We stood at the crest of a lush meadow filled with wildflowers and tall grass that swayed softly in the cool breeze. It felt more like spring here than it did back in the mortal world, despite us having a warm day there. At the base of the hill on which we stood I could make out an old city made of stone in the distance, its buildings nestled together closely. To the right was the water. At first it appeared to be a lake, but as I looked further, I could see that the mouth of the water opened up into a much larger expanse. Where did it lead?

Behind us were rolling grassy hills as far as the eye could see.

"What is this place?" I turned to Nik, my hand still held in his warm grasp.

"Welcome to Istmere," he said with a smile, watching as I took in the vast landscape before us. Istmere was truly beautiful. It somewhat resembled the mortal realm, but it felt otherworldly, more innately magical. It was as if I could feel the magic deep in my bones, in every breath that I took. It was tingling under my skin, lifting the hair off the back of my neck. This was a place of power, that's for sure. Now I understood how the meadow in Colorado was such a strong magical tether to this world.

"I figured we could practice some magic here," Nik said, turning towards me.

"I can feel the magic here." I placed a hand on my stomach and took a deep breath, my eyes fluttering shut. "It permeates everything."

"It will be the easiest to control your magic here, in Istmere. I thought, why not bring you here to test out those Stormshade abilities of yours?" He grinned as he nudged me in the side.

"Your wish is my command," I teased, forming a ball of flame easily in the palm of my hand.

"I see you've been practicing." Nik raised an eyebrow.

"I have," I replied as I turned the ball of flame into a whirling cell of water, then just as quickly I froze it into ice. "Now how do I call on storm magic?"

"It's going to be similar to how you call on your elemental magic," Nik explained, "you will feel it in your core. I can't exactly say how it will feel because I don't have storm magic like you do. But when I feel my shadow magic, I feel as if I'm tapping into a deep part of myself. My elemental magic is right there at the surface, always ready for me to call upon it. My shadow magic is hidden deeper in my core, it's a spark of energy that has to be tapped into."

I nodded and closed my eyes, trying to find that spark that he spoke of. Now that I had been practicing with my elemental magic I could sense it in my core readily, the feeling becoming familiar. I did as Nik instructed and searched a level deeper, trying to find a spark of magic buried beneath, as if it were hiding.

My brow furrowed as I focused. Just as I was about to give up I felt a spark of magic reach out to me, as if it were saying 'I'm here.' When I touched that magic with my mind I felt a rush of heat across my skin, as if a hot blast of flame was ignited right below the surface. I could feel my storm magic there, tucked away, waiting for me.

"Good, now hold on to that feeling." Nik could see the moment I had found it, the lines on my face creasing in concentration. "Tap into it exactly as you would your elemental magic. It might be a little harder to coax out, but it will come when you call on it."

I pictured the storm magic flowing out in a steady stream, not too much, but just enough. I wanted to start with something small. I had already created a vortex once in the laboratory in my dream, so I tried once again to create a small vortex of wind. I pushed that energy through my fingertips, pushing it left, then right, then left again, until I felt the wind at my fingertips begin to swirl.

I opened my eyes and there, at the tips of my fingers, was a mini tornado, swirling angrily. It couldn't have been more than six inches tall, and it whirled and spun in the palm of my hand. My eyes snapped up to Nik's as his darkened, a mischievous grin on his face.

"More," he coaxed, his eyes focused on the small tornado I had created.

I pictured more energy funneling into the vortex until it bounced off my hand onto the ground, now standing a foot tall and whirling in circles around our feet. It kicked up dust and wildflowers as it picked up speed and intensity.

"Amazing." Nik smiled, his eyes meeting mine.

I had done it. *I had really done it.* I might not be able to call on a powerful storm yet, but I had tapped into my storm magic and created the tornado that now spun at our feet. What else could I do with this magic? With a snap of my fingers the tornado extinguished, and the wildflowers floated back down to the ground at our feet.

I spread my arms wide, the palms of my hands facing up towards the sky, as I called on my storm magic once more. A crack of thunder sounded overhead, and though it was my magic that had created it, I still startled. I jumped as the sound reverberated through me. The clouds began to darken over-head as I funneled more magic into them, they slowly became black and furious. The meadow was no longer blanketed in sunshine, but rather enveloped within the dark clouds I had created.

I felt the first drop of rain hit my cheek as I turned my face towards the sky, a smile on my lips as the storm energy surrounded me in its embrace. I felt another rain drop hit my skin, then another, as the fat droplets began to pour from the sky. Nik's face was lit with wonder, his eyes on me with a heated gaze.

"You're incredible," he breathed, taking a step towards me.

I lowered my hands back to my sides as the rain pelted down on us, the rainstorm taking on an energy all its own. It rained harder, soaking through my hair and my clothes as I turned towards the sky again and laughed.

I was a Stormshade, *and I was powerful.*

I could sense the energy of the storm, calling to me from its place in the sky. If I reached out to that energy, would I be able to harness it as my own? With my face still turned towards the sky I peered at the clouds, reaching out to them with my own magic. They responded instantly. I felt a lightning-like surge of energy fill my core, but it wasn't my own, it was that of the storm.

The storm I had created *had its own magic*, and I was able to use it as if it were my own. The feeling of power inside of me raised the hair on my arms and brought goosebumps to my flesh as the storm whipped the hair back from my face. My clothes stuck to me mercilessly, and I wished that I hadn't worn jeans today. All I could do was laugh as the rain came down around us harder, soaking us through.

Nik took another step towards me, and I could feel my breath get caught in my throat. His gaze was molten lava, and I felt as if I would simply melt under it. His pale hair was darkened from the rain, curls of it plastered to his forehead. His black T-shirt clung to his skin in a way that made my mouth dry up. I could see every muscle, every outline. My eyes traveled back up to his, a wicked grin across his lips.

He raised his hand slowly to cup my cheek, wiping the rain from my skin with his thumb. His other hand found my hip and tugged me close, my hands falling to his chest where I could feel his heart beating heavily.

"Incredible," he whispered again, his mouth so close to mine I could feel his breath on my skin, my stomach tightening.

"I did it," I breathed, unable to believe it myself. I had thought it would be difficult, but it wasn't. It was as easy as breathing. It was as if I was born to wield this storm magic, and it effortlessly responded to me in return. I curled my fingers into the front of his soaked T-shirt, pulling him even closer.

"I knew you could, firecracker," he said before lowering his mouth to mine. His lips were soft and warm, wet with rain as they slid across mine. My lips opened for him as he slid his hand from my hip to the small of my back, pressing himself into me. I could feel every dip and curve of him pressed against me, his other hand moving from my cheek to tangle in my hair. I felt a hot need surge up within me, pooling low in my belly. A small whimper left my lips, and he smiled against my mouth, pressing against me harder.

Kissing Nik was everything I had imagined, and more. His chest was hard beneath my touch, and I moved my hands to explore his abdomen, tucking them beneath the lip of his shirt and feeling the smooth skin there. I ran my hands up his stomach as he let out a low moan against my mouth, biting my lip before pressing his forehead to mine.

"If we keep going, I won't be able to stop," he whispered, his breath hot against my face, the rain still falling around us relentlessly.

"Who says we need to stop?" I asked, rounding my hands to his back beneath his shirt and pulling him closer.

"There's something I wanted to show you," he breathed, closing his eyes and swallowing hard, "but right now, I can't even think of what that something might be." I could feel him laugh against me, our bodies still pressed tightly together, the rain from his wet curls dripping down onto my nose.

"Are you sure about that?" I teased, bringing my lips back to his. I moaned against him as I moved my hands down his back, feeling every taught muscle beneath my fingertips before pulling back again.

"You really had to go and ruin this perfectly sunny day with rain?" He laughed against me, his eyes dark with want as they roamed my face. I had started this storm, and I could stop it just as easily. But I was too distracted with the feel of Nik's hands all over me.

I gently pushed him away, a smirk across my lips as I sprinted down the hill towards the city made of stone off in the distance. I raised my arms to the sky and threw my head back, laughing as a crack of thunder sounded again in the distance.

"Hey, get back here!" I could hear Nik close on my heels as I ran through the tall grass, my wet jeans thwacking against me with every step. I spun beneath the deluge of rain, letting it drip down my face, plastering my hair to the back of my neck. I was spinning when Nik's arms found me, enveloping me, and pulling me against him as I danced in the rain. His hand was in my hair again as he pulled me in for one more fierce kiss before turning towards the abandoned city.

"Come with me." He smiled, his hand held out for me to take. I placed my hand in his as we started walking, focusing on pulling the storm magic back into myself. I pictured the energy as a single point in the clouds, then I imagined it funneling downwards until I could absorb it back into myself.

As we walked, the storm clouds began to dissipate, and the sun started to peak through the clouds once again. The rain had stopped. We were still completely soaked through as we walked towards the city hand in hand, but the sun was once again warm at our backs.

We walked on for several minutes before the city came into clear focus. It was set in ruins, the stone archways were falling apart, rock scattered across the ground where it appeared to have been blasted apart. Nik gave my hand a gentle squeeze as we walked under the first archway, and I could see the city before me clearly. A vision flashed before my eyes, and it was gone just as quickly as it had appeared.

A city in ruin, stone buildings reduced to rubble as smoke rises from the ashes. A woman with blue and white hair, raising a sword high above her head in victory; she turns, and her eyes are endless black pits.

Without Nik having to say anything, I knew this was where the war had occurred all those years ago against the Stormshades and the Dark King. The war where he met his end. This was the site where *so many* Stormshades were slain and lost their lives. I turned to Nik and his eyes were filled with sadness as he gave my hand another gentle squeeze. How many of my relatives fought in this war? Died in this war?

I could see that the city was once beautiful. The sun shone through the archways that framed the stone walkways, winding through the city and between the buildings. I could picture what it had once looked like in its glory, vines of ivy climbing up the stone, flower boxes filled with color. Once the streets had been bustling with witches as the shop owners opened their windows to the noises of the street down below.

"I wanted you to see this place for yourself, to understand what happened here." Nik's mouth was set in a hard line. "This was our capitol, our holy city. The birthplace of our magic."

I could feel my connection to this place strongly in the magic that still dwelled here. In the earth, in the stone, it was *everywhere*. Nikolai was right when he said he was sure this place would be deserted, it appeared as if nobody had been here in decades. It was completely and utterly deserted, a snapshot in time from the end of the war against Stormshades. It was left exactly how it had been after the great war all those years ago. With such a strong connection to our magic, why had the Nightshade army not bothered to rebuild it after they had won the war? Why had they left it to ruin like this?

"The people?" I turned to Nik, a question in my eyes. It didn't look as if anyone had come back for them, but there were no skeletons scattered among the rubble. The only thing that remained were the swords and battle leathers of those that had fallen in battle.

"They returned to the earth from which they came, absorbed back into the magic of this place. Nothing would remain of them," he explained. "A witch's bones can be a powerful thing, a way in which someone might harness the energy they had possessed when they were once alive. All witches return to the earth upon their death, absorbed back into the magic that pulses into the very being of this earth. That is, unless someone takes the bones first," he said ominously.

Nik ducked as we walked under the second, smaller, archway, his sword at his back almost catching on the crest of the arch as he passed through. The remnants of stone were piled so high that it only left a small space for us to walk through. I ducked too, mindful of my own sword at my back. It was so light, I had almost forgotten that I had it.

Nik swept his arm wide, indicating the city beyond. Past him I could see the vast city expanse, buildings as far as the eye could see. This city was huge, much larger than I had initially thought. Rebuilding would be quite the task, but the pulse of magic that ran down my arms and up my spine reminded me that a powerful magic resided here. Bringing this city back to life would be worth it.

One building in particular caught my eye off in the distance. There, nestled under the alcove of a slate rooftop, was a tattered wooden door set in a dark stone archway. If I had to guess, that particular door would lead to a long dark corridor, one that I was quickly becoming familiar with. The same dark corridor from my dreams. Is that where my grimoire had come from? Had it been here, buried in this forgotten city, all these years?

"Welcome to the fallen city, Diana. Welcome to Siraleth."

I felt a sharp pang in my gut as I pictured what Siraleth might have looked like before the war. The homes lined the cobblestone streets so close together that you couldn't tell where one house began and another one ended. The remnants of blacksmith and magic shops alluded to what was once here, their signs still hanging, but their walls reduced to nothing but wreckage and rubble. The city was built on the edge of the water, and I could imagine the port as a bustling thoroughfare with boats and ships as it once had been. How big *was* Istmere?

Nik walked ahead of me and kicked through the rubble as he mournfully took in the scenery. How many times had he come back to Siraleth after the war? Was this where Nik's family had lived before they were pushed out of their home and fled to Akra? Before the witch realm was torn apart? I wanted to ask, but the set of his shoulders suggested he wasn't in the mood to field any questions at the moment.

We wound our way through the streets, closer and closer to the doorway that looked familiar to me. The homes that had been blasted to bits still had furniture inside. It was clear that even for the Nightshades that had lived here, nobody had returned to clean up their homes or shops after the war. Siraleth had been left completely untouched. What remained of the Elixir shops were filled with bits of broken glass and bookshelves that had been turned over, thick tomes scattered among the rubble.

Although I had never been here before, the feeling deep in my core felt familiar. As if I had met this energy before. The magic here was palpable, sewn into everything that had been left behind.

Nik kicked a few rocks away before bending down and pulling a book from the debris. He looked it over quickly, dusting off the cover before tossing it back. His eyes met mine and I could see that it pained him to see the city this way, in such disrepair. I couldn't help but wonder what the other cities in Istmere looked like, and if they had also fallen to ruin after the war.

As we wound further through the twisting streets and neared the door from my dreams, I paused before it, waiting for Nik to catch up. He raised an eyebrow as he came to my side, linking his hand with mine.

"I had seen this place before in a dream, but I don't remember it being in Siraleth..." he mused. "Where do you think it leads?"

"Only one way to find out," I told him, reaching for the door handle with the hand that wasn't clasped in his. As I pushed it open, it didn't creak as it had in my dream, but rather it opened smoothly. As if it had never fallen out of use. What lay beyond was not the familiar, long, and empty corridor from my dreams, but rather a humble cottage that appeared mostly untouched from the battle.

I pulled Nik through the doorway behind me and as soon as my foot stepped over the threshold, I felt a warm rush of magic surge up inside me and skip across my skin. Siraleth itself was a powerful and magical place, but this cottage felt as if it had an energy all its own. What was this place?

The cottage was small, and most of its dust filled rooms could be seen from our place at the front entrance. It had a sitting room off to the left with mauve velvet furniture that resembled an expensive tea set. Beyond the sitting room was a small, but well-appointed kitchen, and a single bedroom off to the right of that. How had this home escaped the war almost completely unscathed, aside from the dust that now settled into every nook and cranny over the years?

"Did you feel that?" Nik asked. He pulled his hand from mine and placed it against his core, as if he, too, was feeling the magic well up inside of him. "It's as if the magic here is...palpable."

I nodded. I had felt it too. A powerful witch must have lived here once. Why was so much tangible energy left behind? As I turned to inspect the bedroom, I heard the faint sound of a voice outside the window. My foot paused on a creaky floorboard as I turned to Nik in alarm. Siraleth was deserted; who else would be here?

Nik motioned for me to be quiet with a finger over his lips as he moved soundlessly to the front door of the cottage. He opened the door a sliver and peered out, listening intently, before closing it again and dragging me into the single bedroom off the kitchen.

"Who is it?" I whispered as he dragged us towards the single closet and pulled me inside.

"Nightshade soldiers," he replied through gritted teeth, pressing me against the back wall of the dark closet, "*in tenebris ambulamus et non videri.*"

I held still, holding my breath in fear of giving away our location. I could hear the front door open and slam against the opposing wall, as if whoever it was had kicked it open. I heard a set of boots against the hardwood floors. Then another. How many of them were there? The boots approached the bedroom and I could hear the floorboards creak beneath them as they drew closer and closer to the closet. My breath caught in my throat as the footsteps neared. There was no way they weren't going to catch us here, but what would they do with us? Would they let us go?

The doorknob to the closet began to turn slowly. They were about to find us. What were we going to do? The door swung wide, and a tall man faced me as Nik continued to press me against the back wall. He had a beard similar to Fletcher's the night I had first met him, but this man's hair was cut much closer to his face. He couldn't have been more than a few years older than us.

He glanced around the closet as if he couldn't see us, even forming a ball of flame in his hand to inspect each and every dark corner, as if something could be hidden there. Satisfied that he had found nothing, he extinguished the flame and closed the door, the sound of his boots retreating across the squeaky floorboards.

I exhaled softly, melting into Nik as he pressed against me. How had he not seen us? I waited until we heard the front door open and the sound of footsteps back on the cobblestone streets before speaking.

"Who were they?" I hissed against Nik's chest, "I thought you said that nobody would be here?"

"Fletcher's henchmen, I recognized them," Nik replied softly, his breath warm on my cheeks. "He must have sent them through the portal after us. I didn't think he was following us that closely..."

"Close enough to see us go through the portal? That was a close call. How did he not see us when he opened the closet door?"

"Because I spelled us to be invisible." He raised an eyebrow at me in the darkness.

"Another Nightshade perk?"

"A Nik perk. Not every Nightshade can control the shadows and the darkness like I can."

Damn him and his talent for manipulating shadows. I moved to reach around him and open the closet door, but he caught my hand with his and pinned it above my head, grabbing my other hand and doing the same. I could still feel the magic of this house as if it were a hot coal deep in my stomach as my magic responded to his, surging up and sparking my hands.

"Hey now, firecracker, that was not very nice," he teased, bringing his mouth down to the intersection where my neck met my shoulder.

"I didn't do it on purpose," I laughed, breathless.

"Mmhmm," he murmured against my skin, his lips moving in a soft trail of kisses up my neck and across my jaw. When his lips finally met mine, I felt as if my skin was on fire, the small closet space warming with the heat of our bodies.

My lips opened beneath his as he pressed his hips into me, driving and pinning me against the wall. The broadsword at my back pressed uncomfortably between my shoulder blades, but that was a passing thought as I felt every inch of him pressed against me, my hands held prisoner above my head.

He deepened the kiss, his lips pressing so hard against mine I was sure they would bruise, but I didn't care. Hot need pulsed between my legs as he pushed into me. I felt as if no matter how close he was, it wasn't close enough. I wanted more of him. I wanted to taste all of him. He parted my lips with his and slipped his tongue inside, mixing with mine. The sensation set my bones on edge. I moaned against him as the intensity of his kiss threatened to devour me and swallow me whole. I laughed against his lips and he pulled away enough to see my face in the darkness.

"And *what* is so funny, firecracker?" He ground into me, causing me to gasp, a smile across his lips.

"I've just..." I started, biting my lip, "never felt this way be-fore," I admitted. He wouldn't be able to see the flush that rose to my cheeks in the darkness, but I could feel it hot beneath my skin. His eyes darkened, and I could see a muscle tick in his jaw as he brought his lips back to mine possessively.

"Me neither," he whispered against my mouth. "You're mine." his words were so quiet they were almost swallowed into the darkness as he nipped at my bottom lip. I bit him back, hard enough to draw a little blood. I licked it off, running my tongue slowly across his bottom lip, savoring the salty taste.

"*Fuck*," he moaned, releasing my hands from above my head and moving his fingers to press into my hips. I gripped his shirt tightly in my fist as I pulled him closer. We had started to dry off since the rainstorm earlier and were only damp now, but I was itching to get out of these wet jeans.

As if reading my thoughts, Nik reluctantly pulled back, letting out a deep sigh. "We better be getting back. Who knows how many witches he sent after us through the portal to spy on us."

I nodded, not trusting myself to speak, my heart beating hard against my ribs so loudly I was sure he could hear it. I ran my thumb across his bottom lip, wiping the bead of blood away before licking it off my finger. Nik's eyes were heated in the darkness.

He reluctantly turned and opened the closet door, careful not to make too much noise in case the witches hadn't gone far. I followed close on his heels, trying my best to be quiet against the creaking floorboards, but I wasn't nearly as graceful as he was. Nik scanned the area in front of the house and when he saw no one, he motioned for me to follow. We slipped out of the cottage quietly as the sun began to set over the water.

"We spent more time here than I thought," Nik spoke in a hushed tone as we made our way back down the winding cobblestone streets. He nudged me gently in the side and it sent a wave of heat over me. I was growing accustomed to the feeling of the sword at my back, and though I had been nervous at first, I was looking forward to learning how to wield it.

We made our way out of the city and back up the hill swiftly, continually checking behind us to make sure Fletcher's men weren't on our heels. When we reached the top of the hill, Nik wasted no time and called the portal forth, taking my hand in his and stepping into the abyss.

The first thing I did when I got home was race upstairs and call Tess. I couldn't believe that not only had I been to Istmere, but I had seen the city of Siraleth. I had felt the magic there, and Nik had kissed me. A few times. I felt hot all over at the thought of it. His body pressed against mine, his eyes darkening, the way he felt under my fingertips. I shook the thoughts of Nik loose and continued dialing, suppressing a giggle at the thought of Tess' reaction.

"It's about time!" Tess answered, a laugh in her voice.

"Who answers the phone like that?" I threw myself down onto the pillows, Waffles jumping up onto the bed to join me.

"I do. Your best friend, in case you forgot," she teased, "I have been waiting all day for an update!"

"Well, I called you as soon as I got home," I assured her, scratching Waffles under the chin until he started to purr.

"I thought you turned your phone off. My messages didn't say delivered."

"That's because I was in a place where there *was* no cell service, or no cell phones at all, rather."

"You *what?* You went to the other realm?" I could imagine her pouting on the other end of the line, feeling left out. I told Tess all about how I had used storm magic for the first time, and how easy it had felt. How natural. I told her how Nik had taken me to Siraleth to see the fallen city. How Fletcher's men had followed us through the portal, but hadn't caught us. I left the best part for last, knowing it would kill her.

"I have some pretty big news to tell you myself," she announced.

"You go first," I told her.

"No, you," she insisted, "because I'm pretty sure I already know what it is." I was pretty sure she had already guessed, too.

"Nik kissed me," I sighed, biting my lip.

"I knew it!" she squealed through the phone. "I need *all* the details."

"It was hot. Like…scorching." I could hear the soft pad of footsteps on the stairs. Was it my mom? Jake?

"Oh, you bad girl," she teased, "what else?"

"I'll have to tell you tomorrow," I told her in a hushed voice, almost positive it was Jake outside my door, eavesdropping. "Want to go to the movies?"

"Want to make it a double date?" she countered, a note of mischief in her voice. "Then I can tell you my big news...or...show you."

"You're going to make me wait until tomorrow?" I asked, knowing patience was a virtue, but one that I never had.

"I sure am. Meet you at the movies at nine. We can catch that new rom-com. Tell lover boy. Love you!" And before I could protest any further, she hung up with a click.

I had texted Nik to meet us at the movie theater, but he had insisted on picking me up instead, even though I hadn't told my mom about him yet. I knew she would question my car being parked in the driveway all night, so I had told her Tess' parents were picking me up.

I waited at the curb for Nik to drive up, hoping my mom wouldn't peek out the window and see. If he kept insisting on coming to my house, I would eventually have to tell her about him. But what would I even say? He wasn't my boyfriend, but he was *definitely* more than a friend. It was complicated.

My phone dinged as I saw the black BMW pull around the corner from Easton Street, the headlights washing over me. I pulled it out of my back pocket to quickly check the text.

Puck and I are inside. See you soon. XOXO Tess.

I wondered what the news was that she had to tell me. Were she and Puck making things official? The BMW pulled up to the curb, and I jumped into the passenger seat, hugging my jacket around me to fight off the chill in the night air.

"Hey there, firecracker," Nik said from the driver's seat. I couldn't see his face clearly in the darkness, but I knew he was smiling.

"Hey," I replied, suddenly nervous. The last time I had seen him, his hands had been all over me. And his mouth...it was all I could think about now, sitting here in the darkness with him. The car felt too small, as if the energy between us would explode at any moment and couldn't be contained. He reached across the console and grabbed my hand, holding it in my lap against my thigh.

"You're freezing," he laughed, rubbing his thumb along my hand as he pulled back onto the road. His hand was warm and rough against mine. I could feel his eyes on me as he seamlessly navigated the roads towards the town center. My eyes met his in the dim light of the streetlamps we passed, and my tongue felt dry in my mouth.

All I could think about was the soft trail of kisses he had left on my neck. The feel of his soft lips, fervent against mine, wanting. How the hell was I going to make it through this entire movie? I had half a mind to ditch it, but I knew Tess would never forgive me for bailing on our first double date.

We pulled into the parking lot and parked next to what I assumed had to be Puck's car, another sleek and expensive looking model I wasn't familiar with. Where did these two get enough money to have such nice cars?

Nik and I walked into the theater hand in hand, instantly spotting Tess and Puck sitting on a bench near the entrance. Tess raised a brow at me, her eyes flashing to our conjoined hands as she got up to greet us.

"Who is ready to watch some sappy, romantic comedy goodness?" She turned to Puck, then me. "We need popcorn."

Tess grabbed me by the arm, all but ripping my hand from Nik's as she dragged me to the concessions stand.

"You need to *spill*," she said, grabbing us a spot in line and looping her arm through mine.

"You said you had something to tell me," I reminded her.

"I will, I will," she assured me as the line started to move and we stepped forwards. "But first...details. You know I need details."

"I already told you about the storm magic, and how we went to Siraleth. What more do you want to know?" I asked.

"Girl. I want to know *everything*. Was he a good kisser? Did it go further? Does his breath smell good?" She ticked each question off with a finger and I gave her arm a squeeze, glancing behind us to make sure Nik and Puck were out of ear shot.

"Shhh, he will hear you!" I hissed, turning back to her. "Of course, his breath smells good," I replied with a smirk. It smelled faintly of cinnamon and coffee, and his mouth tasted like honey, but Tess didn't need to know that much.

"He is a *very* good kisser...and it did not go further than that."

"So, are you guys dating now?" she asked.

"I don't think so...we haven't talked about it. We just kissed. It's not a big deal." I shrugged. Even though we had walked into the movie theater hand in hand, knowing that there would be a ton of people from school here that would see us together. And knowing my feelings for Nik were growing stronger each day.

"Yeah…right…not a big deal. Says the girl who has never shown interest in *any* guy before," Tess pointed out.

"I just want to see where things go. We don't know each other all that well yet. He's helping me with my magic, and things got a little hot and heavy. Who knows, maybe it was only the energy of the magic making us feel something. I don't know." I sighed.

"Not with the way he's looking at you," Tess said with big eyes as we stepped up to the counter. I chanced a glance behind us, and Nik was standing with Puck by the window. His hands were stuffed into the pockets of his black leather jacket, his blue eyes burning as they met mine. I quickly turned back to the counter. He had said I was his yesterday when we were kissing, but it could have been the heat of the moment. Right? I remembered the possessiveness in his voice as he had bit my lip.

"Two large popcorns, and two large diet sodas," Tess told the attendant as she handed him a wad of cash. "Extra butter."

"Puck and I will share a soda so I figured you and Nik wouldn't mind doing the same." Tess turned to me with a wink as the attendant put our sodas down on the counter and turned to get our popcorn.

"Back to you…what is this news you have been so secretive about?" I asked, hoping to turn the subject off me and Nik as I grabbed one of the sodas and two straws.

"Easier if I show you." Tess smiled, reaching her hand out to grab the other soda. Instead of grabbing it, her hand hovered over the glass of the snacks counter and the soda shot forwards, closing the distance between her hand and where the attendant had left it sitting on the counter. She turned to me with a smile, her eyebrows raised.

"What. The. Hell," I whispered, glancing around to make sure nobody had seen. "*I* didn't do that."

"I know. I did." Tess threaded two straws through the top of the cup and took a sip, a satisfactory smirk plastered across her face.

"You—you have magic!?" I asked grabbing her arm as the attendant turning to us with our popcorns. We left the line, but with my hands full, I motioned to Tess to step to the side before rejoining Nik and Puck.

"Now you're the one who needs to spill," I said. "That day at Buttercream when the chair shot out—that was you?"

"I think so." Tess nodded. "I confirmed it with Puck. It's just like with you and Nik, you spending so much time around him awakened your dormant magic. The same thing happened to me. And since you've awakened, I've been around all these magic users. I don't think I'm specialized though, like you or Nik. But it's still pretty damn cool. The question is...which one of my parents is the secret keeper?" she mused. "Or is it both?"

"Are you going to ask them?"

"Hell no. What if they spellbound me, as someone did to you? My magic should have awakened a lot earlier than this. I may be closer to my parents than you are with your mom, but I'm not crazy. They'll think I've lost it and send me to college abroad or something, even if one or both of them is secretly a witch," she replied, bringing the popcorn bucket to her mouth and grabbing a piece between her teeth. "So far, I've only been able to move things, but I have to admit I feel less left out now." She laughed.

"I can't believe it. What are the chances? Nik and Puck come to town, and now you and I both manifest powers. How many other kids at our school are witches that we don't know about? What, is Silver Oaks a secret refugee for witches or something?"

Now that I thought about it…it must be the portal that attracts witches here. Nik had said it was such a powerful magical location that witches would seek it out, even subconsciously. Is the portal the reason for Silver Oaks becoming a hot spot for witches and magic? Were there more witches in Silver Oaks than we ever realized? Had they settled here after coming through the portal after the war?

"What are you ladies talking about?" Puck asked as he crept up behind Tess, plucking the popcorn bucket from her hands and looping his other arm around her waist.

"I was telling Diana about my newfound magic," Tess said, trying to wrestle the popcorn bucket back.

"Your *what*?" Nik asked over my shoulder. Apparently, he hadn't known either. He sounded equally as surprised as I was. I felt guilty that I had been spending so much time with Nik that I hadn't realized Tess was manifesting magic of her own. I had been so wrapped up in my own magic that I hadn't even noticed the times she may have blatantly used magic in front of me, like at the bakery that afternoon. I was happy that Puck could be there for her as she discovered it, the same way Nik had been for me. We had a lot to catch up on later when we were alone.

"You heard right." She smirked, successfully trading the soda to Puck and grabbing the popcorn. "Nothing fancy like you and Diana, but magic nonetheless."

Puck and Nik met eyes, a silent message passing between them.

"Care to fill us in?" Tess asked, glancing from Puck to Nik, then back again.

"It's nothing, darling," Puck replied in his most exaggerated British accent. "If we don't get going, we might miss this movie that Nik and I are *oh so excited* to see." He plastered a fake smile on before escorting her down to the ticket taker.

"You know, Tess isn't my favorite person, but I'm glad you can share this with her," Nik said quietly in my ear as he reached across and grabbed the soda with its two straws. I gave him an exasperated look as we handed our tickets off and entered the theater.

"She will grow on you, I promise."

"Like mold"—he scrunched his face up in mock disgust—"that's what I'm afraid of."

I gave him a playful shove as we took our seats, and he immediately grabbed my hand and brought it into his lap.

"You *are* going to have to share some of that popcorn, you know," he teased as he gave my hand a playful squeeze. The lights dimmed, the movie starting.

We had made it through the movie without a bathroom break, but by the time the credits rolled, Tess and I were about to burst. A large soda had been a terrible idea, even if we had been sharing it. We left the boys in the hallway and ran to the bathroom in a fit of giggles. I had never imagined a time where Tess and I could be on a double date. Tess was always the one with boys wrapped around her finger, and I was always the one with my nose buried in a book.

I met Tess back at the sink and we burst into another fit of laughter as we caught each other's eyes in the mirror. We heard another stall door open and tried to quiet ourselves as we realized we weren't alone.

"Ms. Finch, it's good to see you. We've missed you in art class," Tess said, drying her hands off as she watched Ms. Finch move to the sink through the reflection of the mirror.

It had felt like weeks since we had seen Ms. Finch. Fletcher had been teaching our art class the past few weeks and keeping a close eye on us. We weren't sure when Ms. Finch would be returning, if she was at all. She rinsed her hands off quietly, a quiver in her jaw. Her hair appeared unbrushed and frizzy, her glasses sitting askew on her nose. She didn't look...well. No wonder she had decided to take some time off. Was she having some kind of mental breakdown as Tess had suggested?

"It's...nice to see...you too...dear," she replied, drying her hands off slowly. Her words were short and choppy, as if they were being dragged out of her. "It's unfortunate that it had to come to this." Her eyes met Tess' in the mirror, then mine as she turned towards us.

"Come to what?" Tess asked, confused.

Ms. Finch stood between us and the door. She took another step towards us, her hands behind her back. What was she talking about? Why did she look so…frazzled? So…out of it?

"You see…I had no choice, not really. If it wasn't me, it had to be someone else. But it had to be done, regardless," she started to ramble, taking another step closer and removing one hand from behind her back. That hand now held a sharp hunting knife. Where had that come from? What was Ms. Finch doing with a knife?

"Ms. Finch, what are you talking about? Had no choice about what?" I asked, taking a measured step back and hitting the tiled wall behind me. I shot Tess a panicked glance, but she did not take her eyes off Ms. Finch.

"About what I have to do here. You see…she wouldn't take no for an answer. She would never take no for an answer. And he failed. He was always destined to fail, if you ask me. She knew that. He was too *weak*. Too *soft*. But it has to be done, you see. It has to be me. I thought I could avoid this; I never wanted to hurt you. I've been in hiding for weeks, hoping that if I simply disappeared, I wouldn't have to follow through with these orders. But she found me, she always finds me. She has eyes *everywhere*. I'm sorry it's come down to this."

"Ms. Finch, I don't know what you're talking about, but whatever it is we can help you…" Tess assured her, holding her hands out as if she was trying to calm a scared animal.

"You cannot help me. I tried, I really did, but there is no help for me now." Ms. Finch shook her head violently, her eyes wide.

"Whatever it is, we can figure this out. Put the knife away and come with us," Tess said calmly. Ms. Finch took another step towards us and exploded in a burst of movement. She was closest to Tess, and she leaped for her, but Tess was ready. Tess blocked the arm that held the knife as it arced towards her with her forearm and gave Ms. Finch a rough push back. But she only came back at her, again and again. Tess ducked under her arm and tried to make a dash for the door, but Ms. Finch turned and kicked her hard in the back of the legs, Tess sprawling onto the hard tile floor with a smack.

Ms. Finch turned towards me and there was nowhere for me to go. Could I hide in a stall until Puck and Nik heard the scuffle and came to help? Could I use my magic to protect myself?

I focused on the knife in Ms. Finch's hand and imagined it was hot, as hot as the coals of a burning fire. It was only a second before she was on me, but a terrible screech wrenched free from her throat as she dropped the knife with a clatter. The handle of the knife had turned red hot, her hand cradled to her chest with a hiss.

"Very good. I see he's taught you something, at least. But that won't help you now, I'm afraid," she sneered, taking a step back from me. Tess had made it to the bathroom door and had slipped through it without Ms. Finch's notice. It was only a matter of time before Nik and Puck were here.

Ms. Finch wrenched her neck to the side, and it cracked as the bone shattered and she dropped to all fours, throwing her head back in a snarl. Her fingers had turned to claws, and they now dug into the tile, causing deep gouges. Her teeth sank below her bottom lip as they extended, and her skin turned to fur before my eyes. A wolf. She was turning into a wolf. Ms. Finch was a shapeshifter. She was a Nightshade. Was she working with Fletcher? Is that was all of this was about?

I had backed against the far wall of the bathroom and stared at Ms. Finch in horror as her yellow eyes met mine. Ms. Finch had fully transformed now, her brown fur muddied under the florescent lighting of the movie theater bathroom. She snapped her jaw and licked her lips, slowly slinking towards me. She knew she had me cornered. The bathroom door slammed open, cracking against the tile wall with a fierce bang as Nik, Puck, and Tess poured inside.

"Don't move," Nik called towards me as Ms. Finch snapped her eyes towards Nik, her hackles raised.

"I knew you were a Nightshade, but I never imagined you were working with *him*," Nik spat. "You're outnumbered now. Diana and Tess may be new to their magic, but Puck and I sure as hell aren't. Let us leave, and no harm will come to you."

I could see the indecision in the way Ms. Finch set her shoulders, her ears back. She knew there was no getting out of this now, whatever she had set out to do here. Whether that was to kill me or capture me, she had failed. She gave the slightest nod but stayed in her wolf form, backing away towards the sinks to let me pass. Nik nodded towards the exit and I made a beeline for it, grabbing Tess and dragging her behind me as I went. I did not stop until we were outside the doors of the movie theater and I pulled Tess to me in a tight embrace.

"What the hell was that?" I asked, squeezing her tight.

"I have no idea. Are you ok? I didn't want to leave you in there, but I had to get help." She squeezed me back tightly.

"I'm ok," I assured her as Nik and Puck came bursting through the front doors.

"We need to go, now." Nik's tone brooked no argument as he grabbed my hand and we started towards his car.

"My place," he called over his shoulder at Puck and Tess as they made their way to Puck's car on the other side of us.

We jumped in, and before I even had a chance to fasten my seatbelt, Nik had taken off, peeling out of the parking lot without looking back.

As it turns out, Nik lived right in the downtown area in one of the apartments over the new shops. We parked in a back parking lot and made our way down a narrow alleyway to a side door in the building.

We climbed the two flights of stairs to his apartment, and he unlocked it quietly before we slipped inside. He turned, locking the door and securing the deadbolt into place. He also secured the door chain. I doubt that could hold the door against a giant, shapeshifting wolf, but it made me feel better to know that Nik was *also* a giant, shapeshifting wolf.

Tess and Puck had only been a few minutes behind us and would be here any minute. Nik turned the lights on and the dark apartment was illuminated. He moved quickly to the wall of windows to pull the blinds shut. Nik had a view of the downtown streets, and he could see all the storefronts from his living room window. The walls were painted a dark and moody navy, and the fixtures were modern and industrial. It looked like a bachelor pad, if I had ever seen one. Did he live here alone?

The apartment was small, but well-appointed. The living room was furnished with a large, comfortable looking sectional. The room was open to an equally dark and moody kitchen with black cabinets and a large island accompanied by sleek barstools. There only appeared to be two other doors in the apartment, and they were closed. I imagined they were the bathroom and the bedroom.

Nik ran a hand through his hair and turned to me, his jaw set.

"Are you ok?" he asked.

"I'm ok," I assured him as he wrapped his arms around my shoulders and pulled me towards him. I could feel his lips on my forehead as he held me close.

"I didn't think...I didn't think she was a threat to you. This is my fault, this entire thing is my fault." He sighed against me, shaking his head.

"It isn't your fault that Fletcher came to town, or that Ms. Finch has completely lost her mind and might be working with him. You couldn't have known this would happen." I pulled away so I could see his face.

A line creased his forehead between his eyebrows as he looked down at me, his eyes roaming my face. What was he thinking? Was this some kind of retribution for whatever it was that he and Fletcher had been arguing over? It unsettled me that we didn't know what they wanted, and that it was escalating.

A knock sounded at the door and I jumped in Nik's arms, startled. He gave my arms a squeeze before moving to the door and peering through the peephole. Satisfied that it was only Puck and Tess, he undid the three locks and cracked the door open, letting them in.

"That was crazy back there, brother," Puck said as he entered the apartment, clapping Nik on the back. He made his way to the refrigerator and turned back to us with a beer in his hand, popping the top open against the countertop.

"Want one?" He looked to Tess, then me, both of us shaking our heads.

"Sure, help yourself," Nik said as he dragged out a barstool and sat down, motioning for me to join him.

"What was that?" Tess asked, dragging out a bar stool of her own and settling down.

"You tell me," Puck responded, taking a sip of his beer. "What the hell did she say in there?"

"A whole lot of nonsense," I replied, propping my chin on my hand. "She kept saying she didn't want to, but that she had no choice. That there was no help for her. She said...she said 'she' would never take no for an answer. Whoever 'she' is."

Nik and Puck met eyes across the counter, another silent conversation taking place.

"What?" Tess asked. She had caught it, too.

"Nothing," they replied in tandem. What weren't they telling us?

"Does this have to do with your beef with Fletcher?" I asked Nik, "because if so, you need to loop us in. It involves us now."

"It isn't about that." Nik swallowed. "I told you, I was taking care of that."

"But did you? Because Fletcher is still creeping around school and now Ms. Finch, who was always weird but never 'attacking people in public' weird, came at me with a knife in the movie theater bathroom. Then she turned into a wolf to try and maul me to death. So, I think I'm missing something here," I pointed out.

"I know as much as you do. I have no idea what she could have been talking about. Fletcher's beef is with me and Puck, not with you. I don't think this incident with Ms. Finch was related," he replied.

"Then what could it possibly have been about? And how many God forsaken witches reside in this ridiculously small town, anyway?"

"At least six that we know of," Tess said absently.

"As I told you before, the meadow with the portal to Siraleth is a hot spot of magical energy. Witches are drawn to this area. They can sense the energy residing here and they will seek it out, even subconsciously." He took a deep breath before continuing. "The question is, what do we do now? There is a lot of heat on us right now, with Fletcher breathing down our necks. Until we figure out what tonight was about, Diana and Tess are in danger."

"I say we get out of dodge," Tess offered with a shrug.

"Like that's so easy to do with school and, oh, this little thing called our parents," I pointed out.

"Actually, it might not be that hard," Tess mused. "I was supposed to go on a college tour next weekend. That's the perfect excuse to get out of town."

"And our parents?" I asked.

"I'll tell my parents I'm going with your family, and you can tell your mom you're coming with mine. They will have no reason to find it suspicious."

"Will we truly go on the college tour? There's so much going on right now. School is the last thing on my mind to be honest." I sighed, burying my face in my hands.

"Me too," Tess agreed, her shoulders sinking in defeat.

"I have a crazy idea," Puck offered with a mischievous grin.

"Do we even want to know?" Nik said, propping his elbows up on the countertop and running a hand down his face.

"I say we go to Istmere." He shrugged, as if he was suggesting we go grab a coffee or something.

"Istmere," Nik replied, deadpan.

"Yes, Istmere. You already showed Diana the city of Siraleth, but that's all ruins and ghosts. Tess has never been. Why don't we bring them to Prins? They've never seen an actual city of witches before," he offered. "We can keep a low-key presence and only stay a day or two. Just to get away. You have to admit, it would be pretty damn hard for Fletcher or Ms. Finch to find us there."

"Won't it be dangerous for me to go there and be around other witches? Being a Stormshade and all..." I pointed out.

"I don't think so," Puck replied with a shrug. "Nobody knows you exist. Stormshades are supposedly extinct, and as long as you don't use your storm magic, nobody has any reason to suspect. If you don't use your magic, you won't have a recognizable magical signature that anyone can detect. They'll think you are a regular old witch like the rest of us."

"That might be true. When we first met, I could smell it all over you. But you had been using your magic, even if you didn't know it yet," Nik agreed. I could see him running the possible scenarios through his head, thinking of every possible way this might go wrong. "And anybody looking for a Stormshade would be in The Stone City anyway, they wouldn't be in Prins."

"What is Prins like?" Tess asked, a wistful note in her voice.

"Well, we will just have to show you, won't we." Puck winked at her as he took another sip and Tess practically melted off the bar stool.

"A weekend in Istmere? It would be good to get away, even if only for a little while," I agreed.

"We just need to lay the footwork with our parents," Tess said.

"Agreed. We need to have a bulletproof plan." I nodded.

"So, it's settled. We'll go to Istmere next weekend and travel to Prins through Siraleth," Nik said.

"Where should we stay?" Puck asked, "Not like we can make a reservation ahead of time." He laughed, taking another swig of his beer.

"We have a few options, but we should stay at our favorite inn if they have a vacancy," Nik replied, and Puck agreed with a nod and a smile. From the looks on their faces they had made trouble the last time they had been there, no doubt.

"Is Prins close to Siraleth?" I asked.

"Close enough," Nik responded with a shrug. How close was close enough? I would wear my most comfortable sneakers, just in case. What do you even pack to spend the weekend in the witch realm? What would it be like? The excitement of returning to Istmere was burning in my veins and I couldn't wait for next weekend.

"Pack *light.*" Nik gave Tess a pointed look, and she rolled her eyes at him. "Whatever we carry with us, we carry on our backs."

"I am so excited." Tess squealed clapping her hands together. "Now I get to be a part of your witchy little group."

"We can practice your magic while we're there, if you want," Puck offered, finishing off the beer and placing the empty in the sink.

"Obviously," Tess replied. "I am leagues behind all of you, including Diana. This is so exciting!"

"It's settled then," I said, pushing out from my barstool. "We tell our parents we are going on a college tour, and we take the portal to Siraleth. Then travel to Prins on foot."

"Isn't it a little late in the year to be taking a college tour?" Puck pointed out, "Shouldn't you all be decided by now?"

"Tess and I are both late bloomers," I conceded with a laugh. Neither of us had exactly figured out what we would be doing after high school yet, even though most of our class had already chosen their schools. "I could say the same for you."

"Nik and I are going back to Istmere after...school." Puck trailed off as he met Nik's glare. Was that something I wasn't supposed to know? Were there colleges in Istmere? There was still so much that I didn't know about that realm.

"We had better get back tonight before my mom suspects anything." I stifled a yawn with the back of my hand. "She thinks Tess' parents were picking me up, remember?"

Nik pushed out his bar stool and wrapped his arm around my waist from behind, resting his head on my shoulder. "Ah, good point. Let's get you home, firecracker. I'll have you all to myself next weekend."

The past week of school sped by in a blur, the excitement of traveling to Istmere taking up our every waking moment. Tess and I had packed as light as humanly possible, making sure that everything we brought would be comfy and easy to walk in. Well...as light as Tess could ever be expected to pack.

I had filled my backpack and kept it to the essentials, knowing we would only be gone for two days. My mom easily bought the story that I was going on a college tour with Tess, and so did her parents. We had planned to have Nik drive, that way we only had to leave one car at the meadow over the weekend.

Fletcher had been relatively nonconfrontational all week, and he and Nik had largely ignored each other in class. I was half expecting there to be a scene when Nik had first walked in and seen Fletcher at Ms. Finch's desk, his feet kicked up. Nik had only sat down quietly, his back to him. Fletcher didn't say anything about Ms. Finch, which made me wonder if they were involved with each other after all. Surely, he would have taken the opportunity to gloat, or at least taunt us with the run-in if he had been behind it.

We hadn't run into Ms. Finch again, and there had been no sign of her in town. It appeared nobody else at the movie theater had heard anything out of the ordinary, or else school would have been buzzing with the gossip. How they hadn't heard our art teacher turn into a giant wolf and try to tear our heads off was beyond me. She must have changed back into her human form in the theater bathroom before slinking off. Why did she want to hurt me? And most importantly...would she be back?

I imagined Fletcher's substitute position was only temporary, and that he wasn't staying in Silver Oaks forever. He would have to return to The Stone City at some point. Would Ms. Finch resume her position as our art teacher after he left?

I was happy to be going somewhere Ms. Finch wouldn't be able to find me, and get away from all of this craziness for the weekend. I had to admit, I was a little jealous that Tess would get to practice her magic in Istmere and I couldn't. I knew it was safer this way, but I still relished the feel of harnessing my magic in Istmere. How it had been so much easier than conjuring it in this realm. How much more powerful my magic had felt at my fingertips when I was there. There were no Stormshades in Istmere, and I couldn't exactly go parading it around. I would have to keep all of my magic, even simple spells, locked down over the weekend.

I couldn't help but wonder if it was my mom or my dad who had magic lineage, and which of Tess' parents passed it down to her. I wished it was something I could talk to my mom about, but we were so entirely *opposite*. We never connected on the same page. If I ever tried to explain any of this to her, she would never believe me.

I slept at Tess' house on Friday night to further the ruse with my mom that I would be going along with Tess and her family for the campus tour. On Saturday morning Nik picked us up with Puck already riding shotgun, and we took off towards the meadow. Towards the portal that would bring us to Siraleth. Would Fletcher be following us again, like he was last time? I hoped we were able to slip off unnoticed, the last thing we needed was Fletcher following us around all weekend. The whole point of this trip was to avoid him. I left the grimoire safely tucked away in my dresser drawer. The only people who knew I had it were Tess and Nik, and I wanted to keep it that way.

Tess was just as confused as I was the first time I had arrived at the meadow to find it largely empty with nothing but a serene lake and the pine trees surrounding us. She, too, could sense the energy radiating out of this place, as if it were a beacon to fellow witches. Nik showed us to the portal and Tess and Puck went through first, disappearing in the blink of an eye. Nik took my hand as we stepped through the portal, and just like last time, stepped into nothingness.

Siraleth was different from the last time I had seen it. We had come on an unseasonably warm winter day and the sun had been shining bright and high in the sky. Before I conjured the storm, that is. Today, Siraleth was covered by thick and angry clouds that threatened to burst open and soak us in a deluge of rain at any moment. Normally I would be tempted to try to shield us with my storm magic like an umbrella, but I knew that I couldn't touch my magic at all on this trip.

Tess and I weren't sure exactly what to bring, so we had stuck with jeans, t-shirts, and thermals for the most part. Nik and Puck donned their standard issue black jeans and leather jackets. I couldn't help but wonder if we would stick out like a sore thumb in Prins. What did the people there dress like? Istmere was another realm entirely, they didn't have the same stores that we did. I imagined they had quaint little shops with tailors where they could get their blouses and dresses custom made, but I wasn't entirely sure what to expect. There was no cell service, no cars, no modern technology at all.

I had noticed an array of weapons in the packs Nik and Puck had brought with us, and wondered if they were expecting to run into any trouble. Nik had packed the light broadsword with the scabbard that he had let me use the other day, and I wondered if maybe we would have time to do some more sword training while we were here.

We started off towards the ruins of Siraleth, checking behind us frequently to ensure nobody followed us through the portal. We walked the cobblestone streets through the dense fog that had descended upon the fallen city's center, keeping close to one another. We passed the familiar cottage Nik and I had visited last week, and continued on through the city until we reached what appeared to be the edge of the city of Siraleth. Nothing stood before us but snow-capped mountains and vast, grassy, landscape.

"From here, we keep walking across the plains," Nik started, "we could have portaled directly into Prins, but that portal is being monitored. I didn't want to draw any attention to us as we traveled through."

"Good idea." Puck confirmed with a nod. "It isn't too much farther, only a few miles. The cities are fairly close together by your world's standards. Of course, you do have cars..."

"Hopefully this rain holds off," I peered up at the sky, watching the angry clouds move swiftly across the plains, "I didn't bring a raincoat."

"We will have to change once we get there, anyway. To blend in more," Nik replied, gesturing towards his outfit. "Some people dress like this in Prins, but we want to stay completely off the radar if possible. Best to completely blend in."

Just as I had suspected. "But we packed clothes, what will we wear?"

"Don't worry, we've got you covered." Puck's hand moved to my shoulder, giving it a gentle squeeze. "We have to blend in with the other witches. Nik and I were raised in Istmere, but you guys will stick out like a sore thumb."

What would it have been like if I had been raised in Istmere, too? Would I have full control of my powers by now? How powerful would I be? I couldn't help but wonder if Jake was a witch too, and if my parents had known about this side of my life and never told me. It felt like a betrayal, to be so enthralled with and drawn to the supernatural all my life, but to be kept from it. Only to find out it was a part of me all along, and it always had been. Would I have gone to a school here in Istmere? Would I still be planning to go to college? If I had been raised here, my life would be completely different.

"We will have to travel through The Shadow to get to the pub and inn. It's a seedy part of town, and we'll need to stay close together or someone will try to sell you a potion that will turn you into a frog," Nik interrupted my thoughts.

"A what?"

"Magic can be…tricky. We have to be careful in The Shadow. There might be witches there who can sense your Stormshade energy, though they're uncommon. We will have to do our best to mask it, and make it through unnoticed," he replied.

"But on the bright side, if you ever want to shrink yourself down to the size of a lime, or find someone to sell you a brew that'll erase your most embarrassing memories, The Shadow is the place to do it." Puck laughed.

"The bright side?" I asked, raising a brow at him.

"I think I'll pass," Tess chimed in, giving me a wide-eyed glare.

Be careful in The Shadow. Got it.

"Will we run into any of your friends while we are here?" I asked.

Nik and Puck exchanged a glance before replying, "Probably," in unison. I wondered if they had the same bad boy reputation here as they did back in our realm.

We walked for what felt like hours in silent anticipation. My mind was reeling with thoughts of what Prins would be like and who we would meet there. We eventually came upon two large stone columns that stood about twenty feet apart from each other. The towers were so tall that their spires disappeared up into the growing fog and the angry clouds above.

"This marks the formal entrance to Prins. From here on out, stay close," Nik told us as he pulled us to the side of one of the pillars. He opened his pack, shucking off his leather jacket and stuffing it inside.

"Take these," he said, offering Tess and I both a thick swath of black fabric that we quickly unfolded.

"A *cloak*?" I asked.

"We need to blend in. So yes, a cloak. Put it on, and fasten it," he replied. We did as we were told, and the cloak was large enough that it almost swallowed me entirely. It hid my arms and legs with only the toes of my sneakers peeking out at the bottom. The hood safely hid my red hair within its silhouette, and someone would need to be standing close to me in order to see my face beneath it. I guess the cloak *was* a good idea, to keep us inconspicuous.

Nik looked as if he was born to wear his, only the tiniest wisp of his blond hair sneaking out at the top of his hood. You could still see his muscled frame and his cloak only fell to his calves. These cloaks must be his, I realized.

"I need to scout, give me a minute." Nik turned and grabbed the pillar as if it was the trunk of a tree. With remarkable agility, he ascended the pillar as if he were climbing a rope, and disappeared into the fog.

Puck saw the expression on my face and turned to me. "Not all those tattoos are for show, you know. Some of them are spells. They give him extra strength, speed, and better eyesight."

"And yours?" Tess asked as she peered through the fog, trying to make out Nik's frame through the dense mist.

"A combination of the two as well." Puck gave her a playful nudge. "But there are only so many spells that can work on the skin."

"Could a Stormshade get some of those?" I asked.

"Skin spells? Of course, I don't see why not." Puck smiled as Nik's outline appeared on the pillar through the fog, quickly descending. There must be handholds, I realized, but the fog was so dense they were invisible to us. He dropped the remaining fifteen feet to the ground and landed in a crouch, a grin spread across his face.

"All clear," he announced, "I see Saanvi, I only wish I could send her a raven. We will have to greet her the old-fashioned way."

"Saanvi?" I asked, I hadn't heard him mention that name before.

"An old friend. She will guide us through The Shadow, she just doesn't know it yet. No way to send her word ahead of time that we were coming."

I nodded as he picked his pack back up and we continued on walking between the two pillars.

As soon as we had passed through, everything before me changed. What had appeared as nothing but long expanses of grass and uncut wildflowers was in reality a bustling city set on the edge of a busy port. The docks full of people coming in and out with their goods. The buildings were mostly made of stone or brick, with cedar shingles and small windows. They were multiple stories, some with thatched roofs, and they looked worn, as if they had withstood the test of time.

The townspeople were dressed in long cloaks and breeches with tunics and boots. Some women wore muted dresses outfitted with layered skirts and floral designs, but most were dressed in working gear. Horse-drawn carriages hurried back and forth as people outside their storefronts called out to those passing by, trying to hawk their wares on the busy street.

"It's a glamour"—Nik smirked—"the city is hidden to those who don't know where to find it." Nik caught the attention of a man in a cap and boots pushing a wheelbarrow full of sage. He appeared to ask him for directions as the man began pointing and gesticulating.

"I'm pretty sure I know where to find Saanvi, I just wanted to be sure," Nik said as he rejoined us, adjusting his cloak to hide most of his face. Nik had been right, we did blend in with these cloaks.

We started down one of the city streets, evading the pushy shop owners and keeping our heads down as to not draw any attention to ourselves. Tess stuck close to my side as Nik and Puck led the way through the spiraling cobblestone streets. The city was nestled between the port to the right and the sloping cliffside to the left. There were streets that twisted and turned up the cliffside, and we could see the larger, more affluent, houses nestled along the cliff higher up. The city appeared as if it was constructed in layers, and there was something to see no matter which direction you looked.

Nik caught sight of what must have been Saanvi ahead of us and he pushed ahead, greeting her with a tight embrace. A tingle of jealousy crept up my spine as she turned to give him a lingering kiss on the cheek.

She was gorgeous, naturally. Her long black hair was fastened into a tight braid down her back and her terra-cotta complexion was unblemished, her eyes darkly lined with kohl. She wore a cloak fastened at her neck with the hood thrown back. Beneath it she wore tall boots, breeches, and a white tunic tightly secured with a blue velvet corset.

"Saanvi!" Puck called out as he caught up to them, pulling her into an equally deep embrace. It appeared they hadn't seen each other in quite a while.

"What the hell are you two knuckle-heads doing back in Prins so soon?" she asked, taking a step back and examining them at arm's length.

Nik nodded towards me, and Saanvi's eyes went wide. "We found some newbie witches in the human realm and wanted to show them a day in the life of an Istmere witch."

"Well, aren't you going to introduce me?" she asked.

Saanvi was tall and lithe, but with a feminine and athletic silhouette. One I would kill for. I felt like a short, frizzy, thing next to her and I pulled my cloak tighter around myself self-consciously.

"Saanvi, this is Diana." Nik grabbed me by the hand and pulled me closer, wrapping an arm around my shoulder. Well, that was a good sign at least. Maybe this Saanvi was more like an old friend, or a sister to them.

"And this is Tess." Puck shot Nik a pointed glare as Tess stepped into our circle, nearly as tall and just as lithe as Saanvi.

"Ah, yes. Tess. How could I forget," Nik replied tartly.

I nudged him in the side playfully. "Be nice," I uttered under my breath through a clenched smile.

"So, what do you lot need? You *always* need something." Saanvi laughed.

"We need you to take us through The Shadow," Nik answered.

"The Shadow. Of course, I should have known. And you'd like me to take you right now, I presume?" she asked.

"If you can." Nik nodded. "We want to make it to Eight Bells with enough time to reserve a few rooms before the tavern fills up and they're all booked for the night."

Saanvi nodded and turned to glance down the road both ways, "Well then, come along."

She led us deeper into the city and I could see ahead of us that Prins sloped sharply downwards into what must be The Shadow, then rose again on the other side. There were multiple sets of steep staircases that lead down into the pit, and from here all you could see were the rooftops of the buildings below.

The Shadow appeared almost as if it were a bowl, set down into the middle of the city. It was full of cramped and narrow soot covered streets and unkempt dilapidated buildings, not like what we had seen of the city so far. Many of the buildings and walkways were covered with dark sheets pulled tightly across rooftops to shield the people below from the prying eyes above. It obscured most of the view from here. We approached a staircase that would lead us down into The Shadow, and Saanvi knelt to adjust the laces on her tall boots.

She glanced both ways, then in the blink of an eye her tall boots and long braid disappeared as she turned into a small black cat with a green emerald hanging from her black collar. I had seen Nik shift before, but Tess held back a small gasp as she watched. Saanvi was a Nightshade. A shapeshifter, like Nik.

"I thought shapeshifters could only turn into wolves?" I whispered under my breath as I leaned into Nik.

"It's true that wolves are a common form, but they're not the only form," he replied quietly.

"You can turn into a cat?" I asked, amused at the idea of Nik turning into a furry little kitty as I suppressed a laugh.

As if he could read my mind, he shot me a glare. "No, we can only shift into one animal form, not any creature at will. I like to believe my form is a wolf because I am a fierce fighter and protector. Saanvi is stealthy and has nine lives, it makes perfect sense that her magic chose a cat for her shifted form."

Saanvi turned towards our hushed conversation and me-owed at us once before heading towards the stairs, quick-ly descending them as we followed. Once we reached the bottom it appeared even darker, despite the ominous dark clouds threatening to bring a storm down over all of Prins. It was as if the darkest of those clouds hovered over The Shadow, helping to conceal it.

We stayed close together and Tess looped her arm through mine as we followed Nik and Puck. Saanvi was quick, and it took some effort to keep up with my shorter legs. The storefronts here were not open to the street and overflowing with wares for sale like they had been higher up in the city. Here they were hidden behind boarded-up windows and closed off doors. A few of the shops appeared somewhat normal, whereas others appeared almost sinister as we walked down the city streets. I remembered what Puck had said, about this being a place to experience questionable, tricky, magic if that's what you were in the market for. Maybe even dark magic.

The Shadow had winding and twisting streets, making it easy to get lost if you weren't familiar with its layout. Nothing was laid out in a straight line. Patrons slipped into the shops quickly with their caps turned down low over their faces. Those passing us on the street either ignored us entirely or glowered at us from beneath their cloaks, their expressions dark and unwelcoming. The store fronts that were not boarded up appeared to sell Elixirs and other enchanted items. The only patrons that lingered on the streets were those outside the pubs, laughing and leering with their drinks in hand at passersby.

After a few minutes of walking, we reached a dead end that had a closed and chained door. We continued down the alley despite it appearing to lead to nowhere. Saanvi briefly turned back into her human form and passed her hand over the chained lock, whispering a few words under her breath.

The lock came free with a pop and Saanvi glanced behind her before turning back into a cat and passing through the door. Puck closed it behind us, and we could hear the lock snap shut on its own on the other side of the door. It must have been some type of self-locking spell.

We were inside a dark and windowless tunnel, and the floor beneath us was slightly damp. My sneakers squeaked against the wet stone as we pressed forwards into the darkness. The tunnel wasn't terribly long, and when we reached the other side Nik pulled the door open. This one had not been locked from the other side. This door led us directly onto a steep staircase leading upwards, presumably out of The Shadow.

When we reached the top of the staircase, the sun was clearer, the air not as heavy. We were on the other side of Prins, we had safely made our way through The Shadow unscathed. I could see the other side where we had come from across the pit. Saanvi turned back into her human form and stretched her arms high above her head, letting out a catlike yawn.

"All in a day's work," she said, cracking her neck.

"Thank you, Saanvi." Nik placed an arm on her shoulder and squeezed it with a grateful smile.

"Anything for you." She smiled in return. "Where are you lot off to now?"

"Straight to Eight Bells, of course," Puck answered. "It's been too long since I've had a pint of Dragon's Ale."

"Dragon's Ale?" Tess questioned with a raised eyebrow.

"It's light, you'll love it. Only problem is, it goes down like water and half the time we end up getting kicked out. Don't worry, there's no drinking age in Istmere," he replied with a laugh as he saw her eyes go wide.

"We are planning to spend the weekend here, so no getting kicked out tonight," Nik warned Puck with a pointed look.

"It was great seeing you, and it was nice meeting you both." Saanvi nodded towards us. "I've got to get back to work before they notice I'm gone. You'll need to learn your own way around The Shadow someday, though I'm afraid you *do* stick out like a sore thumb. Send me a message if you've got any fun plans before you head back. Now you know where to find me." She winked.

"Will do." Nik smiled, and just like that Saanvi turned back into the little black cat, and disappeared back down the staircase.

Eight Bells Pub & Inn was nestled between a row of buildings adorned with a cobblestone street front and a big gold sign hanging out front. It had both a bank, and a bookstore located on either side of it, the building deeper than it was wide.

The narrow pub had a long wooden bar running the length of it, dusty wooden tables and leather booths situated opposite it. A long spiral staircase at the back of the pub led up to the inn, and the kitchens were located beyond that. I hadn't realized how hungry I was until my stomach gave a soft grumble as we entered and my nose filled with the smell of bar food.

"Let's check in and ditch these bags first," Nik suggested, making his way to the counter at the back of the pub where a short, stout, woman with wild dark curls and an apron manned the desk.

"Can I help you?" she asked without glancing up from her notebook. She continued to scribble into it, uninterrupted, as she leaned over the desk.

"We'd like to book a few rooms at the inn," Nik replied.

"Only got two rooms left," she answered, still not looking up. There was a pause as we all glanced at each other. Would Tess and I share a room while Nik and Puck shared one? I couldn't imagine them sharing a bed, or rather, fitting in the same bed.

"How do you want to do this?" Nik asked, pulling his hood back to reveal his swath of pale golden hair.

"I don't mind sharing a room with Puck if you don't mind sharing a room with Nik." Tess nudged, a fake innocence in her expression. Of course, she wanted to share a room with Puck. Or did she think she was doing me a favor, pushing me to share a room with Nik? I hadn't thought this far in advance, and I hadn't exactly packed the right pajamas for such an encounter. I imagined I'd have my own room or that I'd be sharing one with Tess.

I opened my mouth to reply but Tess pushed her way to the front of the desk. "We'll take them, thank you," she told the clerk and grabbed the two bronze keys from her. Without looking up she held her hand out for payment and Nik plopped a few large golden coins into her palm.

"Rooms 310 and 317. Enjoy your stay," she said as she finally gazed up, her eyes vacant. She said it in a way that implied she *certainly* didn't hope we enjoyed our stay. Why did Nik and Puck like this place so much?

We made our way up the spiraling wooden staircase to the second floor which opened onto a landing with a long row of guest rooms. We continued upwards to the third floor which appeared much the same. We made our way down the hallway, the thick wooden planks creaking beneath our feet as we reached Room 310.

"We can take this one." Puck snatched the keys for the rooms out of Tess' hands and passed the other room key to Nik. "Meet you downstairs in ten?"

"You got it." Nik nodded and looked to me, a question in his eyes. I swallowed hard before starting down the hallway again. Tess gave me a wicked grin and wiggled her eyebrows before disappearing behind the heavy wooden door to their room. I followed Nik down the hallway to Room 317 and paused, taking a deep breath, and swallowing the lump in my throat as he unlocked the door. I quietly followed him inside.

The room was much larger than I'd expected. It was appointed with a queen size bed on the left side of the room made out of cast iron, with a comfortable looking mattress and heavily layered cream linens. To the right was a brick fireplace set into the wall, two red upholstered chairs sitting before it. Next to the fireplace was a door to a separate washroom with a sink, tub, and shower. It appeared they did have running water here in Istmere, *thank God*. The windows on the far wall bathed the room in light and looked out onto the rooftop of the bank. I could see the rest of the city beyond in the distance.

"I can go if you need some time alone to wash up," Nik offered, dropping his pack down next to the bed. "It was a long trip to get here if you aren't used to it."

"No, that's ok." I moved to the opposite side of the bed, dropping my pack down as well and crossing my arms awkwardly.

"Are you ok with this? Because Puck and I can share a room, it's no big deal," Nik said as he ran a hand through his hair.

"No, it's ok." I paused. "Are you ok with this?" I asked, meeting his eyes across the bed. It hadn't even occurred to me until now that maybe *he* didn't want to share a bed with *me*. Sure, we had kissed a few times, but that might not mean anything to him. Not the way it did to me.

His eyes were smoldering with heat, and I could see a muscle tick in the line of his jaw. "I am ok with this," he answered softly.

The silence felt deafening as he held my eyes, a dangerous glimmer in them. What would happen tonight, if anything? Was I ready for something to happen? A flush of heat rushed to my cheeks and Nik grinned.

"It's almost as if I can read your thoughts, firecracker."

"If only." I laughed, but it sounded hollow in my own ears.

"Let me get a fire started, so the room is warmed up for when we get back," Nik offered as he moved to the fireplace and crouched before it. "Nights in Istmere can get pretty cold."

"Ok, I am going to freshen up."

I moved towards the washroom and closed the door quietly behind me, my nerves on edge. This would be my first time sharing a bed with a guy, and I was *nervous*. I felt it creeping up my chest and into my throat as if it were a powerful flame I couldn't douse. My stomach flipped as I gripped the sink and saw my reflection in the mirror. My cheeks were flushed, my soft blue eyes framed by my falling auburn curls. I took a deep breath through my nose and let it out through my mouth, splashing some water onto my cheeks and pushing my hair back from my face.

Tess had done this a million times, and so could I. Nothing had to happen if I didn't want it to...but did I want it to? I thought of how it had felt to have Nik pressed against me, the stifling heat of him consuming me. His fingers running across my skin, his mouth on my neck. I *did* want something to happen tonight. I wanted him. I swallowed hard as the realization settled in my stomach and I splashed more water on my face, turning to grab the towel hanging on the rack.

Maybe I would change my mind after a few Dragon's Ales. I needed to not overthink this, as I did everything else. I stepped back from the sink and sat on the edge of the claw-foot tub, steadying my breathing until I felt calm enough to join Nik back in the bedroom.

By the time I had collected myself, Nik had a roaring fire crackling in the fireplace. He was lying on the bed with his legs crossed at the ankles, his head resting on his bent arms.

"Did you use magic to do that?" I asked, gesturing towards the flickering flames.

"Only a little," he confessed with a shrug. "A man should know how to start a fire, and trust me, I *know* how to start a fire."

"Sure, you do." I nodded with a demure smile. "Let's go grab some of these famous Ale's you've been talking about." I moved towards the door as Nik got up from the bed.

"If you're a lightweight, which I assume you are, we should keep it to two. *Maximum.*" He smirked.

"And what makes you think I am a lightweight?" I asked with a raised eyebrow. He reached out and grabbed a lock of my curly hair between his fingertips, examining it.

"Just a calculated guess," he answered as he twirled it around his finger. Truth be told I had only ever had a few drinks in my life, mostly wine coolers when my mom had friends over and she let me have a few. I'd had a few beers at one of the college parties Tess had dragged me to and I'd had wine on a family vacation to Napa Valley once. But that was a long time ago. The truth was, I had no idea how I would handle the Dragon's Ale, but I didn't want Nik to know that.

"I guess we will have to see," I said, turning the knob and starting down the hallway. When we reached the bottom of the spiral staircase, we could see that Puck and Tess had already grabbed a booth. Our mugs of ale were already waiting for us on the wooden tabletop. I slid into the booth first, and Nik followed.

"This tastes nothing like ale in the other realm," Tess told me as she took another gulp. I lifted the wooden mug to my nose first and took a whiff. It sure smelled like beer in the other realm, for what it was worth. I took a small taste and realized she was right, this was nothing like ale in the other realm. It had a smooth, but earthy flavor. Almost Buttery.

"That's actually really good," I conceded, "What's in it?"

"Don't ask," Nik and Puck replied in unison with a laugh. They had been doing that a lot lately since we'd arrived in Istmere.

"Just enjoy it," Nik told me before taking a gulp himself and resting his mug back on the table. "Oh, Eight Bells. How I have missed you."

"Can we order food?" Tess asked, practically reading my mind.

"Of course." Puck flagged down a waitress to grab us a few menus.

Within the hour we had devoured two dozen chicken wings, and nearly half a dozen mugs of Dragon's Ale between me and Tess. Nik and Puck had consumed much more than that, but you wouldn't know it. The only difference in them was that they were more flirty than usual, which was really saying something because Nik was incorrigible. As we sat in the booth and watched the other patrons, I noticed people using subtle magic around me. It was absolutely fascinating. What would it have been like to grow up in a place such as this, where easy magic was commonplace?

One gentleman used his magic to send an ale down the bar to a beautiful woman who thanked him with a smile. Another used magic to grab his coat from the rack by the door and bring it to his chair, never having to get up to go and grab it. My favorite had to have been the woman who had used her magic to spill a heavy pitcher of water that a waitress had been carrying past on a man who wouldn't leave her and her friends alone.

I felt my own magic impatiently at my fingertips, itching to get out. It was crazy to think I had lived my whole life without this magic, but never a moment passed now where I didn't feel it. Ever since I had started practicing, it had become second nature to me. It felt as if it were such a deeply rooted part of me, I have no idea how I had ever lived without. Maybe it was the three mugs of Dragon's Ale, but I vowed that when I got home, I would ask my mom about my magic. If she had no idea about any of it, then it had to have come from my dad. Then I would know for sure. I needed answers.

I was so at peace here in Prins, sitting in this worn leather booth with Tess, Nik, and Puck, a wooden mug in my hand. I couldn't remember a time I had felt this happy, this light. This...*at home*. I loved it here. It was only my second time visiting Istmere, but it already felt as if it were home to me. More than the other realm ever had.

As I watched the people of Istmere, admiring their clothing and their easy ways of magic, the door to the pub jingled open. A sharp spike of dread shot down my spine before I even saw who it was that had entered. It was as if my magic noticed something...wrong, something sinister, and responded without me having even noticed. My eyes snapped to Nik's and in his expression, I could see that he had felt it, too.

I peered around the booth to see who had entered, but it was not a man that I recognized. I had never seen him before, but somehow, he felt familiar. He had a familiar set to his jaw, but I couldn't see his eyes. He had his newsboy cap pulled down low over his brow to obscure his face. He wore a fitted jacket and clean, pressed slacks. Who did he remind me of?

"Time to go," Nik whispered in my ear as he kicked Puck under the table and nodded towards the front door.

"Shit," Puck replied as he gathered his cloak and Tess did the same.

"Who is that?" I asked quietly, sliding out of the booth behind Nik.

"Fletcher's brother. We can sneak back later, but for now we've got to get out of here. Before we're spotted," Nik replied.

No wonder he looked so familiar. He had the same strong jaw, the same firm set of his mouth. The likeness was so uncanny they could be twins, and I wondered how I hadn't put it together initially. What was Fletcher's brother doing here? Had Fletcher known we went through the portal? Had he sent him to search for us?

We kept our eyes on the ground and quickly moved to the door, slipping through it and starting down the cobblestone street away from the pub.

"That was a close call." Nik let out a sigh of relief as we rounded a corner out of sight of the pub. We continued to walk down the road until we came to a crossing.

"Where are we going now?" I asked as we paused at the corner, letting the horse-drawn carriages barrel past on the busy street.

"To kill some time before we go back. Kane can't stay there forever. He's not a frequent patron of the esteemed Eight Bells, so I have to assume he was looking for us. They don't like him there, it's only a matter of time before he gets kicked out. How he might know we are in Prins, now that is the question."

"Maybe a little fellow that looks exactly like him just a smidge taller, and younger, and more annoying, tipped him off..." Puck ran a hand through his shaggy brown hair, his shoulders moving as he laughed silently.

"You don't think he saw us?" Tess asked, nervously shifting her weight from one foot to the other.

"No, I don't think he saw us. He would have been on us by now. But it couldn't hurt for us to pick up a few glamour vials while we're here. Hopefully we don't have to use them," Puck told us. "I'm out anyway, and they work great on humans in the other realm."

"Glamour vials?" I asked. Were they similar to the glamour we had encountered when we approached the pillars that led to Prins? The one that hid the city from those that didn't know it was there?

"It's a potion that makes you look like someone else. It obscures your obvious features and changes little things about you such as your hair color, or the shape of your nose. Not a long-term solution, and kind of expensive, but good to have on hand just in case," Nik replied.

"Alastir's?" Puck asked Nik, pulling the hood of his cloak over his mess of curls.

"Alastir's," Nik confirmed with a nod before turning to me to explain, "An old friend. He owns a charm shop here in town."

Nik led the way, and we turned left at the corner, deeper into Prins and further away from the steep staircase that had led us up from The Shadow. This part of the city was much livelier than that of The Shadow, but not quite as chaotic as the port we had encountered when we first arrived in Prins. The clouds continued to cover the city, it had been threatening to storm all day but so far it had remained clear. The shops had their doors propped open and their merchandise could be seen in the windows or on the tables set up outside. Many shops had long open awnings with the shop owners sitting in rocking chairs out front, talking with patrons as if they were old friends.

The cobblestone street wound left and right through a maze of alleyways and houses. Many of the houses were four or five stories tall in this part of the city, housing many different families on each level. The buildings were set close together with Juliet balconies leading out onto the streets below. Most houses appeared to be shotgun style, short one way and long the other. The houses were stone and brick here, exactly as they were at the port where we entered Prins. Many shop keepers and residents had colorful tapestries strung out on their balconies or had painted the stone or brick something bright and colorful.

At the top of a rounded hill, we stopped in front of Alastir's Charm shop. It was a narrow building wedged between a blacksmith and a cobbler. A thin alleyway separated each building.

"Stay here, and don't move," Nik told me as he and Puck turned to open the door.

"We can't come in?" I asked, my brow furrowed. I was desperate to see the types of wares a charm shop in Istmere might sell, and see if there was anything I could get my hands on to bring back with me to the other realm.

Nik shook his head. "Not a good idea, Firecracker. Alastir is a very old, and very powerful witch. He might be able to sense you are a Stormshade, even if you haven't been using your magic here. I trust him...but not with this. Not something I'm willing to risk. Stay with Tess."

I nodded as he and Puck turned the knob and left us alone on the street outside the shop. I peered at the sky, wondering if it would continue to *threaten* rain, or if it would storm at some point tonight.

Now it made more sense to me, but I had *always* loved storms. There was something so peaceful about falling asleep to the patter of rain on my windowsill and the soft roll of thunder off in the distance. The excitement I would feel when I would catch lightning spark over the barn at Tess' house. Or the feeling of comfort I would get when the dark clouds would roll in. As if they could wrap me up and keep me safe. I had never met anyone who loved thunderstorms as much as I did. I had always said it felt as if they were re-charging me, and once they had died off and dissipated, I always felt refreshed. Renewed.

This part of the city was more along the outskirts, and it was much quieter than the city center that housed Eight Bells. The streets here on the top of the hill were too narrow to allow for travel by horse and buggy. Patrons remained either on horseback or on foot.

"How are you doing?" Tess asked, leaning her back against the stone wall behind her and propping her foot up against it, "I have to say, Istmere is quite incredible."

"I love it here. It feels like...home," I told her, and she nodded in understanding.

"For me, too. The energy here...it feels...connected to me somehow." She rested a hand over her heart and took a deep breath.

"That's exactly how I feel. As if I was always meant to be here. Nik said it's probably the magical tether Istmere holds, the latent magic in the very being of the earth here. It's tied to everything. The trees, the dirt, even the water. When we get back home...I'm going to ask my mom about my magic," I told her, setting my jaw in determination. It was not a conversation I looked forward to, but after seeing this place and everything it held, it was something I knew I needed to do.

"I am too," she agreed with a nod, her voice thick with emotion. "Seeing this...I can't believe they kept this from us. Why would they do that? Hide this from us our entire lives?"

I nodded, meeting her bright green eyes under the dark shadow of the clouds. "I know there is a dark side to magic, and from what Nik has told me there have been dark times here recently. I understand why my family may have had to flee, if I wasn't the only Stormshade in our lineage. To keep us safe and protect us from the queen and her hatred of us. But I still would have wanted to know who I was. Where I came from. That this place even existed at all."

"I wish we were staying longer than the weekend. I'm not anxious to get back to our realm and deal with school, Fletcher, Ms. Finch and everything else," Tess said with a heavy sigh. I couldn't agree more. It felt as if we were free of those problems here, at least for now. I desperately wanted it to last longer than two days.

While Nik and Puck were inside Alastir's the sky had begun to darken, and night had started to descend upon Prins. I could hear the soft roll of thunder off in the distance, moving towards us. Perhaps we were going to get a storm after all.

How much longer would Nik and Puck be? I was anxious to get back to Eight Bells before we were soaked through our cloaks, this being the only one I had. I couldn't wear the clothes I had packed without the cover of the cloak, I would stick out too much.

"Are you ok sharing a room with Nik? Because if you aren't, I can share a room with you. Nik and Puck can duke it out for the second bed. I thought you might want to spend the night with him," Tess asked, meeting my eyes with a question in them.

"I do"—I swallowed hard—"want to spend the night with him." My voice was thick. "I'm not saying anything is going to happen—" I started as I saw her mouth curve into a smirk, "but I am ok sharing a bed with him. And I'm sure you *can't wait* to get your paws all over Puck." I laughed.

"I can't. You know me so well," Tess laughed. "I am going to ruin that boy. He is surprisingly...innocent."

I raised an eyebrow at that, and we both burst into a fit of laughter.

Tess was glancing over my shoulder with a confused expression, and I turned to see what she was looking at. A young man was approaching us quickly, a stern expression creasing his brow. He couldn't have been more than fifteen, and he was heading right for us. Was he going to check out Alastir's shop? He appeared awfully angry, the set of his jaw tight.

He came to a stop right in front of me, his cloak whirling around him. Tess stood up straight, coming to stand by my side.

"How dare you," the young man snarled, quickly glancing down the street each way to make sure we were alone. "I happened to have been *using* that grimoire."

"Grimoire?" Tess echoed from my side.

"Yes, grimoire," the young man replied through his teeth, not sparing Tess a glance. "You entered that lab and just...took it. Maybe it *was* yours to begin with, but I was in the middle of deciphering a spell. A very important spell, mind you."

Who was this person? I had never seen him before. How could he have seen me? How could he know I had the grimoire?

"I know what you're thinking," he started, growing more frustrated by the second, "I am a dream walker too. And now that you took the grimoire, it is...*gone.*"

"If it's mine to begin with...what's the problem?" I asked, crossing my arms over my chest. I remembered seeing a beaker full of bubbling liquid, as if someone had been in the lab when I had entered. Had he heard me coming, and hidden? Or left the dream entirely to avoid being caught?

He lashed out faster than I could respond, his hand around my throat, dragging me into the alleyway between the charm shop and the blacksmith. He pushed me back, my head cracking against the stone wall behind us hard enough for me to see stars.

"I need that spell, and you are going to give it to me," he snarled, his face inches from mine, his hand tight around my throat. I was racking my brain but couldn't think straight with his hand pressing down on my windpipe, cutting off my air. The grimoire had required a spell to open it, and not just *anybody* could open it. Tess couldn't, only *I* could. How had this young man opened it himself? And what spell was so important that he was willing to *strangle* me for it?

His hand left my throat as abruptly as it had lashed out in the first place, and I could hear his body slam against the wall opposite us.

"You'd better start talking. Now." Nik's voice was cold dread, suffocating and terrifying all at once. I couldn't imagine being on the other end of that wrath.

The young man sputtered and tried to speak, but Nik held him against the wall so tightly with his forearm that he couldn't move. The young man's hands came up to claw at Nik's arm, but he didn't so much as flinch. He pushed him harder into the wall, his jaw tight.

"How dare you touch her," Nik snarled into his ear, the young man's face was quickly turning a deep shade of purple.

"He can't exactly answer you if he's dead…" Puck called from the mouth of the alley, Tess safely at his side. Nik let up only enough for the young man to take a gasping breath, his eyes flashing from me to Nik.

"I only want the grimoire," he spit out, gasping down as much air as he could manage.

"Wrong answer," Nik pushed against his throat once more and the young man started flailing wildly, pulling and clawing at Nik's arm with all his strength.

"Let him talk, I want to know what he knows. He told me he was a dream walker," I told Nik as I came up behind him, resting my hand on his shoulder. Nik released him with a push and the young man doubled over, loosening the cloak at his neck and coughing to catch his breath.

"Time to talk. What do you want with Diana? And make it fast, I don't have a lot of patience left with you." Nik's eyes were hard as the young man glared up at him.

"I'm a dream walker, the same as her." He nodded towards me while he rubbed at his neck. "I was in the lab, transcribing an incredibly important spell, when I heard someone coming. I left the dream, but not before I saw her. I saw her walking down the spiral staircase to the lab." He fell into another fit of coughs before finally catching his breath.

"When I went back into the dream, the grimoire was gone," he finished.

"It's *my* family's grimoire. What do you want with it?" I asked, "And how were you even able to open it? It doesn't open for just anyone."

"That's right, *it doesn't open for just anyone.* Only for *your* blood. For Kotova blood."

"Kotova blood?" I asked, confused. Nik didn't turn from the young man but I could see his mouth was set in a hard line. Had he heard of this before?

"That's right. It is the Kotova family grimoire, after all..." the young man said slowly, as if he was stating the obvious.

"But my last name is Barnes," I told him.

"Maybe in the mortal realm your last name is Barnes, but here, in Istmere, it's Kotova. You wouldn't have been able to open the grimoire otherwise. You are a direct descendant of the Kotova bloodline. The grimoire has never picked someone who isn't of the Kotova bloodline. *Never,*" he told me, pressing back against the stone wall and taking a deep gasping breath, his hands braced on his knees.

"Then how did you open it? You must be of Kotova blood as well?" I asked, raising an eyebrow.

"Of course." He shrugged, as if this was common knowledge.

"Well then, who are you?" I asked.

"If I tell you who I am, will you let me finish the spell I was transcribing?" he asked, hopeful.

"No," Nik and I both replied in unison. This time he did turn to meet my eyes with a gaze I couldn't read.

The young man's shoulders sagged as he released a heavy sigh. He expected this answer.

"The grimoire didn't *choose* me, it didn't come to me. I found it while I was dream walking. Because it didn't choose me, I couldn't take it out of the dream with me the way you did. I could only open it because of the blood that runs through my veins. The Kotova grimoire has been hidden for over a *decade*. It's a miracle I ever found it, even if it was only in a dream. I have been searching for it for *years*."

"You are not getting your hands on that grimoire," I sighed, exasperated. "I will ask you again, who are you?"

"The name's Tyr, nice to meet you." He grimaced, running a hand down his face in defeat.

"And how, exactly, do we both have Kotova blood, Tyr?" I asked.

"I'm fairly certain I'm your cousin."

21

"**M**y *cousin*?" I asked, incredulous. My dad had been an only child. My mom had both a sister and a brother, but my uncle never had children. My aunt had a girl that was *certainly* not this young man that stood before me now.

Tyr responded with a nod, glancing quickly at Nikolai whose face remained unchanged. "Your mother was my mother's sister," Tyr spit out, untying the cloak at his neck to reveal a deep red mark forming across his throat from Nik's arm. I shook my head back and forth furiously. None of this made any sense.

"Aunt Ellorie only had one child, my little cousin Maggie. It's not possible," I told him.

"Afraid I've revealed some family secrets then, haven't I?" Tyr appeared uncomfortable as he rubbed at the sore spot on his throat. "Not my intent. Nor was it my intent to…harm you. I only want to borrow the grimoire so I can finish the spell. It's exceptionally important, and I lost my temper a bit. That's all."

"The next time you lay hands on her," Nikolai seethed, "will be the last time you have hands. Or breathe, for that matter. Do you understand, boy?"

"Yes, sir." Tyr nodded enthusiastically. "As I said, not my intention. I saw her over here and I lost my temper. I only need the grimoire if only for a minute—"

"You're not getting your hands on that grimoire," I interrupted, "ever." There was a long pause as Tyr glanced from me to Nikolai, then to Puck and Tess, who still stood in the mouth of the alley.

"There are dangerous spells in that grimoire. It called to *me*. It came to *me* in a dream. It is *mine*," I snapped.

"Yes, that's all true. The grimoire chose you, but if I could just—"

"The lady said no. Now if I were you, I would be on my way. Run along now, and don't speak a word of this. To *anyone*. She was never here, you never saw her," Nik said as he pinned him with a cold stare.

Tyr gathered his cloak around himself and, with one last look at me, he took off for the mouth of the alley. We followed him out to the street, but by the time we reached Puck and Tess, Tyr was gone.

"What the hell was that?" Tess asked.

"I was thinking the same thing. I didn't know I had any magical *cousins*. Family secrets, indeed," I replied. "Did you get the glamour?"

"Yes, enough for each of us," Nik replied, grabbing my shoulder and turning me towards him. "Are you alright?"

"Yes, I'm ok," I replied, rubbing my throat. It would be a little sore from where Tyr had pinned me. I believed Tyr when he said he hadn't meant to hurt me. He was young, and Nik had scared the ever-loving magic right out of him.

"I fear that won't be the last we see of him," Puck said as he tucked the vials of glamour potion into the inner lining of his cloak pocket.

Thunder cracked loud overhead, the storm having moved much closer during the scuffle. I felt a single drop of rain fall on my cheek and I moved to wipe it away. My magic surged forwards again, as if it was begging to come out and play in the oncoming storm. It was buzzing right at the surface. I wouldn't even have to dig deep into my well of magic. It was right there, ready to be called upon.

"We'd better get back before this storm descends," Nik peered at the sky before starting back down the cobblestone street towards Eight Bells, and we all followed.

By the time we had reached the inn we were soaked through, having been caught in the deluge of rain. Without being able to use my storm magic, we hadn't been able to outrun the storm. It had grown late, and we were all tired, retiring to our rooms for the night.

The first thing I did was claim the washroom for myself and strip out of my sopping wet clothes, indulging in a hot bath to warm my skin. The inn had left little bubbling, scented soaps on the edge of the tub and I let the hot water wash away the cold chill from deep in my bones. The thunder rolled forcefully overhead as I scrubbed my skin clean in the light of the lantern I had placed at the head of the claw-foot tub.

Was Tyr truly my cousin, or was he bluffing? There had to be some truth to it, because he had been able to open the grimoire himself. But the Kotova bloodline? What was my mom keeping from me? We had a long conversation ahead of us when I got back, that was for sure.

I washed my hair in the rich decadent shampoos and conditioners the inn provided and toweled myself off, sure that Nik would need to use the washroom, too. He must be freezing in his wet clothes.

From the appearance of the pub downstairs, I had never imagined the inn would be so tidy and comfortable. The rooms were spacious and clean, a stark contrast to the dark and sticky pub found below. I wrapped myself in a long white robe and exited the washroom to find Nik bent over the fireplace with a poker, a stern expression of concentration on his face. He had ditched his wet shirt and cloak and was barefoot and shirtless, his black jeans sticking to him as if they were a second skin.

"The fire should help warm things up," Nik said as he stood, his defined muscles and tattoos on full display in the light of the fire. I had imagined his tattoos ran the length of him, but with his entire chest exposed I could see that they covered his chest. They peeked out at the top of his neck, then moved down his arms to stop above his elbows. His abdomen was left bare of markings.

His eyes turned molten under my gaze, and I suddenly felt self-conscious in only a robe. I wrapped it tighter around my frame. Nik was so confident. So arrogant. So cocky. I was the complete opposite, and I couldn't help but wonder what he might see in me in this moment. As if he could see the thoughts playing out on my face, he returned the fire poker to the mantle and moved towards me in slow, measured steps. His feet were light against the hardwood floor.

"Don't you want to wash up?" I asked, my voice cracking and betraying me. He reached out and grabbed the knot of my robe at my waist and pulled me flush against him, his skin still wet from the rain. He was flushed warm from the fire, his wet hair falling into his darkening eyes.

"That can wait," he said, lowering his face towards mine, our noses only inches apart. His jaw was faintly lined with stubble, his full mouth pulled into a smirk.

"What are you thinking?" he asked.

"No chance," I replied with a nervous smile.

"Ohhh, come on now, firecracker. I won't tell," he purred.

"That's not what I'm worried about." I swallowed hard. I could feel his warm breath on my face, and I could practically taste the cinnamon and Dragon's Ale on his lips. Only a few inches between us. If I leaned up on my tiptoes, I could easily bring our mouths together and close the distance. But I was...afraid. Afraid he wouldn't feel the same way about me. That he wouldn't find my body as attractive as I found his. That I wasn't *enough* for him. But the way he was looking at me now...as if he could devour me whole. There was no way I could misinterpret that. His eyes were molten lava. His calloused, battle-worn hands were gentle as they caressed the soft skin of my jaw.

I leaned up and pulled his mouth down to mine, erasing any thoughts of inadequacy from my mind the second his lips found mine. He kissed me back hungrily, like a man starving and I was the *exact* flavor he craved. He pulled my lower lip between his teeth and gave it a soft bite before sucking on it. I could feel my knees buckle, but his arms were around me, pressing me to him. He pushed me back towards the bed and as I lay against the pillows, his lips quickly found mine again, tracing the line of my jaw and moving down my neck.

He pulled back when he saw the slight bruise that now graced my throat, courtesy of Tyr. I had noticed it in the mirror in the washroom, the skin yellowing and purpling slightly. His expression heated as he met my gaze, and he covered the bruise with the sweetest kisses, his tongue licking the skin in agonizing slowness. He pressed his body into mine, but I could barely feel him through the thick cushion of the robe. I suddenly wanted to be rid of it entirely.

He continued to kiss down my neck and over my collarbone, his hand slipping inside the robe and pulling it aside to reveal my shoulder. I pulled eagerly at the loopholes on his jeans, hoping to peel them off.

"Impatient, are we?" he whispered against my lips, a laugh in his voice. He pulled back long enough to let me unbutton his pants and unzip them, his eyes on mine. The only sound in the room was the soft crackling of the fireplace and the sound of his zipper. He let out a groan as his mouth found mine again, but his jeans were stuck to him from the rain. We both dissolved into a fit of laughter as he tried, unsuccessfully, to shuck them off.

"Incredibly sexy," I teased as he tossed the pants to the floor with a wet thud. His underwear and the fluffy robe were the only things between us now. Before tonight, I wasn't entirely sure what I wanted. But here, in this moment, the only thing I wanted was Nikolai. The feeling of his mouth on mine, the heat of his skin, the pulse between my legs that tightened every time he touched me. I wanted to take things slow, but I wanted this. I couldn't feel any doubt in his affections when I met his eyes, and all I saw there was desire and warmth, like a slow, wanton burn.

He pressed back over me, and I could feel the hard length of him through the material of the robe. I wrapped my arms around his hips and pulled him closer as he ground into me. I threw my head back with a soft gasp. I had never, *ever*, felt *want* like this. He grabbed the knot of my robe and glanced up at me with a question in his eyes. I nodded fervently, and he loosened the knot gently, pushing the top of the robe aside to expose the hardened peaks of my pale breasts. His eyebrows raised as he realized I wasn't wearing any undergarments.

Once the knot was loosened, the bottom of the robe slipped open as well, and I could feel him pressed against me. Almost skin to skin except for those damned boxer briefs. His hair was still wet from the rain and it dripped onto my chest as he hovered over me, admiring. His lips were parted slightly, and he held me tightly around the ribcage, his hands warm against me. I made an impatient noise that broke him from his trance with a wicked grin.

"I love that sound," he breathed as he lowered his mouth to my body, taking my full breast into his mouth and the other in his hand. I gasped as he sucked on it and bit down gently, his hand massaging the other. The pulse between my legs grew into a strong need as I ground myself into him, groaning at the feeling of friction. His mouth made his way up my breast to my neck, and finally captured my mouth again with his.

"I know what you want…" he spoke softly against my mouth, "but I want to take things slow with you. I've…" He broke off, blinking fast. "I've never felt like this…about someone before," he confessed.

"Me neither," I whispered against his mouth.

"But I won't leave you with nothing…" he teased.

He spread my legs with his and slipped his thigh between them until his knee hit the center of me. Stars exploded behind my eyes at the feeling of his skin meeting my core. I threw my head back as I ground into him, his thigh moving against me.

"Does that feel good?" he asked, knowing the answer before even having to ask.

"Yes," I spit out, unable to concentrate my thoughts on anything but the sensation of his leg between mine, his mouth on my neck, his hand at my breast.

"Do you want me to stop?" he asked, pulling back to meet my eyes.

"Don't you *dare* stop," I told him, grabbing the back of his neck and bringing his mouth back down to mine. I bit his lower lip with a hiss as he took my breast between his fingers, massaging in time with the movement of my hips.

There was a point of pleasure I was *dangerously* close to, and soon I would go tumbling off the edge. I panted against his mouth and he let out a groan, moving back down to take my breast into his mouth.

"Like this?" he asked, grinding his thigh harder against me.

"Just like that." I nodded.

I threw my head back and cried out, my hand curled into his mess of wet hair, my legs shaking, as I fell over the cliff and was consumed by a pleasure I had never known before. My body contracted, my back arching off the bed into him as everything tightened and released. My breathing was hard as he kissed me again, this time more softly. If he could do that with just his thigh, I could only imagine...

He fell to my side and pulled me close, my back nestled against his chest, his mouth at my ear.

"How was that?" he asked, his voice low and sultry.

"It was...amazing." I closed my eyes and enjoyed the feel of him cradled against me. "But what about you?" I asked, moving to turn around, but his tight grip held me in place.

"I'm just fine, Firecracker. That wasn't only for you," he assured me with a gentle kiss on the back of my neck.

"Did you want to wash up?" I asked, realizing he had never had a chance to when we had gotten back in from the rainstorm. I could still hear the rain battering heavily against the windowsill of our room, the thunder echoing directly overhead loud enough to shake the floorboards. I hadn't even noticed.

"That can wait," he repeated his sentiment from earlier.

I liked the idea that he didn't want to waste one second with me, that he couldn't get enough of me, as I couldn't get enough of him. Somehow, I felt giddy and sated at the same time. I curled deeper into him, his leg slipping between mine as he cradled me against his chest. He slid the duvet over us and I fell asleep wrapped in his arms, the warm fire crackling, his wet hair dripping onto the pillow we shared.

When I woke the next morning and rolled over, Nikolai wasn't in the bed next to me. The blankets were still warm, and I raised my head to see the door to the washroom was closed. The room was filled with the soft sound of a running shower.

I turned over and pulled my robe with me. It had slipped open again in the middle of the night. I couldn't help but flail my legs and giggle. Last night had been *amazing*. The feel of Nik's skin against mine. His mouth on my body. I suppressed a squeal as I rose from the bed, pulling on the only other pair of pants I had brought with us to Istmere and a long sleeve navy sweater.

My stomach grumbled, and I wondered if Puck and Tess had gone down to grab breakfast yet. I felt a pang in my chest as I realized this was our last day in Istmere, and we would need to return to our own realm by nightfall. I dreaded the conversation I would have with my mother, and returning to school to see which Nightshade would be after me this week…Fletcher or Ms. Finch.

As I tugged my sneakers on, I heard a knock at the door.

"You better be decent!" I heard Tess call from the other side.

"Of course, I am." I opened the door with a laugh. Tess quickly surveyed the room, and when she realized Nik was in the washroom, she threw herself down onto the unmade bed. "Spill. How was last night?" she asked with a raised brow.

"You spill. I want to know how *your* night was," I told her as I joined her across the crumpled duvet.

"No way, you first," she insisted with a shake of her head.

I relented with a sigh and told her all about last night. How Nik and I had hooked up, but it hadn't gone any farther than that. How it had been *amazing*, and I had never felt like this about anyone before.

I could hear the shower turn off and Tess met my eyes before bursting into a fit of giggles. I shoved her off the bed to quiet her, but she kept laughing, curled up on the floor.

"I knew it. It's always the 'innocent' ones that *love* the bad boys," she choked out between laughs.

"Well, now that you know all about *my* night, what about you?" I asked.

As Tess got up to join me back on the bed, Nik sauntered out of the washroom, squeezing his wet hair in a towel. He wore the same black jeans as yesterday, but with a white T-shirt that hugged his muscled frame. It showed off the tattoos at his neck and those peeking out below the shirt at his bicep.

"Care to let me in on the joke?" he asked, moving to the bed to put his boots on.

"It wasn't that funny," I told him as Tess shot me a glare. I would have to wait to hear about her night until we were alone again.

"What do you say we hit up one of Puck and my favorite breakfast spots before we start heading back to the portal?" he asked.

"Sounds good to me. Will Saanvi be escorting us back through The Shadow?" I asked.

"I think so," he nodded. "I'm going to send her a message once we get to breakfast."

"Good, because I am *starving.*" Tess tossed her hair over her shoulder and moved towards the door while Nik and I followed. "Puck is already downstairs waiting for us. We will come back for our bags?" she asked.

"Yes. I definitely need at least one more pint of Dragon's Ale before we hit the road," Nik replied with a laugh.

I took one last glance around the room before shutting the door behind us and heading downstairs to meet Puck.

The breakfast place was a few blocks away from Eight Bells and the cool morning air sent a shiver through me despite the sweater I had chosen this morning being rather heavy. The rest of Prins was already awake, the busy streets filled with people and covered in a thick layer of fog from last night's storm.

The cobblestone streets were still damp, but from what we could see of the sky overhead, it appeared that it would be a clear day today. Tess grabbed my arm, and we walked together, both of us grinning. This weekend trip to Istmere had been exactly what we needed. A little time away to unwind, and I hoped it wouldn't be the last time we snuck off to have a weekend to ourselves. I wish we had more time. There was so much of Istmere I wanted to explore and so much about my magic and my heritage that remained a mystery.

I could see the spot we were headed to about a block down, The Giddy Griddle. It had a red and white striped awning with tables set out on the street. The inviting smell of hot cakes wafting down to us made my mouth water.

A stranger walking too close bumped my shoulder hard enough to make me lose my balance; Tess' arm looped through mine was the only thing keeping me upright.

"Hey, watch where you're going!" Tess called after him, but the stranger didn't spare us a second glance. He just kept walking.

"Nice. I don't think yelling at strangers falls under 'lying low' and 'not drawing attention to ourselves,'" I told Tess as I gave her arm a playful squeeze.

"I couldn't help it. He was rude." She shrugged.

I could see Nik's spine straighten out of the corner of my eye as another set of strangers approached us from the direction of the restaurant. Their cloaks billowed behind them, and their hoods were pulled up so we couldn't see their faces. There were three of them.

"We need to get out of here. *Now.*" Nik grabbed my hand, and all but tore me out of Tess' grip, pulling me back the way we had come.

"What are you talking about? What is going on?" Tess asked, turning to Puck, who had grabbed her as well and was dragging her down the street behind him. Neither Nik nor Puck answered. They kept walking faster and faster, making it difficult for me to keep up with my much shorter legs.

"The glamour vials?" Puck asked, shooting Nik a sideways glance.

"It's too late, we've already been spotted," Nik replied.

"Seriously, what is going on?" I asked as Nik turned to me, his eyes focused on something behind me. He paused briefly, his eyes searching.

"Diana, listen to me. I need you to run." He grabbed both of my hands and pulled me towards him. "I need you to run as fast as you can. It doesn't matter where you go, I will find you. Just *run.*"

Nik pulled an obsidian dagger from his belt, his jaw set. A question bubbled to my lips, but his expression stopped the words before they could come out. I didn't question him. I did as he asked. I *ran.* Tess was on my heels as we raced through the streets, not knowing where we were going. We stopped at a busy intersection where we needed to wait to cross, and I turned to Tess as I tried to catch my breath.

"I'm with you," she told me, breathless. "Let's go."

We tore across the intersection, our sneakers slapping hard against the stone, twisting and turning around carriages and carts. The shouts of the store merchants telling us to slow down buzzed in our ears as we ran past. I never was terribly athletic, and now I cursed myself for it as I heard the cloaked strangers chasing us, their footsteps growing closer and closer. How many of them had Nik and Puck been able to take down? How many of them were there, and what did they want with us?

"Where do we go?" I asked as we turned a corner towards Alastir's, the charm shop we had visited the day before. I pumped my arms at my sides and focused on my breathing as we ascended the round hilltop, then started to make our way back down on the other side.

"No idea. All I know is we *avoid* The Shadow." Tess panted at my side. She was in much better shape than me, and I could tell she was holding herself back to not leave me behind. Tess would never leave me behind.

We turned another corner, but the way was blocked by two cloaked figures, their hoods pulled up over their heads to conceal their faces.

"Shit," I muttered as I started to turn back, completely out of breath.

Before I could turn and try to run the other direction, I was hit *hard* by something from behind. I couldn't see Tess anymore. I couldn't hear the hard footsteps of our pursuers. I couldn't see the misty morning air. My vision swam with black spots before I fell to my knees on the cobblestone and a grain sack was pulled over my head. That was the last thing I remember before the world went dark.

When I came to, my head was pounding to the rhythm of my own heartbeat. I had a sharp headache in the back of my skull and as I peeled my eyes open, I realized my head was still covered with the grain sack. All I could see was the faint light seeping through the gaps in the burlap.

I was jostling back and forth, and I could hear the clop of horse hooves on stone. I must be in a carriage of some sort. My hands were bound tightly behind my back, so tightly my shoulders ached, and my fingers felt numb and cold. I tried to move my legs and realized that my feet were bound at the ankles as well.

I listened quietly, motionless, to see if I could hear anyone nearby. Was I alone? Where was Tess? Where were these people taking me? I listened closely but heard nothing, not even the sound of shifting or breathing from anyone else who might be in the carriage with me. After a long period of silence, nobody had spoken.

I braved the silence and softly called out to Tess, but there was no answer. I half expected to be knocked in the back of the head again the second I opened my mouth, but as I called out once more, louder, there was still no response.

I couldn't hear the sounds of the busy road outside, or the rough shouts of people on the streets. All I could hear was the sound of the horses trotting along and the carriage bouncing back and forth mercilessly over the uneven road. It took everything in me to keep myself upright with how tightly I was bound and how hard I was being jostled back and forth by the movement of the carriage. My head pounded harder. The only reprieve was to squeeze my eyes shut against the faint light seeping through my hood.

"Nik?" I whispered, "Puck?" But nobody responded.

I was alone.

I must have dozed off at some point because when I woke again I was no longer in the carriage. I was being carried over someone's shoulder like dead weight. I could no longer hear the sounds of the horses' hooves or the carriage wheels against the cobblestone. The only sound filling my ears was that of the heavy footfalls of the man who carried me.

I remained limp against him, pretending that I was still passed out to buy me more time to assess where we were going. We were traveling down a long flight of stairs, arms holding tight around me as we descended. We came to a stop at the bottom and the man holding me turned abruptly. I was hot under the hood they had placed over me, my hair sticking to my forehead and plastered to the back of my neck.

"Where do you want me to put this one, commander?"

"Next cell down," a gruff voice replied.

We were walking again, but it was a short distance before I was thrown down and dragged the rest of the way by the bindings at my feet. I stifled a grunt and tried my best not to cough as I was dragged against the stone floor, dirt flying up into my face, causing my eyes to sting and my lungs to burn. I was tugged over a cold threshold that caught me hard in the stomach before I heard iron bars closing behind me with a reverberating clang. I was pulled off my stomach and thrown against the back of the cell unceremoniously before the sack was ripped off my head and I could see my surroundings for the first time.

I was in a dark, windowless cell, a soldier staring down at me with a sneer on his face. He was older, but strong. His black metal armor was so tight it appeared painted on, the crest of a dark sword etched onto his chest plate. He scratched his grey beard with a gloved hand before turning and exiting the cell, locking it behind him.

"Wait—" I started, trying to move towards the door, but my arms and feet were still tightly bound. "Where am I? What do you want with me?" I pleaded.

The soldier sneered before spitting at my feet and turning to disappear down the long corridor.

"Wait! You can't keep me here! You have to let me out!" I called after him, "This has to be some mistake!" But I received no reply, my voice echoing down the empty corridor. I wiggled in the dirt to try to move towards the iron bars, but my legs were numb. My shoulders felt as if they would dislocate if I tried to move them anymore. I had been tied for too long.

"It's no use," a familiar voice called from the cell next to mine.

"Tess?" I asked, peering into the darkness of the adjacent cell, my voice breaking. "Tess, is that you?"

"Yes," she replied softly. "I tried breaking free, too. It's no use. I've been here for hours waiting to see if they would bring you down." *Hours?*

The prison was dark and damp, the cells only divided by iron bars which I could reach through if my hands weren't bound. It was so dark I could only make out the silhouette of Tess' body slumped against the back wall of her cell. There were no windows to provide any source of light, and the cell floors were packed with dirt. The corridor across from us appeared to stretch on forever, and beyond the long corridor was an impenetrable concrete wall.

"We need to get out of here," I told her, glancing around to see if there was anything that could help me to loosen my bindings.

"It's ash," Tess sounded defeated. "They told me the bindings are made of ash...there's no way we can get out of them ourselves. Not until they let us out. And the iron bars are infused with ash, too. We can't use our magic down here."

"Shit." I hung my head in defeat. I didn't have any weapons on me, and if I couldn't use my storm magic, I had no idea how I was going to break us out. I dove into the deep well at my core to see if she was right, and I felt nothing. Absolutely nothing. There was no warm energy waiting for me to call on, there was nothing at all. *Shit.* We were screwed.

"Who are these people? What do they want?" I asked, leaning my head back against the cold concrete of the tiny cell. It was much cooler now that I didn't have the hood suffocating me, but my hair was still plastered to me. I was desperate to shake it out. There was nothing worse than an itch you couldn't scratch.

"I don't know. They haven't spoken to me at all, other than to tell me about the bindings. I overheard them calling this the Stormvault."

"Stormvault?" I asked.

"It's the name of this prison. I don't think we are in Prins anymore…" Tess replied.

I had to agree. I remember waking in the carriage and not hearing the busy sounds of Prins outside. It had been quiet. *Storm*vault…did these soldiers, whoever they were, know I was a Stormshade? But how could they? I hadn't used my magic in days. I hadn't even so much as reached out to it or dipped into it since arriving in Istmere. Not to mention there *weren't* any Stormshades. Not anymore.

"Where are Nik and Puck?" I asked.

"No clue. I don't know if they were captured, too. I haven't heard them being mentioned by the guards, and they sure as hell aren't down here."

"It's just us?" I took a deep breath, closing my eyes against the darkness.

"It's just us," Tess confirmed. I could hear the chains at her wrists jingle as she tried to shuffle closer to the edge of my cell. I used the wall for leverage and did the same. At the corner where our two cells met, I could finally see her face in the shadows. Her normally perfect hair was mussed and hanging over her shoulders, a mascara tear stained her cheek. I couldn't imagine what I looked like after having a burlap sack placed over my head, for God only knew how many hours, and being dragged down here in the dirt.

"Do you know how far down we are?" I asked.

"About three flights down is my best guess. I didn't see or hear anything that would suggest our location," she replied.

"How the hell are we going to get out of here?" I racked my brain for ideas, but was coming up short. They needed to unbind us. Without magic, it seemed utterly impossible. Would they eventually take off our restraints? My fingers had gone numb, and it was becoming difficult to wiggle my toes.

"Your guess is as good as mine." Tess sighed, leaning her shoulder against mine through the bars. "I'm just happy you're safe."

"Me too. When I woke in the carriage and you weren't there...I was so worried. I was alone."

"I think they separated us on purpose," Tess replied. I swallowed the lump in my throat and leaned into her. I could hear her stomach grumble and she let out a humorless laugh. "I never got my pancakes."

Leave it to Tess to be upset about pancakes while we were being held captive in a prison somewhere in the witch realm.

"Once we make it out of here, I will make you a short stack that will knock your socks off," I promised her.

"With chocolate chips?" she asked in a small voice.

"Of course."

I could hear the sound of boots clapping against the stone corridor and I straightened, peering through the darkness. All I could see was the shape of the two soldiers as they approached our cells.

"Who are you?" I asked into the darkness as I heard the cell unlock with a click. "What do you want?" But the soldier did not respond. Instead, he moved towards me with a handkerchief held in his gloved fist. I shot a glance towards Tess, but in the darkness, I couldn't see her anymore.

"Lights out, princess," the soldier sneered before pressing the cloth to my mouth. I struggled and tried to kick out, but my legs were bound too tightly. I tried to roll over onto my stomach, but the soldier was stronger than I was, and he wrestled to keep the cloth over my mouth. It wasn't long before the world went dark...again.

When I woke this time, it was with a start, shooting upright. My hands and feet were no longer bound, and I was lying on a cold marbled floor in a room lined with windows. The windows were draped with blood red curtains, a dais with a single throne on the far side of the room. To my right lay Tess, her limbs at odd angles, as if they had simply dropped her there. We were alone.

"Tess, wake up." I crawled to my knees and put my hand on her shoulder to shake her. "Tess, I need you to wake up now."

This would probably be our only chance at escape. I moved to the set of double doors behind me and when I pushed them, I could hear the sound of chains clinking together on the other side. The door was chained shut. Great. At least this room was full of windows.

I ran to the nearest window and peered out, my fingers clawing at the windowsill to pry it open. The wall of windows led out to a steep, shingled rooftop. When I glanced down, I could see we were at the top of a tower, in a castle made of stone. The roof dropped off to a terrace far below. Far too high to jump from and live to tell the tale. I would have to break the window and hope for the best if this was truly our only way out.

As far as the eye could see, there were buildings made of the same natural colored stone, set into the side of the snow-covered mountain. The only way down were the narrow roadways that switched back and forth down the mountainside, heavily guarded by uniformed soldiers. Of course...we were in The Stone City. We were in Akra. I had never seen it myself, but I had heard Nik talk about it. This was where he grew up. But what were we doing *here*?

I knelt by Tess' side again, shaking her with more fervor this time. My legs and arms were tired and sore from being bound for so long.

"Tess," I hissed. "Tess, if you are planning on waking up, now would be a good time!"

The doors behind us burst open, and I fell to Tess' side with a start. I hadn't even heard anyone fumbling with the chained lock. In filed a set of six soldiers, three on each side of the door, their hands on their swords.

"I think there's been some kind of mistake..." I started, but their faces were covered by their armored helmets. None of them turned at the sound of my voice. My eyes found the marble floor and I could feel tears welling in them. I couldn't make a run for it, not without Tess. I wouldn't make it far if I went out those windows, or with these armed soldiers here. Could I use my magic to get us out? I wasn't bound anymore, and that meant I should have access to my storm magic. I blinked back the tears that had threatened to fall and swallowed, determination replacing the moment of despair.

As I started to search my core for that familiar energy, a heel stomped against the floor at the door's entrance.

"Tsk, tsk, tsk. I wouldn't do that if I were you," came a sultry voice. I slowly raised my eyes from the tile, and through the swell of unshed tears I saw her.

A woman with blue and white hair, raising a sword high above her head in victory, she turned, and her eyes were endless black pits. A war, witches slaughtering witches, fire burning down an empire. The blue-haired woman sitting on the throne of shadows, a pack of black wolves at her side. A city in ruin, stone buildings reduced to rubble as smoke rises from the ashes.

It was *her*. It was the woman from my vision. It was the Shadow Queen. The Black Heart. I swallowed hard, fighting back more of the tears that welled in my eyes, and raising my chin defiantly towards her. She would not see me cry.

"What do you want with me?" I asked, sitting back on my heels, my hand squeezing Tess' tightly.

"Do not speak unless you are spoken to," she warned, and for the first time, her eyes met mine. She had no sclera, no iris or pupil. Her eyes were black tourmaline, empty and endless. She sauntered into the room and on her heels were three prowling black wolves.

On her head was a crown of iron spikes ornamented with black gems. Her dress was a blue grey that matched the streaks in her hair, with a low-cut neckline that dipped to her waist. It had big silver jewels adorning the shoulders and blue beads down the arms and bodice before it cascaded into a spill of soft ruffles down her legs. There was a slit that reached up to her hip, and I could see her black stilettos as they clicked against the marble. Despite her eyes, she was breathtakingly beautiful.

She parted the dress to one side and climbed the dais, sitting on the throne. She crossed her long spidery legs and tapped her black painted nails against the arm rest impatiently.

"We will begin soon. I'm only waiting for our boys."

Our boys. So, they had captured Nik and Puck, after all. We were in deep shit, and the longer this went on, the less I could see a way out of this. We were supposed to return to our realm today, and I had no idea how much time had passed already. It appeared to still be light out, but did time pass the same here in Akra? How long had I been knocked out for? I had no idea. Tess' hand was still limp in mine, but her chest rose and fell in a steady rhythm. I choked back my bubbling emotions and stood before the Shadow Queen, waiting.

She glared down on me from the dais with scorn, her emotions plain on her face, despite her lifeless eyes. Did she know I was a Stormshade? Is that why she looked upon me with such...disgust? Did she plan to kill me? Another armor-clad soldier entered the throne room and knelt before the queen before rising and whispering something in her ear. The queen nodded, and the soldier shuffled out as quickly as he had come in.

"We might as well get right down to it, Diana. Can I call you Diana?"

I didn't answer her. Instead, I leveled her with a cool stare, despite the fear slowly crawling its way up my throat. *How did she know my name?* I held my hands behind my back to hide their shaking and dug my nails into the palm of my hand hard enough to draw blood. With the other hand I started to pick away at the nail bed, focusing on that pain. It was the only way I knew to keep my emotions in check when they were swirling out of control.

"You see, Diana, you have something that I need. Something that is *far* too powerful to be in the hands of someone such as yourself. If you give it to me, this will all be over, and you can return to your monstrously boring life. Are we in agreement?" she asked, her tone deceptively pleasant. As if this whole scenario was a simple transaction, and not that she had kidnapped me and dragged me here against my will to throw me in a dungeon.

"I'm not sure I understand what you want," I replied tightly.

"You know *exactly* what it is I seek," she accused. "The grimoire."

How did she know I had it? The only people who knew of it were Nik and Tess. And Tyr. *Crap.* Tyr had seen me with the grimoire, and we had let him go. The queen could see it on my face as I unraveled the truth.

"That's right," she crooned, "innocent little Tyr came running to his Shadow Queen the moment he saw you in Istmere. He told me all about you."

I swallowed hard. How much had he told her? That I was a dream walker? Did Tyr know I was a Stormshade? Some cousin he was...turning me in at the first opportunity.

"I don't have it," I replied.

"Obviously. I would sense it on you. But you will retrieve it for me."

"And if I don't?" I asked, my shoulders tensing.

"There will be dire consequences," she replied in a cool tone.

What, exactly, was in this grimoire that everyone wanted to get their hands on? I had looked at most of it...some of it had appeared innocuous and the rest I hadn't understood. There must be something incredibly precious in there for everyone to want to take it from me the moment they found out it was in my possession. But the grimoire had shown itself to *me*. It had chosen *me*. It was *my* family's grimoire, I couldn't simply hand it over. There had to be a reason that it came to me in that dream...

"Ah, just in time," she said as she rose from her throne and sauntered down the dais steps, the wolves following closely on her heels. I turned, and in the arched doorway between the armed soldiers were Nik and Puck. A wave of relief flooded through me, and my breath released in an exhausted huff. They were safe. They were here. Despite everything, I was sure they would be able to find us a way out of this mess. I expected Puck to rush to Tess' side as she remained limp on the cold tile, but he stopped in the doorway, his eyes tight. He avoided my stare, his eyes downcast. My brow raised in confusion and Nik continued forwards, his gaze on the dais.

"Donika." He nodded with a smile as he walked past me.

He joined her at the base of the steps, and she wrapped her arm around his waist, bringing him into a tight embrace. I shot a glance back at Puck, confused, but he remained head down in the doorway. Tess began to stir at my feet.

I turned my head back towards Nik and Donika. He stepped towards her, taking her in his arms, and she cupped the back of his neck before pulling his mouth down to hers in a passionate kiss.

B ile rose up the back of my throat and I tried my hardest to swallow it back down. I was going to be sick. I felt hot all over. My ears and cheeks burned as if they were on fire. Nik's lips parted easily for hers as if they were familiar to him. As if he had memorized the way she felt against him. His arms tightened around her as she swept her tongue against his, and she laughed softly against his mouth.

"I know I was passed out...but I think I missed something," Tess spoke from the floor. She had sat up and was cupping the back of her head with her hand, her expression confused, squinting at the display before us.

"Same," I breathed as they broke apart. "What the fuck is going on?"

"I'm simply welcoming my boyfriend back home, I haven't seen him in *months*," Donika replied with a sinister smile.

"Boyfriend?" my voice cracked as my eyes fixed on Nik. He didn't so much as stir under my gaze. He met my eyes with his chin held high, his hand in Donika's.

"I sent Nikolai to your realm a few months ago, so he could infiltrate your little group and get me what I needed," she said.

"Is that true?" I asked him as Tess stood and looped her arm through mine, giving it a tight squeeze.

He didn't answer, his expression unreadable.

"But I didn't even have the grimoire when Nik came to school..." I protested. "I didn't even know I was a witch." None of this made any sense. Had this been his intention all along?

"Well, that was the other part of the deal. I knew you were out there, even if you didn't know what you were yourself. I could sense you. I knew you were hidden in the human realm, and I knew that Nik, being one of the strongest Nightshades in my army, would be able to coax you out. *Stormshade*." She hissed the word like a curse.

He was in her army? He was *with* her? She knew I was a Stormshade, and she sent Nik to bring me back here, to her, all this time. None of it had been real. From the very beginning, all he had wanted was to bring me to Istmere. To surrender me to the Shadow Queen. What would she do with me, now that she had me? Would she kill me, like she had all the Stormshades that had come before me? Would she let Tess go?

I felt sick. I felt so hot it was as if my skin was melting. Without Tess holding me up I was sure I would collapse into a pile of limbs at her feet. There was a lump in my throat as

I remembered last night. The feel of Nik's skin on mine. His mouth on my mouth. His hands all over me. Even then, he had known he was going to hand me over to Donika. He had touched me, kissed me, knowing he was going to betray me. How could he lie to me so easily? How could he hand me over to her? I could see a muscle tick in his jaw, but he was still as a statue under my gaze. I shook my head back and forth. It couldn't be...it just...couldn't. I didn't want to believe it.

"Nik was taking an awfully long time getting the job done, so I had to send Fletcher. But even he couldn't bring you back here. Just a little Stormshade...I don't get what all the fuss is about. When Fletcher failed, I sent Antonia Finch, but in the end, it was Tyr who came through for me." Tyr. My own blood. Despite the way in which we met, and the reminder he left on my neck, his betrayal still stung.

Nik had betrayed me. He had manipulated me. He had used me. The last few weeks were a total and complete lie. I wanted to wring his neck, to crush him beneath my anger and bring down this castle around us. I felt my magic surge forth without being called upon, as if it had a mind all its own beneath my rage. As I felt flames lick at my fingertips I was kicked to my knees from behind, and a soldier clapped ash shackles onto my wrists. A feral growl left my mouth as I twisted and turned in his grip.

"I'll let you calm down for a bit, this was quite the news. Nik and I have a lot of catching up to do..." Donika trailed her finger down Nik's chest, a smile in her dark eyes. "Take them back to the Stormvault," she called to the soldier, never taking her gaze off Nik. Tess and I were dragged from the room.

The throne room led out onto a large landing with a wide, curved, staircase that descended into the main part of the castle. I was thrown over the soldier's shoulder and carried around like a rag doll through the castle hallways. I memorized the way, and we passed a large set of doors that must be the main entrance to the castle. I would find a way out of here, no matter what it takes. There is no way they can keep me here. I refused to resign myself to whatever fate Donika had planned for me. I wouldn't play into her little charade.

As Tess predicted, the Stormvault was three levels down from the main floor. She must have been mostly conscious when they dragged her down here earlier. At the base of the staircase, the prison was protected by an iron, ash infused, door that appeared to be as heavy as a boulder. *Vault*, indeed. This time Tess and I were tossed into the dirt of the same cell, and I coughed against the cloud of dust as our shackles were removed. The soldiers left, slamming the iron door behind them, leaving us alone together in the dark.

I reached for Tess in the dark and held onto her tight, my head pounding as I laid it against her shoulder. My eyes squeezed shut as tears stained her dirt-covered shirt.

"Diana, I am so sorry. I am *so*, so sorry," she said as she held me, rubbing small circles into my back.

"Me too," I said as I wiped a dirt-stained tear from my cheek with the back of my hand. "I had no idea. I thought it was real. I thought all of it was real. I can't believe he...used me. He deceived me. He betrayed me."

"I know." She continued rubbing soft circles into my back as I cried, finally letting the emotions from the last few weeks pour out of me. "Puck betrayed us too."

He had. Now I knew why he couldn't meet my eyes in the throne room. He had felt guilty. At least, that's how it had appeared. Nik had felt *nothing*. He was as cruel and lifeless as Donika as he stood before me, his hand in hers. Had everything he told me been a lie?

So, this was the 'business' Fletcher had been alluding to all along. Nik was supposed to bring me back to Istmere…back to Donika. He was much stronger than me, and I hadn't even known the extent of my magic before I had started training with him. Why had he taught me how to reach my magic, anyway? If his intent was to always bring me here? Why hadn't he brought me to her earlier? Was he waiting for the grimoire to make itself known to me? And why did he feel the need to…to…seduce me? Was that the only way he could think of getting close to me?

"What a mess." I laughed as I wiped my nose with the hem of my filthy shirt.

"You're telling me." Tess shook her head. We crawled to the back of the cell together and rest our heads against the concrete, my hand in hers, our legs outstretched.

"There's nobody I would rather be locked in a prison with." I gave her hand a reassuring squeeze.

"In a foreign realm, no less," she added. "Our parents are going to *kill* us if we even make it out of here alive."

"*When* we make it out of here," I corrected her.

We could hear the heavy iron door creak open and swing shut with a thud as a soldier made his way down the long corridor. Through the darkness I could make out a familiar silhouette in the shadows as he opened the door, slid a tray inside, and locked it again. He sat cross-legged in the dirt outside our cell, his elbows resting on his knees.

"I need to talk to you. Both of you," Puck said quietly as Tess moved forwards and dragged the tray to the back of the cell with us. It had a jug of water, what appeared to be some type of mysterious grey meat stew, and hunks of stale bread on it. Tess and I passed the water jug back and forth before digging in. We hadn't eaten since yesterday and we would have to keep our strength up if we were going to make it out of here. I had no idea how much time had passed when I had been knocked out in the carriage, and without windows we couldn't see the sun rising or setting.

"Nothing to talk about," Tess said around a mouthful of the stale bread, her jaw working hard to chew it.

"There is a lot you don't understand…I need to explain," he replied, his eyes on Tess in the dark.

"Nothing to explain. You and Nik are scum who used us and lied to us. End of story," she replied as she bit off another chunk. I remained silent.

"There's more to it, things you need to know…"

Tess held his stare as she chewed thoughtfully.

"What Nik told you about the Stormshades growing too powerful…that part was true. The part that wasn't true was that the Stormshades were abusing their magic. Yes, they are inherently more powerful. But it was the Nightshades that were jealous of the Stormshades power. They wanted to be the strongest witches in the realm. They wanted to eliminate the Stormshades—at all costs. It was the greed and jealousy of the Nightshades that started this decades-old war between our kind to begin with."

Tess and I sat quietly and listened, and when we didn't interrupt Puck continued.

"The Dark King *hated* Stormshades and wanted to destroy them entirely. Donika was a captain in his army and agreed with him, backing his decisions fully. But it turns out the Dark King had a Stormshade lover, someone who had deceived him. He didn't know her true nature, not until it was too late. But that didn't stop Donika from exposing the king. Donika *used* this information for her own gain and she quickly grew her own following. Those that would support her in overthrowing him. There was a battle at Siraleth when the city fell. Most of the Stormshades were slaughtered, those that weren't fled to the human realm and were never heard from again. Donika killed the Dark King in her quest for power. They were on the *same side*. She is evil and selfish, and I abhor her actions. I cannot support that. I do not support her."

"You aren't on her side?" I finally spoke.

"*No.* I do not support Donika or her quest to murder anyone who could be more powerful than her or act as a threat to her position. At this point, nobody could become more powerful than her anyway. She is so deep in dark magic it has completely consumed her," he answered. "She does not know that I am against her, otherwise I wouldn't still have my head."

"And Nik?" I raised my chin and met his eyes through the iron bars.

"It's...complicated."

"Hardly," I scoffed, returning to my stale bread.

"He did not *want* to bring you here. He *wasn't* bringing you here. He told you to run. As soon as he saw Donika's men...he told you to run. Fletcher has been up our asses since Nik has been putting this off, over and over. He was supposed to return to Akra with you *weeks* ago," Puck said.

"And?" I pushed, "Is that supposed to make me feel any better? That he…hesitated to turn me over? To someone who would see me dead?"

"Things…changed," he replied with a heavy sigh.

"It doesn't appear that way to me, seeing as only about ten minutes ago he had his tongue shoved down the Shadow Queen's throat. He is her *lover*, it is clear where his allegiance lies."

"Appearances." Puck ran a hand through his mess of curls with a heavy sigh. "If he were to do *anything* but agree with Donika and beg for her forgiveness for taking so long to bring you here, he would be right down here awaiting execution with the two of you. He is trying to stay alive, so he can figure out a way out of this."

"Execution?" Tess coughed, setting the tray down beside her.

"I'm not going to let that happen." There was steel in his voice as he clenched his jaw. "Donika has brought enough strife to this realm, and it needs to end. I am going to figure out a way to get you two out of here."

"Would have been a hell of a lot easier if y'all hadn't brought us here in the first place," Tess pointed out as she dipped some of the bread into the questionable stew. She turned to me as she chewed thoughtfully. "It's not pancakes, but it will do."

"Is the grimoire hidden?" Puck asked.

I paused before answering. Would he try to retrieve it himself, if he knew where it was? Was this only an act, to gain our trust and get the grimoire for Donika?

"As hidden as it can be...I hadn't realized the Queen of Istmere was after it," I replied drily. "But if she won't stop until she has it...my family isn't safe."

"It needs to stay hidden." He nodded to himself. "As long as we get you out of here and the grimoire stays out of her reach, we can still fix this."

"There's no fixing this," I replied coldly. His eyes met mine once again in the dark, and his expression softened at what he found there.

"Eat. Rest. I will be back with a plan. In the meantime, don't harass the guards. Don't draw attention to yourselves. Nik has her plenty busy right now, but her attention can turn back to you at any moment. I need to come up with a plan before it's too late."

"I'm sure he does have her *plenty busy*," I replied frostily.

Puck met my cold stare with one of his own. "She tires of her play-things easily."

"How unfortunate."

How long did we have before she tired of keeping us prisoner in the Stormvault? Until she tortured the location of the grimoire out of us? Would she hurt our families to get it? And how much had Nik and Puck told her about us? One thing was for certain...they could no longer be trusted. Whatever Puck was saying now, he still betrayed me. Betrayed us. He was Nik's closest friend. If he was on our side, he would have to prove it.

"I'll be back," Puck said as he stood, brushing the dust off his dark pants. "Remember what I said." He gave me a stern look before he turned to Tess and his eyes softened. Maybe he did have feelings for her, and he only got caught up in Nik's schemes. It appeared that Donika was after me and the grimoire, Tess only happened to be caught in the crosshairs. She wasn't a Stormshade, Donika had no reason to go after her. Talk about terrible timing.

Puck gave Tess one last glance before disappearing down the corridor and leaving through the heavy iron door.

"Do you trust him?" Tess asked me as she spooned more of the muddy grey stew into her mouth.

"Not a chance in hell," I replied around a mouthful.

"You always did know how to hold a grudge," Tess laughed.

"There's a difference between holding a grudge and having your trust broken. Nik and Puck have broken my trust, and it will take a hell of a lot more than pretty lies and stale bread to change that."

"I'm with you on that," Tess agreed. "Where did you leave the grimoire?"

I shook my head. "I can't tell you. I trust you with my life, but this will be easier if only one of us knows its location. It's safer this way," I told her. It wasn't hidden too well, and the thought of Donika rifling through my underwear drawer brought a small laugh bubbling to my lips.

"You're probably right." She nodded. "I know that whatever is in that grimoire that Donika wants, we need to make damn sure she doesn't get it. If she's this deep into dark magic, it can't be anything good."

"We are in agreement on that." I placed the finished stew bowl on the ground next to me and rest my head against the wall. "But the grimoire is spelled to begin with. Tyr was only able to open it because he's...family. I'm not sure Donika could open it, even with the spell. Unless she's planning on using Tyr to open it."

"Probably," Tess replied, "appears he's her little lapdog."

I rest my head against her shoulder, and with a sigh she rested her head back against mine.

"Puck was right about one thing, we need to get some rest if we have any chance of getting out of here. If I have the opportunity, unshackled, outside of this cell, I am going to call on my magic like never before and get us the hell out of here."

"I wish I could help," Tess replied.

"You can," I told her. "Any way you can distract the guards...do it. I only need a second before they restrain me with the shackles. Just one second to pull on my magic and surrender to it."

"I'll do what I can," she assured me. I wasn't sure they would be letting us out of this cell unchained any time soon, but we had to be prepared for if they did. If Puck was able to get us out, we had to take that chance. Even if I planned to ditch him at the first reasonable opportunity that presented itself. Tess and I drifted off quietly, hand in hand, leaning against each other for support. Just as we always had.

I woke with a start as I heard the iron door slam shut at the end of the corridor. Tess and I were tangled together on the packed dirt floor, and she lifted her head and peeled her eyes open as footsteps sounded against the stone.

I pushed my back against the wall, as far from the iron door as I could get. The tray and dishes had been removed at some point while we had slept, I wondered if Puck had snuck back in to retrieve them. How long had we been asleep? There was a chill deep in my bones from sleeping on the packed earth without anything but Tess to keep warm with.

The dark silhouette approached, a lantern swinging in his grip, his golden hair illuminated by the flickering flame. Nik appeared different from the last time I had seen him. His hair was swept back as if he had been pushing it out of his face over and over again. His eyes were ringed with dark circles, his mouth set in a thin line before the glow of the lantern. His hood was pushed back away from his face. A black face covering hung loosely at his neck. He wore a black tunic with a leather strappy breastplate, a broadsword nestled between his shoulder blades. He looked every part the shadow witch, down to his laced knee-high boots and his chilling stare.

"What do you want?" I called before he had the chance to say anything.

"I have to explain, and I have to make it quick. Donika doesn't know I'm down here. If she caught me..." He trailed off, glancing towards the heavy iron door at the end of the corridor. As if he expected her to appear there at any moment. It was the only way in or out of the Stormvault.

"I don't want to hear what you have to say." I raised my chin and met his stare with a cold, defiant, one of my own.

"I am trying to *help* you." He ground his teeth together.

"We don't need help from you," I shot back. His eyes were dark and despite myself my eyes drifted down to his mouth. Just last night those wicked lips had kissed me, tasted me. A flash of heat ran over me as I remember the feel of his body against mine, his knee between my thighs. I shook my head trying to shake loose that traitorous thought. My mind was saying one thing, my body another.

"Better the devil you know than the devil you don't," he hissed through the iron bars.

"The devil...how fitting," I seethed back.

"Can you stop being so stubborn for *one second* and listen to me?" he breathed, pressing up against the iron bars. I couldn't imagine how we looked, curled in the back of this dank cell, dirt in our hair and under our fingernails. I had quite literally been dragged through the mud and tossed around like a rag doll for the past day, both emotionally and physically. The sting of his betrayal was so fresh it was hard to even look at him. Had he told Donika what had happened between us last night? It felt as if so much time had already passed since then.

My eyes drifted down as I swallowed the hot feeling of shame. How had I let him touch me? How had I let him in? How had I not seen the truth? Nik took my silence as an answer, and he knelt on one knee before the iron bars bringing himself down to eye level.

"Everything is not as it seems. I did not want to hurt you. This was the very last thing I wanted..." he pleaded, his eyes on mine. Tess sat at my side silently, her freezing glare searing into him. "I know Puck came to see you."

I nodded in response, and he continued.

"What he said was the truth...I lied about the Stormshades. They never exploited their power over the other witches. They never abused their power. That was the Nightshade army. That was Donika."

"Your lover?" I asked with a raised brow.

"No, not my lover. Not anymore."

Not anymore. The words cut into me like a knife, and I couldn't bring myself to meet his eyes again. I could feel tears rushing to the surface and stinging the back of my eyelids, but I bit my lip and pressed my head back, willing them away. I would not cry in front of him or his Shadow Queen.

"How long? How long have you been with her?" I asked, fearing the answer as I dug my fingernails into the palm of my hand hard enough to assuage the sting of tears at the back of my eyes.

"Almost two years," he replied, voice quiet.

"How old does that make you?" I asked, slowly piecing things together.

"Twenty-two," he answered. That confirmed that he had only joined Silver Oaks to get close to me, to complete his mission of bringing me *and* the grimoire back to Donika. Was there anything he *hadn't* lied about?

"Oh, how the lies and secrets continue to pile up," I sneered, meeting his eyes again. No wonder he and Puck had been able to drink at battle of the bands.

"I will admit, I came to Silver Oaks with the intention of securing the grimoire and bringing you back to Donika, but things changed."

"Things changed…" My voice sounded small in my own ears. "How did anything change?"

"You know how." He swallowed hard as he leveled me with a blistering gaze.

"No, I don't," I replied. I needed to hear it. I needed to hear him say it, even if I didn't trust him. Even if I didn't believe him. Even if it wasn't true.

"I…fell for you. I didn't mean to, but I did. My feelings for you are *real*, and that is the honest truth."

"Bullshit. There's not one honest thing about you, Nikolai."

"Don't say that." His eyes softened in the glow of the lantern as he gripped the iron bars with his other hand.

"You used me. You betrayed me. You brought me to the *one person* that would see me and my kind *dead.* You lied to me. How could I ever trust a word you say?" a hot, traitorous, tear spilled down my cheek and I hastily wiped it away with my dirt-covered sleeve.

"I will earn your trust again," he whispered softly.

"I highly doubt that." I laughed humorlessly. I wanted nothing more than to rip that broadsword from his back and slice him open with it, right here and now. My emotions mixed inside of me as if they were swept up in a tornado, threatening to overwhelm me. Sadness. Anger. Embarrassment. Longing. I had never felt anything like this before. I was drowning in it. How could one person elicit so many feelings inside of me, all at once? How could I want to both kiss him and kill him at the same time?

"What good could you possibly see in her?" I asked as my eyes continued to sting from unshed tears.

"She wasn't always like this," he replied. Of course, his first instinct would be to defend her. My eyes narrowed, and I pinned him with a seething glare as he gripped the iron bar tightly.

"In the beginning...she was different, I hadn't seen this dark side of her. She hid it from me, lured me in. Yes, I had wanted power, I was hungry for it. But she deceived me, too. If I could rule this kingdom, no matter the cost, that is what I wanted. Even after she showed me her dark side, that she had lied to me about who she was, I was determined to rule beside her. I was willing to overlook it. I can see that I was wrong. That there are things far more important than power," he said.

Tess scoffed beside me, mimicking my exact thoughts.

"Let's say for one second that I believed you, which I don't. Do you love her?" I asked, my jaw clenched tight, bracing for his answer and expecting the worst.

"No," he breathed.

"Did you ever love her?" I asked.

He paused. "No."

"It didn't look that way to me, you two had *quite* the re-union," I reminded him.

"That is the last thing I wanted...for you to see us that way. I couldn't refuse her. Not now. Not when she has you in the Stormvault and your life is in danger. I would never let her hurt you."

"And me?" Tess replied curtly.

"...And you," he conceded. He knew I would never leave here without Tess, no matter what. No matter the cost.

"How does Donika look so...young? She appears to be our age and yet, she fought in the War at Siraleth?" Tess asked beside me, her unforgiving gaze locked on Nik's.

He nodded. "Dark magic. Blood magic. She was young during the war, only fifteen, but her appearance has been frozen in time for ten years or so. Many believe her to be immortal."

Great. If Donika was truly immortal from her abuse of dark magic, we had no hope in this, no hope in getting out of here and defeating her. We would be trapped in this cell until she tired of us and decided to kill us.

"And if your feelings have changed, and you never intended for this to happen, then why did you still bring me here?" I asked.

"I didn't," he swore, shaking his head back and forth. "I was *never* going to fulfill my half of the deal. I was never going to bring you or the grimoire back here. If we hadn't run into Tyr, she never would have known you were in Istmere at all, let alone that you had the grimoire in your possession already."

Was that part true? Could I trust him on this?

"I was going to handle Fletcher and Ms. Finch myself, no matter what it took. I was going to kill them if it came to that. I tried to find Ms. Finch, but she had disappeared entirely. Fletcher or his men got to her first. I was going to break my deal with Donika and find a way to keep you safe. I was never going to come back to Akra."

"That's all well and good except I am sitting in a cell in the Stormvault *right now*. No access to my magic, no idea what is going to happen to me or to Tess, and no foreseeable way of getting out."

"Leave that to me and Puck," he replied, his jaw tight.

"I don't see how you could expect me to trust you, after everything," I said.

"I don't expect you to," he replied. "I will earn your trust back."

"Good luck with that," I said tightly.

"Whether you believe it or not, I am telling you the truth. I will find us a way out of this," he said.

"There is no more *us*. There never was," I spit out. "And if I get out of this *cage*, I am going to unleash a storm on this city the likes of which nobody has ever seen before. And I will hunt you down, and you will be sorry you ever crossed me."

"Good." The ghost of a smirk crossed his lips. "There's my firecracker."

"I am not *yours*. I never will be," I snapped.

A sadness passed over his expression, but it was gone just as quickly as it had appeared, replaced with the steely expression I was familiar with.

"Now run off to Donika and *keep her busy*," I said, my voice dripping with disdain.

"I promise you, nothing has happened between me and Donika since we arrived back here. And nothing will."

"Whatever you need to tell yourself," I replied coldly.

His gaze shot to Tess and then returned to me before he pulled himself up by the iron bar of the cell.

"Trust that Puck and I are working on it, we will be back as soon as we can. I am trying my best to stall her. At some point, she will call you back into the throne room for another interrogation. And she won't be so nice this time."

"I *trust* nothing."

How was he going to get us out of this prison if he was *constantly* under Donika's watchful eye? He could barely sneak away to come down to the Stormvault in the first place. If what he said was true and he wasn't on her side any longer, how was he planning on getting away from her himself? She was the most powerful witch in the realm. With dark magic in her arsenal, she would be impossible to deceive, and even more impossible to defeat.

Nik gave me one last glance filled with angst and longing, his emotions warring on his face. He pulled his hood over his swath of golden hair and dragged the black face covering up over his nose, disappearing down the long corridor, the light vanishing with him.

When the guards came to retrieve us, I was almost certain it was the next day, despite there being no windows in the Stormvault to aid in the passing of time. My mother had to be going out of her mind wondering why we hadn't come home. Surely, she had already called Tess' parents, and they had uncovered our web of lies by now. I desperately wanted to get out of here.

Even if we managed to break out of this cell and out of the castle, how would we make it back to the portal without Nik and Puck's help? I had no idea how to get back to Prins from Akra, and traveling through The Shadow to get to the portal by ourselves would be risky. Our only choice now was to trust them, despite every cell in my body telling me otherwise.

As soon as they got us out of here, we could cut them out of our lives for good and forget about this mess. I would have to find a better hiding spot for the grimoire, but even if we escaped, would Donika ever stop coming after me? Would I ever be safe from her? Maybe there was a concealing spell in the book of shadows that could hide us from her, so she could never find us.

I felt hopeless, and the longer we spent in this prison cell the bleaker things were starting to look. Tess and I had slept a good chunk of time, and Puck had sent a servant with another tray of food and water to keep our energy up. Neither Puck nor Nik had returned themselves. Thinking of the ways in which Nik was *distracting* Donika made my stomach turn.

Tess and I had been discussing our options when the iron door squealed open, the heavy sound of multiple sets of boots on the stone ringing down the corridor. Four soldiers appeared before the cell door, two for each of us. They shackled our wrists in front of us with the same ash shackles they had used before. This time they added a chain before pulling us from the cell like dogs on a leash.

We went willingly this time, knowing where we were head- ed. Donika had called us back to the throne room for inter- rogation, and Nik had warned us she wouldn't be as nice this time. What would she do to me when I refused to give up the location of the grimoire? Was I more use to her alive, than I was dead? We walked up the steep set of stairs that led to the prison before twisting through the palace, ascending two more sets of stairs to the main floor. There were more people bustling about the castle today, both soldiers and servants alike. Everyone avoided our eyes as we were led through the hallways and up the final curved staircase to the elongated throne room.

Donika sat on the dais, her leg thrown over one arm of her throne. Today she wore a black tunic tucked into leather riding pants and knee-high riding boots. Was she heading out of the palace? As we were led into the room, the heavy doors were pulled shut behind us, leaving us alone in the room with Donika and her guards. Her wolves were nowhere to be seen.

The soldiers led us to the middle of the room before they pushed us down onto our knees before her.

"After your little stunt yesterday, I think I'll keep you shackled...for now." She grinned, as if this was a game to her.

"Afraid of me? What had you said yesterday...'Just a little Stormshade, I don't get what all the fuss is about," I mocked. The soldier behind me kicked me in the back with a heeled boot for my insubordination. A grunt left me involuntarily before I regained my composure. Tess shot me a warning glare at my side.

"Oh, I am not afraid of you little Stormshade. You are weak and powerless. You are under *my* control," she scoffed. As if this weren't obvious.

I swallowed down my next response, hoping to avoid being kicked in the back by the lumbering guard again. She didn't appear to be in as forgiving of a mood today, and I had a bad habit of running my mouth when I shouldn't.

"You know why you are here, little Stormshade. Let's talk about the grimoire."

"There's nothing to talk about," I replied honestly, the chain at my wrists jingling as I shrugged.

"There isn't?" She feigned innocence, tapping her chin. "I already told you, there will be consequences if you do not give me what I desire, and I desire the grimoire."

I was prepared to suffer those consequences. The grimoire had chosen *me*, it had belonged to *my* ancestors. I wasn't about to give it up so easily, and to the Shadow Queen, no less. Who knew what dark and powerful spells there might be in there. I could never let her get her hands on it.

"So be it. Have it your way." Her voice was cold as ice. I braced myself as she centered herself on her throne, raising her hands as dark shadows appeared at the tips of her fingers. No, not fingers...claws. They shot towards me, filling the room with their smoke, the sun from the windows quickly eclipsed by her darkness. I squeezed my eyes shut against her as I felt her magic lick at my skin, but it was Tess at my side who cried out.

"What are you doing?" I asked, the darkness obscuring my vision. I couldn't see Tess but she cried out again, the chains at her wrists clanking together as she hit the floor with a heavy thud.

"Motivating you," she raged.

"Stop it!" I cried as I felt around for Tess, finally finding her limp body in the darkness. The shadows cleared just enough to reveal her face, twisted in agony as she curled into herself on the floor.

"Tess doesn't know anything! Stop hurting her!"

"Only if you tell me where the grimoire is…" Donika bargained. Is this what she planned to do? Torture everyone I cared about until I revealed its location? I was prepared to face the consequences myself, but I couldn't put that on my loved ones. My family. I couldn't put that on Tess.

"Stop!" I could sense my magic rising to the surface of my skin, but with the ash shackles bound tightly at my wrists the magic fizzled out with nowhere to go. My magic hit a wall, over and over again, quickly draining me as it tried to burst forth, but failed each time.

"This could all be over just like that." Donika snapped her fingers together as her shadows parted, her lithe body descending the stairs of the dais to come and stand before us. Tess was motionless on the floor before me, her face still warped into a mask of pain. "It is all up to you, little Stormshade."

"Stop calling me that," I shot back, rising to my feet before her. "You would leave me alone? You would release me and let us go if I gave you the location of the grimoire?"

"Well, I didn't say that…" Donika's voice was smooth as silk, a master manipulator.

"Then what motivation do I have to give it to you?" I asked.

"For starters, I will stop torturing your friends. Eventually I would move on to your family…then I would move on to torturing you. That would be a last resort. I find it much more motivating to eviscerate my victims *emotionally* first, then physically. It's always oh so much fun…" Her black eyes met mine. "I've heard you've taken a liking to my Nikolai."

My Nikolai. The words rang hollow in my ears, and my stomach turned as my mouth went dry.

"I could arrange for you two to speak," she offered, examining her perfectly polished nails. So, she didn't know he had already come to visit us in the Stormvault, then.

"I don't want to see him. He betrayed me. Used me. He brought me to *you*," I spit out.

"There are other things I can offer you…" she started.

"Why do you even care? It is *my* family's grimoire. You wouldn't even be able to open it. The grimoire made itself known to *me*, it chose *me*. It is spelled against intruders. Why do you want it?"

Donika's laugh rang out through the throne room, echoing off the stone walls endlessly.

"Oh, you really don't know, do you?" she asked, her dark eyes bewildered.

"—know what?" I hesitated. The energy in the room had changed, and a cold chill ran up my spine as Donika's shadows danced at my feet.

Donika took a step towards me, then another, until she was right before me. She was so close I could reach out and touch her if my hands hadn't been bound and shackled. The cold metal rubbed into my wrists, and I bit the inside of my cheek to keep my composure. This close to me, I could feel the energy rolling off her in waves despite the ash around my wrists choking my connection to all magic. Her magic called to me, and with everything in me I wanted to reach out and grab it. It had been days since I had tasted magic, and I *craved it.*

Donika's smile was wicked as it spread across her face, and a sensation of cold dread settled over me. What piece of the puzzle was I missing?

"It's *my* families grimoire too." She smiled. How could that be? Donika and I were related? The back of my throat burned as I glanced down, trying to piece this together.

"My mother was a *filthy little* Stormshade, just like you. Though I would never dare to claim her family name, her blood still runs through my veins. When the grimoire didn't make itself known to me or to Tyr, I knew it would make itself known to someone else in the Kotova bloodline," she started. She used her shadows to turn my chin up until my eyes met hers. "She and my father had me, and we were all one happy little family together. But that wasn't enough for her. *It was never enough.* She and my father remained friends, but my mother moved on to bigger and better things. She left me behind." Was this why she hated Stormshades so much? Because her mother was a Stormshade, and had left her when she was young?

"That Stormshade traitor tricked the Dark King of Istmere into taking her into his bed. He had no idea what she was at the time, and when he finally found out what she truly was, he cast her out of the castle. Exiled her. He was *weak*, he should have murdered her where she stood while he still had the chance. Little did he know, she was already pregnant with his child," she spat. How could she speak this way about her own mother? How could a love like that have been twisted into such blinding hate?

"What does this have to do with me?" I asked, my voice small.

I had a pit in my stomach that threatened to bring me to my knees before her. Even as she spoke, I already knew.

"She fled to Siraleth, back to me and my father. She gave birth to another worthless little Stormshade. An abomination. A disgrace. She knew she couldn't keep the baby in Istmere, she would never be safe. She stashed her in the human realm to keep her away from prying eyes."

My throat felt so thick I could barely swallow down the tears that sprang forth from my eyes. I didn't dare use my shackled hand to wipe them away. I met Donika's cold stare with one of my own as she continued.

"We went on about our lives. When I had grown and trained and joined the king's army, I was able to deceive him and steal the throne for myself. My first act as queen was wiping my traitorous mother's existence off this planet. Everything was going my way. That is until I heard a rumor about a little Stormshade who had been hidden away in the human realm. A Stormshade that shared my blood. At that point, I had almost forgotten all about it." She laughed.

"Do you feel that?" she asked.

"What?" I asked, my voice cracking. Another tear spilled down my dirt-stained cheek. *I had promised myself I wasn't going to cry in front of her.*

"My magic. It calls to you, doesn't it?" Her mouth turned up into a smirk. "Like calls to like. The moment I walked in here and saw you for myself for the first time, I knew the truth. Your magic calls to me too, after all."

"What do you mean?" I breathed.

It couldn't be...I didn't want to believe it. But some part of me, deep down, knew that she was telling me the truth. I had never fit in, never belonged. I was always searching for something without knowing what it was, and when I found my magic, I thought that *must* be it. I had never felt understood by my parents, but they had been hiding the truth from me all these years. They weren't my parents at all. Did they know that I had magic? Did they know about my mother? Had they been spelled to forget all of it?

"That's right." Donika nodded as she saw the truth unfold on my face. "That little Stormshade was *you*, and now that I have you, I am *never* letting you go."

Donika was my family. Tyr was my family. There was a whole life for me here that had been *stolen* from me. Everything that had come before this was a lie. I had never belonged in the human realm, I always belonged here. How could my mother have lied to me all these years? I would never get the chance to meet my birth mother because she was *already dead*, at the hands of Donika no less. The chance at a different life had been taken from me. How could she have done this? If she hadn't hidden me to keep me safe...

I swallowed back my tears as another thought occurred to me. If what Donika said was true...I was the daughter of the Dark King. *I* was next in line to inherit the throne. Donika had murdered both my mother, *and* my father. My sadness was replaced with a seething rage as I ground my teeth together and met Donika's lifeless eyes. Did Nikolai know any of this? Had Donika told him who I truly was? My magic pushed against the iron shackles at my wrists even harder now, begging to be set free. This witch standing before me had taken *everything* from me, and I would not let her take *anything* else.

"So, you see little Stormshade, that grimoire is just as much yours as it is mine, *sister*."

Acknowledgements

Writing and publishing this book has been a dream come true! I first thought up this story when I was nineteen years old, and fourteen years later it is finally complete. I wasn't sure this story would ever be finished, and I am so thankful to you as the reader for giving it a chance.

I could never have done this without the support of my friends and family. A special thanks to my Mom and Dad for always supporting me in every endeavor, and indulging my creative side. I want to thank my Grammy Frohman who is always on my shoulder, embracing everything that I do. My sister Jennifer, and my brother Eric for understanding why I've spent all these nights holed up with a blanket and my computer. My nieces Layla and Lexi for providing much needed writing breaks in the form of entertaining facetime calls.

A special thanks to my friends who ride or die for me. Jenn, Brian, Lisa, Laura, Cat, and Katie, my Kickstarter preorders could never have been a success without you. A special shout out to Lisa for being my #1 beta reader and listening to all of my crazy ideas. You are the only one to have read this manuscript in its most raw and unedited form and I am forever thankful.

I also need to thank my incredible book team, without them this wouldn't have been possible. Emma Jane at EJL Editing for her amazing editing skills (I'm sorry about all the improper dialogue grammar), Fran at MerryBookRound for this incredible cover that everyone is drooling over, and Hillary Bardin for bringing my babies to life in her amazing character art.

And lastly to you, the readers. Thank you for taking a chance on When Storms Awaken. None of this would be possible without you, and I am forever thankful for your support.

ABOUT THE AUTHOR

Michelle Frohman is an avid reader, writer, and animal lover. She writes young adult and new adult fantasy and paranormal romance and has a B.S. in Animal Science and an M.B.A. Michelle resides in Connecticut with her three cats Kasha (the spicy one), Kiwi (the sensitive one), and Peach (the fluffy one). When she's not reading or writing you can find her obsessing over her cats, drinking unhealthy amounts of peach tea, working on her interior design blog, or riding horses.

instagram.com/michellefrohmanauthor

tiktok.com/michellefrohmanauthor

facebook.com/profile.php?id=100094541655815

www.ingramcontent.com/pod-product-compliance
Lightning Source LLC
Chambersburg PA
CBHW030625310726
48979CB00003B/893